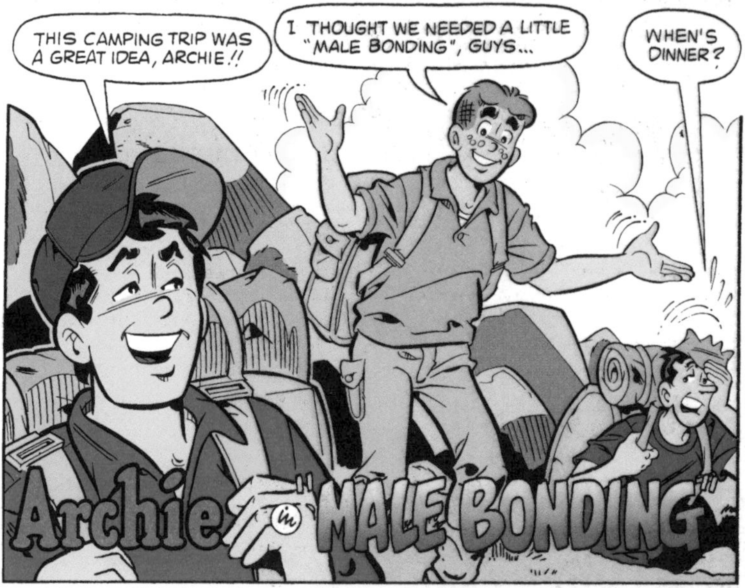
THIS CAMPING TRIP WAS A GREAT IDEA, ARCHIE!!
I THOUGHT WE NEEDED A LITTLE "MALE BONDING", GUYS...
WHEN'S DINNER?
Archie in "MALE BONDING"

Script: George Gladir / Pencils: Tim Kennedy / Inks: Ken Selig / Letters: Bill Yoshida / Colors: Barry Grossman

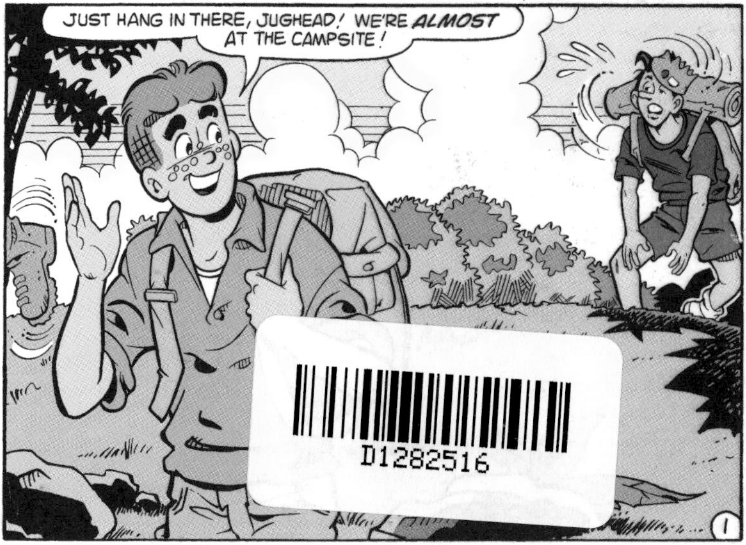
JUST HANG IN THERE, JUGHEAD! WE'RE *ALMOST* AT THE CAMPSITE!

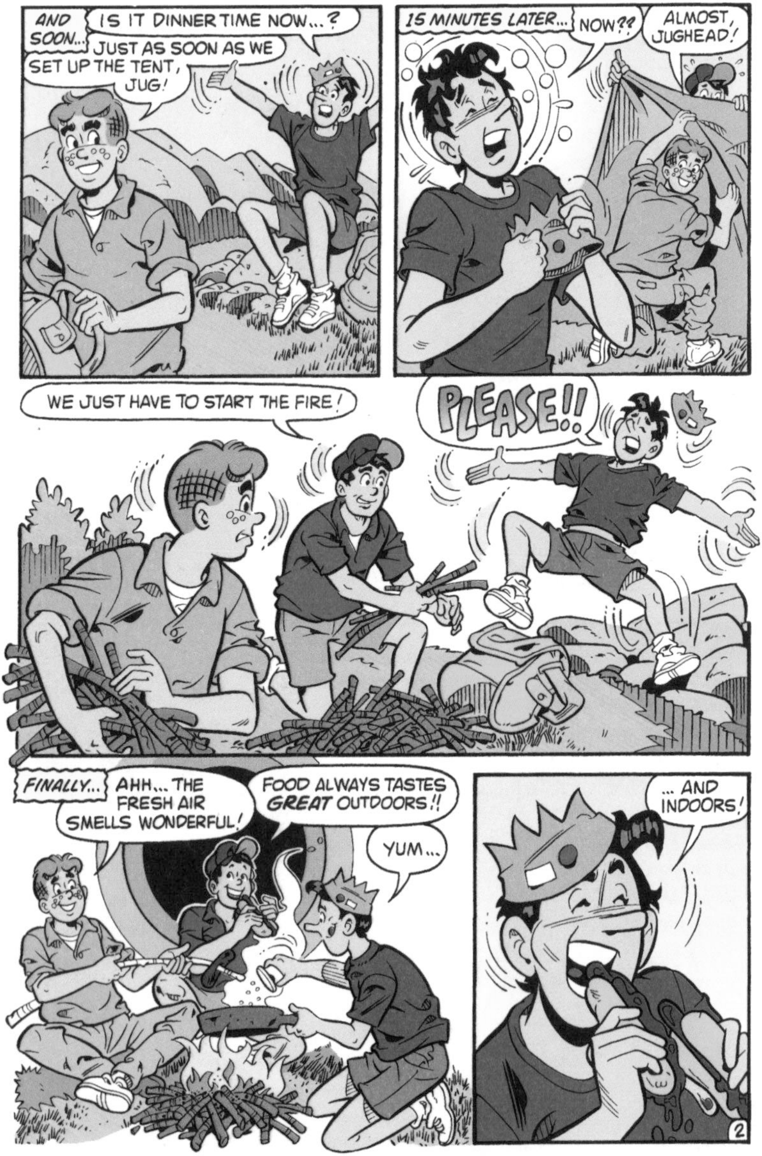
AND SOON...
IS IT DINNER TIME NOW...?
JUST AS SOON AS WE SET UP THE TENT, JUG!
15 MINUTES LATER...
NOW??
ALMOST, JUGHEAD!
WE JUST HAVE TO START THE FIRE!
PLEASE!!
FINALLY...
AHH... THE FRESH AIR SMELLS WONDERFUL!
FOOD ALWAYS TASTES *GREAT* OUTDOORS!!
YUM...
... AND INDOORS!
2

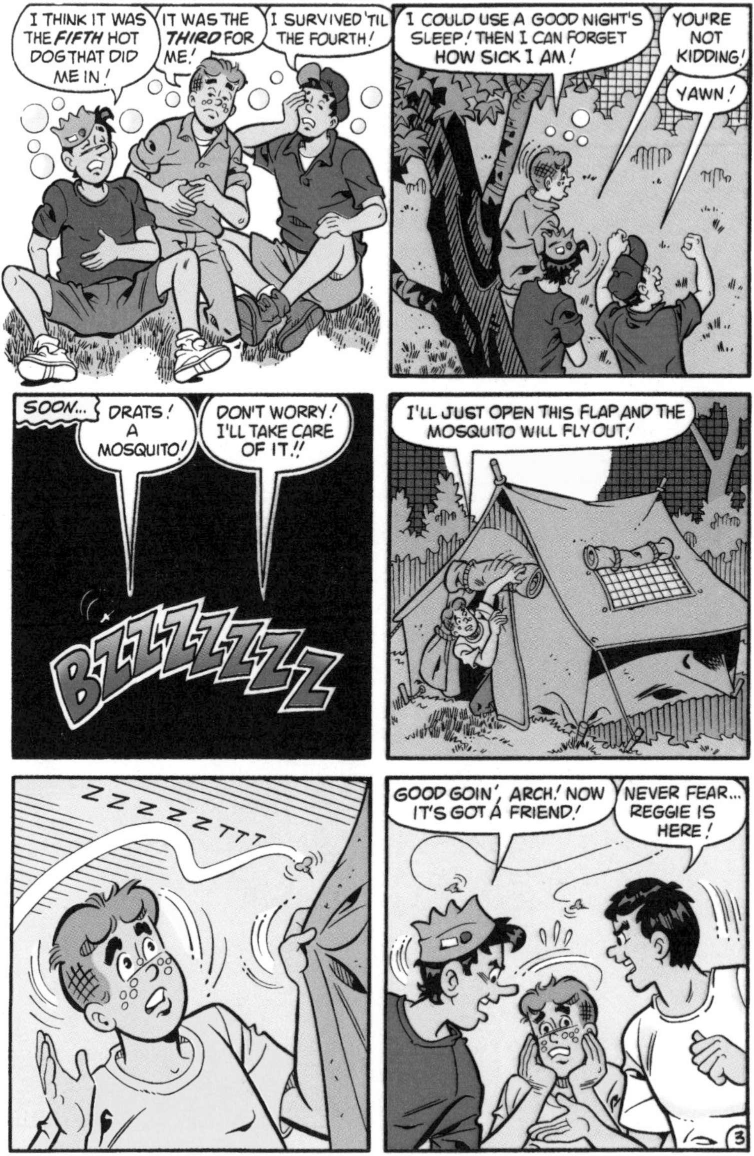
I THINK IT WAS THE FIFTH HOT DOG THAT DID ME IN!
IT WAS THE THIRD FOR ME!
I SURVIVED 'TIL THE FOURTH!
I COULD USE A GOOD NIGHT'S SLEEP! THEN I CAN FORGET HOW SICK I AM!
YOU'RE NOT KIDDING!
YAWN!
SOON...
DRATS! A MOSQUITO!
DON'T WORRY! I'LL TAKE CARE OF IT!!
BZZZZZZZZ
I'LL JUST OPEN THIS FLAP AND THE MOSQUITO WILL FLY OUT!
ZZZZZZTTT
GOOD GOIN', ARCH! NOW IT'S GOT A FRIEND!
NEVER FEAR... REGGIE IS HERE!
3

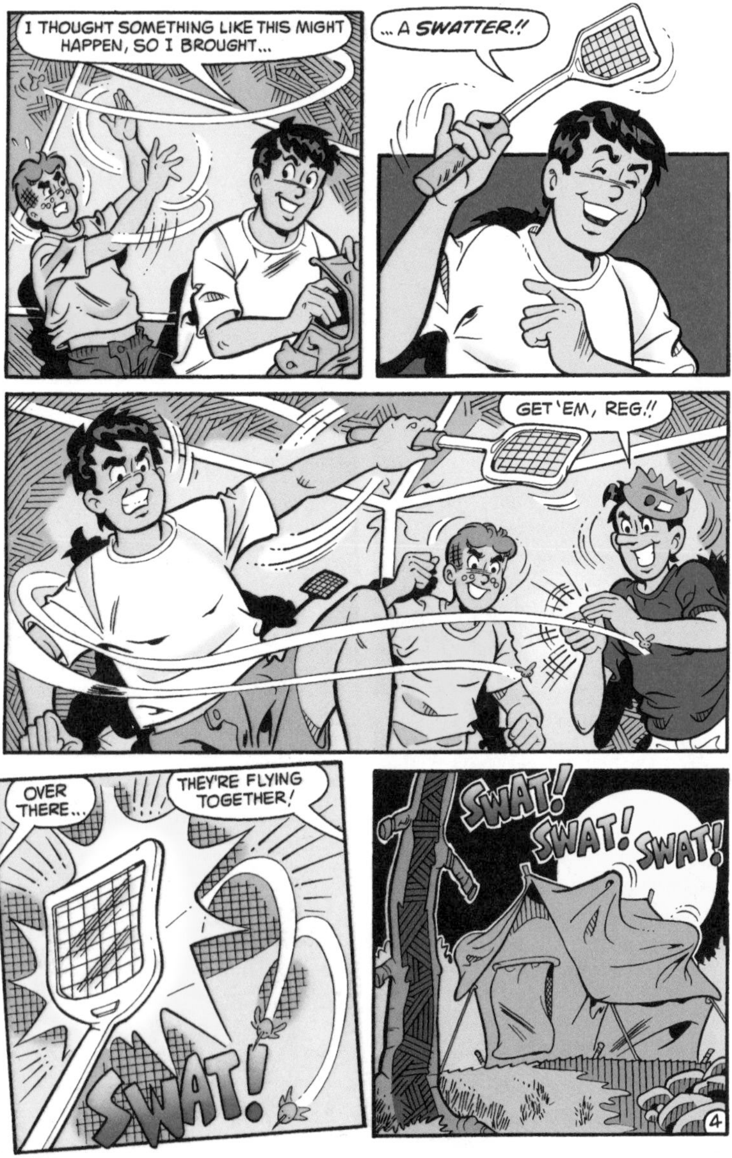
I THOUGHT SOMETHING LIKE THIS MIGHT HAPPEN, SO I BROUGHT...
...A SWATTER.!!
GET 'EM, REG.!!
OVER THERE...
THEY'RE FLYING TOGETHER!
SWAT!
SWAT! SWAT! SWAT!
4

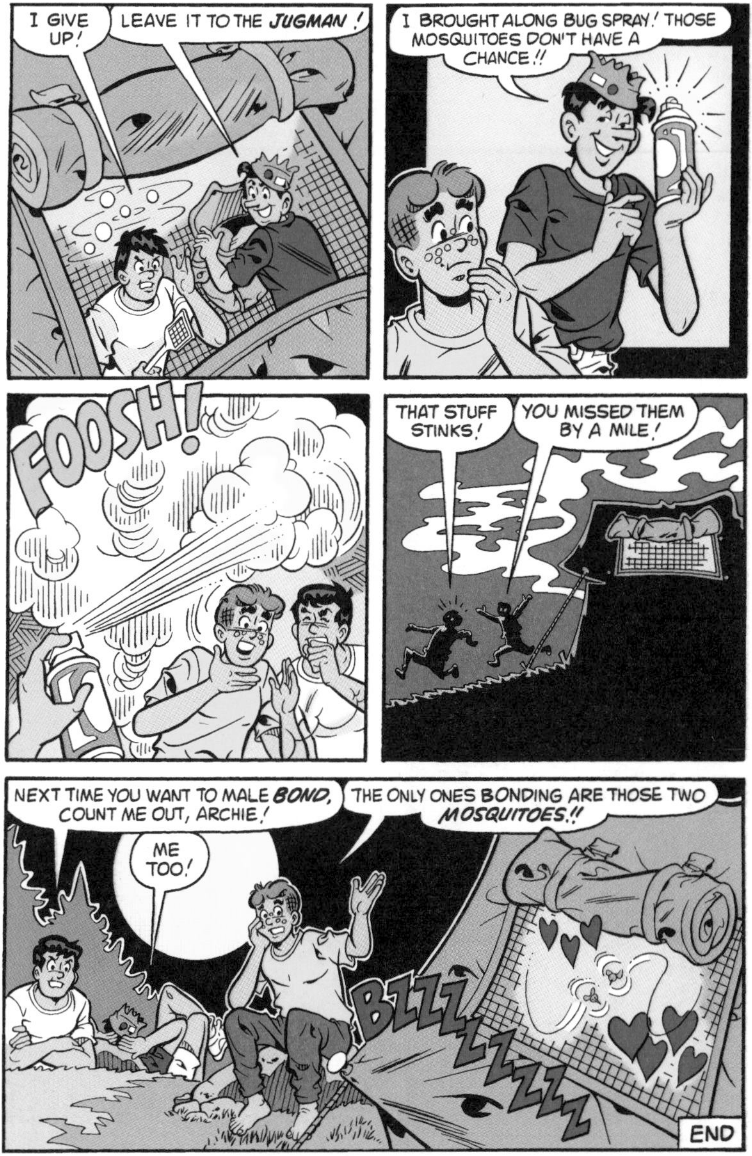
I GIVE UP!
LEAVE IT TO THE JUGMAN!
I BROUGHT ALONG BUG SPRAY! THOSE MOSQUITOES DON'T HAVE A CHANCE!!
FOOSH!
THAT STUFF STINKS!
YOU MISSED THEM BY A MILE!
NEXT TIME YOU WANT TO MALE BOND, COUNT ME OUT, ARCHIE!
ME TOO!
THE ONLY ONES BONDING ARE THOSE TWO MOSQUITOES!!
BZZZZZZZ
END

# Archie in ABSENCE MINDED

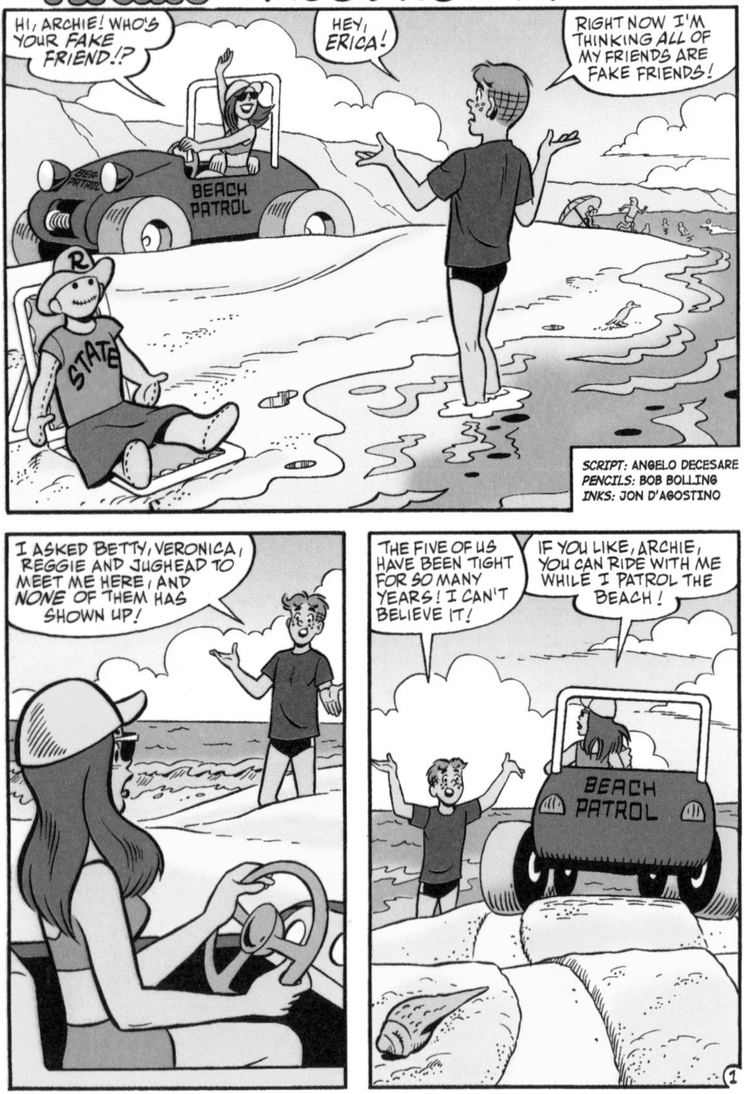

HI, ARCHIE! WHO'S YOUR FAKE FRIEND!?
HEY, ERICA!
RIGHT NOW I'M THINKING ALL OF MY FRIENDS ARE FAKE FRIENDS!
BEACH PATROL
STATE
SCRIPT: ANGELO DECESARE
PENCILS: BOB BOLLING
INKS: JON D'AGOSTINO
I ASKED BETTY, VERONICA, REGGIE AND JUGHEAD TO MEET ME HERE, AND NONE OF THEM HAS SHOWN UP!
THE FIVE OF US HAVE BEEN TIGHT FOR SO MANY YEARS! I CAN'T BELIEVE IT!
IF YOU LIKE, ARCHIE, YOU CAN RIDE WITH ME WHILE I PATROL THE BEACH!
BEACH PATROL

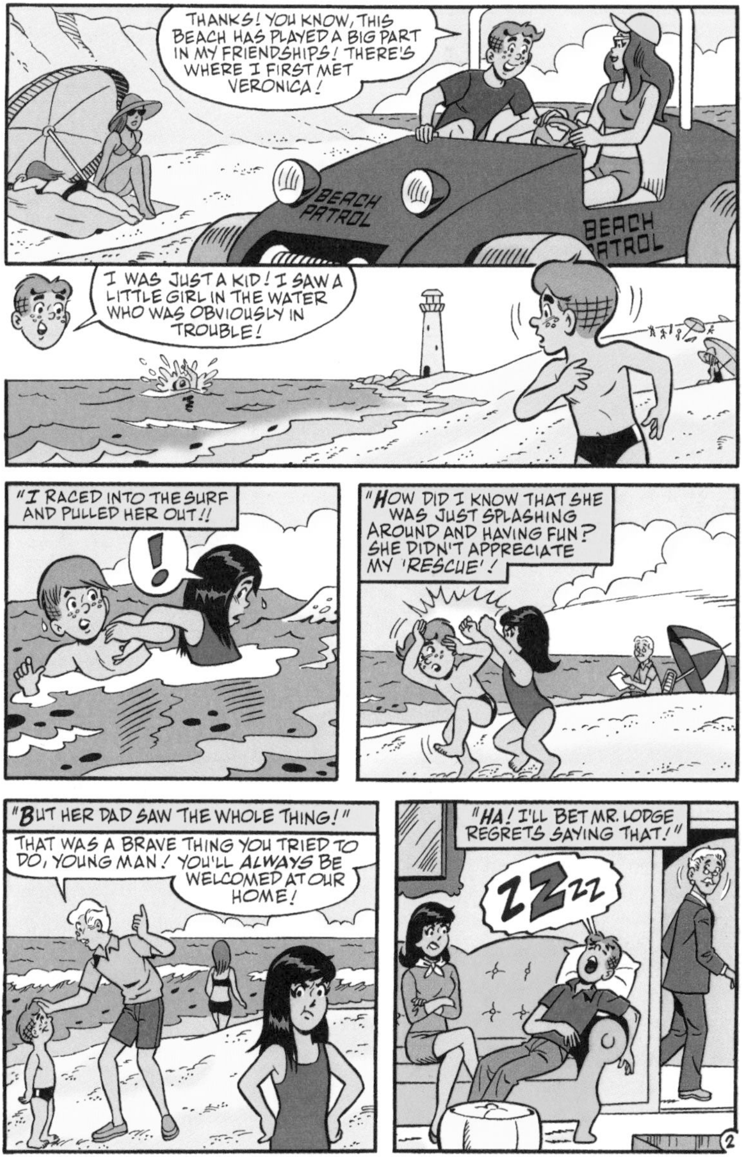
THANKS! YOU KNOW, THIS BEACH HAS PLAYED A BIG PART IN MY FRIENDSHIPS! THERE'S WHERE I FIRST MET VERONICA!
BEACH PATROL
BEACH PATROL
I WAS JUST A KID! I SAW A LITTLE GIRL IN THE WATER WHO WAS OBVIOUSLY IN TROUBLE!
"I RACED INTO THE SURF AND PULLED HER OUT!!
!
"HOW DID I KNOW THAT SHE WAS JUST SPLASHING AROUND AND HAVING FUN? SHE DIDN'T APPRECIATE MY 'RESCUE'!
"BUT HER DAD SAW THE WHOLE THING!"
THAT WAS A BRAVE THING YOU TRIED TO DO, YOUNG MAN! YOU'LL ALWAYS BE WELCOMED AT OUR HOME!
"HA! I'LL BET MR. LODGE REGRETS SAYING THAT!"
ZZzz

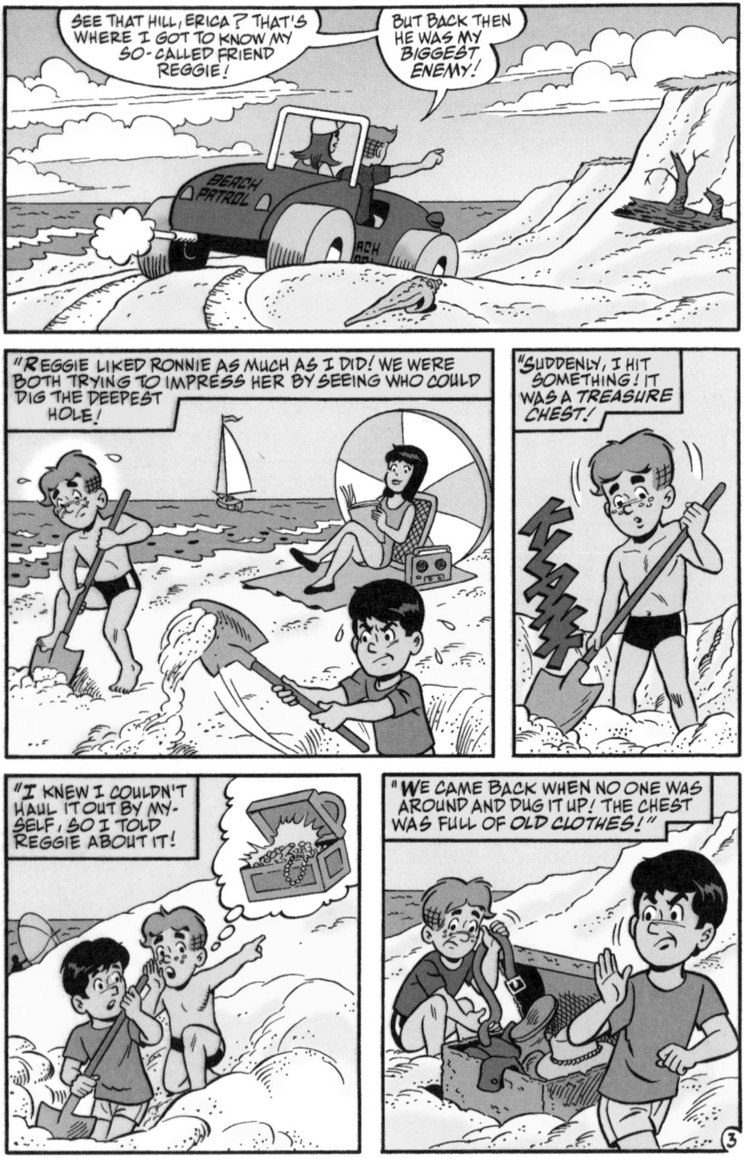
SEE THAT HILL, ERICA? THAT'S WHERE I GOT TO KNOW MY SO-CALLED FRIEND REGGIE!
BUT BACK THEN HE WAS MY BIGGEST ENEMY!
BEACH PATROL
"REGGIE LIKED RONNIE AS MUCH AS I DID! WE WERE BOTH TRYING TO IMPRESS HER BY SEEING WHO COULD DIG THE DEEPEST HOLE!
"SUDDENLY, I HIT SOMETHING! IT WAS A TREASURE CHEST!
KLANK
"I KNEW I COULDN'T HAUL IT OUT BY MY-SELF, SO I TOLD REGGIE ABOUT IT!
"WE CAME BACK WHEN NO ONE WAS AROUND AND DUG IT UP! THE CHEST WAS FULL OF OLD CLOTHES!"
3

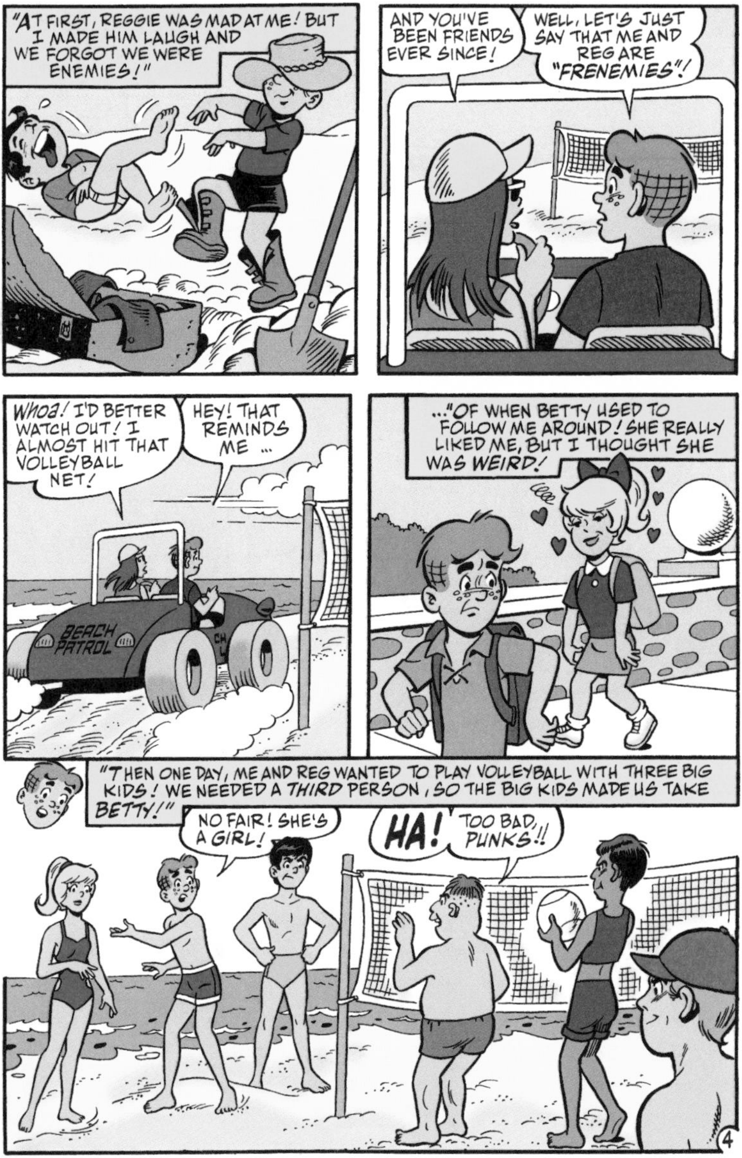

"AT FIRST, REGGIE WAS MAD AT ME! BUT I MADE HIM LAUGH AND WE FORGOT WE WERE ENEMIES!"
AND YOU'VE BEEN FRIENDS EVER SINCE!
WELL, LET'S JUST SAY THAT ME AND REG ARE "FRENEMIES"!
Whoa! I'D BETTER WATCH OUT! I ALMOST HIT THAT VOLLEYBALL NET!
HEY! THAT REMINDS ME ...
BEACH PATROL
..."OF WHEN BETTY USED TO FOLLOW ME AROUND! SHE REALLY LIKED ME, BUT I THOUGHT SHE WAS WEIRD!
"THEN ONE DAY, ME AND REG WANTED TO PLAY VOLLEYBALL WITH THREE BIG KIDS! WE NEEDED A THIRD PERSON, SO THE BIG KIDS MADE US TAKE BETTY!"
NO FAIR! SHE'S A GIRL!
HA!
TOO BAD, PUNKS!!

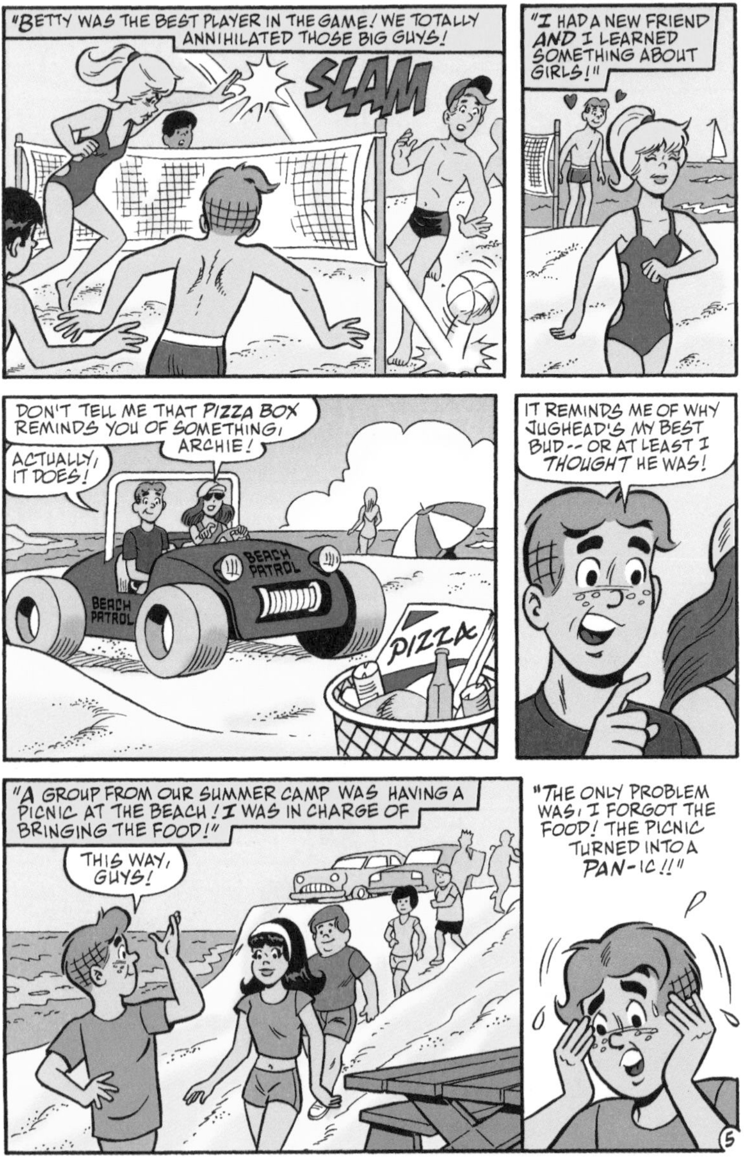
"BETTY WAS THE BEST PLAYER IN THE GAME! WE TOTALLY ANNIHILATED THOSE BIG GUYS!
SLAM
"I HAD A NEW FRIEND AND I LEARNED SOMETHING ABOUT GIRLS!"
DON'T TELL ME THAT PIZZA BOX REMINDS YOU OF SOMETHING, ARCHIE!
ACTUALLY, IT DOES!
BEACH PATROL
BEACH PATROL
PIZZA
IT REMINDS ME OF WHY JUGHEAD'S MY BEST BUD -- OR AT LEAST I THOUGHT HE WAS!
"A GROUP FROM OUR SUMMER CAMP WAS HAVING A PICNIC AT THE BEACH! I WAS IN CHARGE OF BRINGING THE FOOD!"
THIS WAY, GUYS!
"THE ONLY PROBLEM WAS, I FORGOT THE FOOD! THE PICNIC TURNED INTO A PAN-IC!!"
5

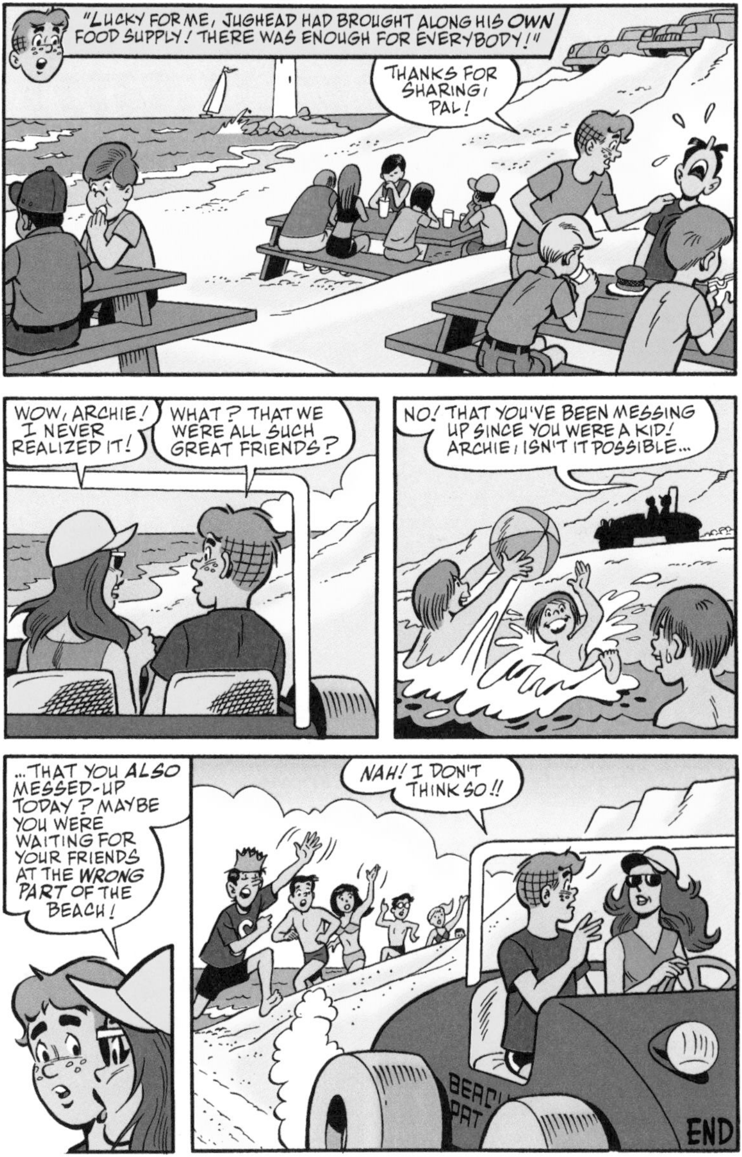
"LUCKY FOR ME, JUGHEAD HAD BROUGHT ALONG HIS OWN FOOD SUPPLY! THERE WAS ENOUGH FOR EVERYBODY!"
THANKS FOR SHARING, PAL!
WOW, ARCHIE! I NEVER REALIZED IT!
WHAT? THAT WE WERE ALL SUCH GREAT FRIENDS?
NO! THAT YOU'VE BEEN MESSING UP SINCE YOU WERE A KID! ARCHIE, ISN'T IT POSSIBLE...
...THAT YOU ALSO MESSED-UP TODAY? MAYBE YOU WERE WAITING FOR YOUR FRIENDS AT THE WRONG PART OF THE BEACH!
NAH! I DON'T THINK SO!!
END

# Archie
## "MY BETTER BUDDY, BETTY.."

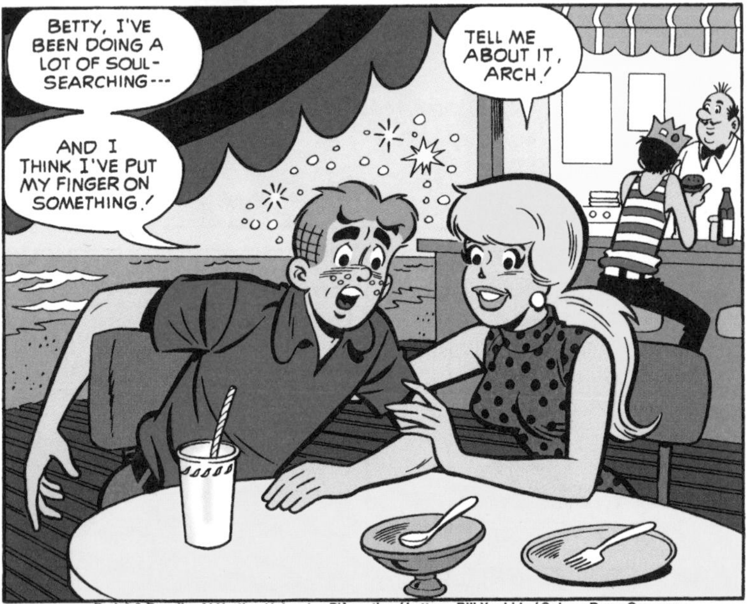
BETTY, I'VE BEEN DOING A LOT OF SOUL-SEARCHING---
AND I THINK I'VE PUT MY FINGER ON SOMETHING!
TELL ME ABOUT IT, ARCH!

Script & Pencils: Al Hartley / Inks: Jon D'Agostino / Letters: Bill Yoshida / Colors: Barry Grossman

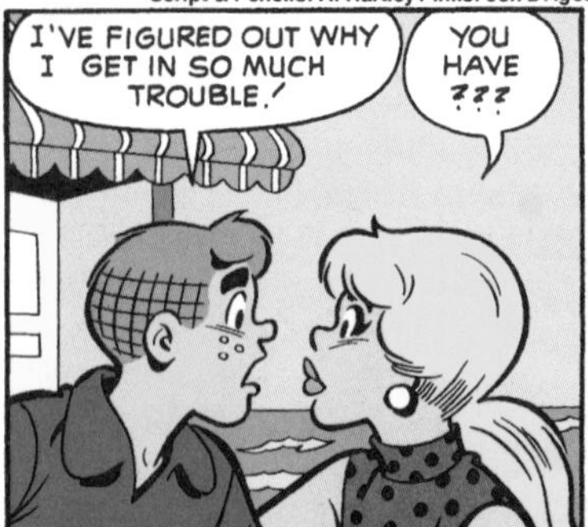
I'VE FIGURED OUT WHY I GET IN SO MUCH TROUBLE!
YOU HAVE ???

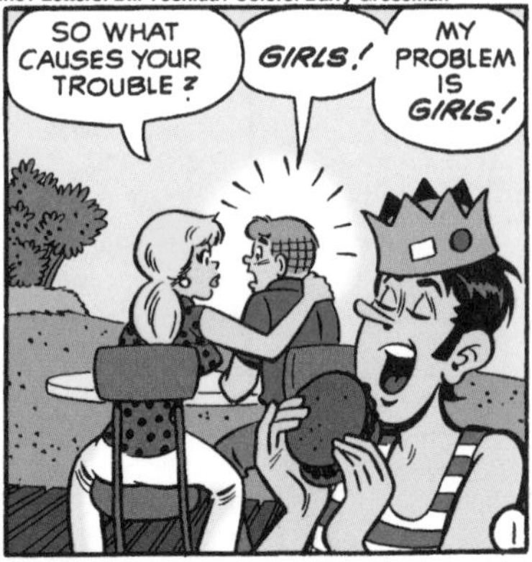
SO WHAT CAUSES YOUR TROUBLE ?
GIRLS!
MY PROBLEM IS GIRLS!

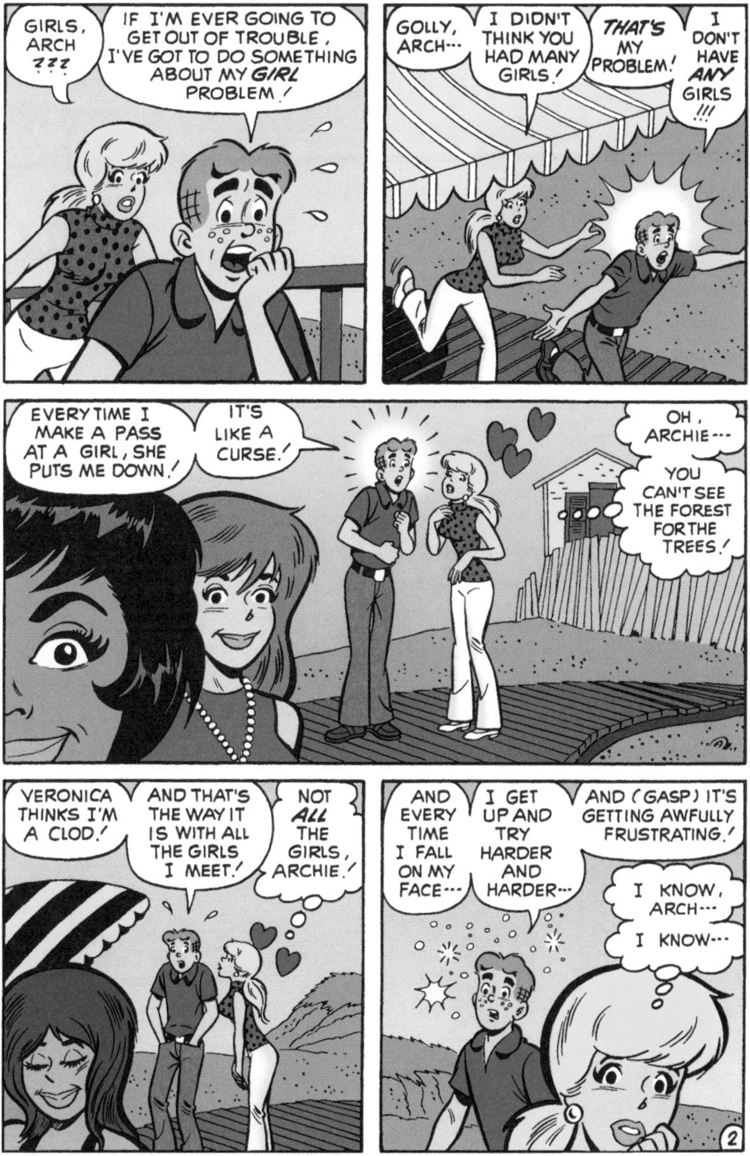
GIRLS, ARCH ???
IF I'M EVER GOING TO GET OUT OF TROUBLE, I'VE GOT TO DO SOMETHING ABOUT MY GIRL PROBLEM!
GOLLY, ARCH---
I DIDN'T THINK YOU HAD MANY GIRLS!
THAT'S MY PROBLEM!
I DON'T HAVE ANY GIRLS !!!
EVERY TIME I MAKE A PASS AT A GIRL, SHE PUTS ME DOWN!
IT'S LIKE A CURSE!
OH, ARCHIE---
YOU CAN'T SEE THE FOREST FOR THE TREES!
VERONICA THINKS I'M A CLOD!
AND THAT'S THE WAY IT IS WITH ALL THE GIRLS I MEET!
NOT ALL THE GIRLS, ARCHIE!
AND EVERY TIME I FALL ON MY FACE---
I GET UP AND TRY HARDER AND HARDER---
AND (GASP) IT'S GETTING AWFULLY FRUSTRATING!
I KNOW, ARCH---
I KNOW---
2

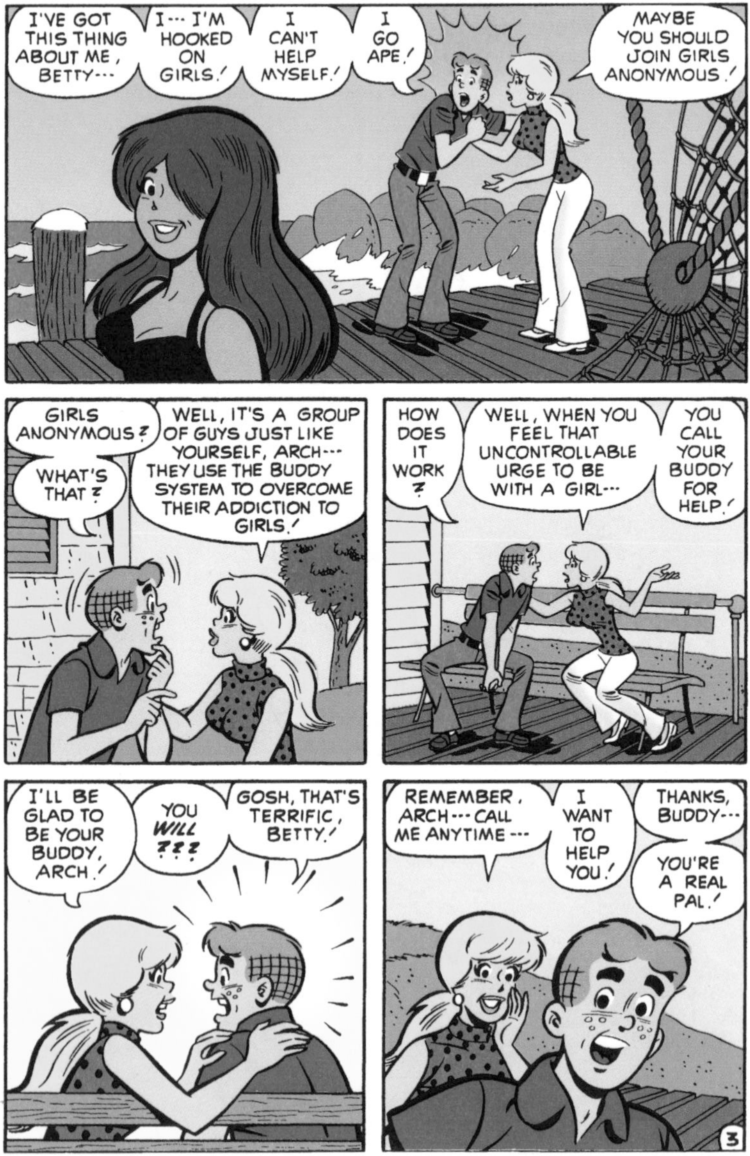

I'VE GOT THIS THING ABOUT ME, BETTY---
I--- I'M HOOKED ON GIRLS!
I CAN'T HELP MYSELF!
I GO APE!
MAYBE YOU SHOULD JOIN GIRLS ANONYMOUS!
GIRLS ANONYMOUS?
WHAT'S THAT?
WELL, IT'S A GROUP OF GUYS JUST LIKE YOURSELF, ARCH--- THEY USE THE BUDDY SYSTEM TO OVERCOME THEIR ADDICTION TO GIRLS!
HOW DOES IT WORK?
WELL, WHEN YOU FEEL THAT UNCONTROLLABLE URGE TO BE WITH A GIRL---
YOU CALL YOUR BUDDY FOR HELP!
I'LL BE GLAD TO BE YOUR BUDDY, ARCH!
YOU WILL???
GOSH, THAT'S TERRIFIC, BETTY!
REMEMBER, ARCH--- CALL ME ANYTIME---
I WANT TO HELP YOU!
THANKS, BUDDY---
YOU'RE A REAL PAL!

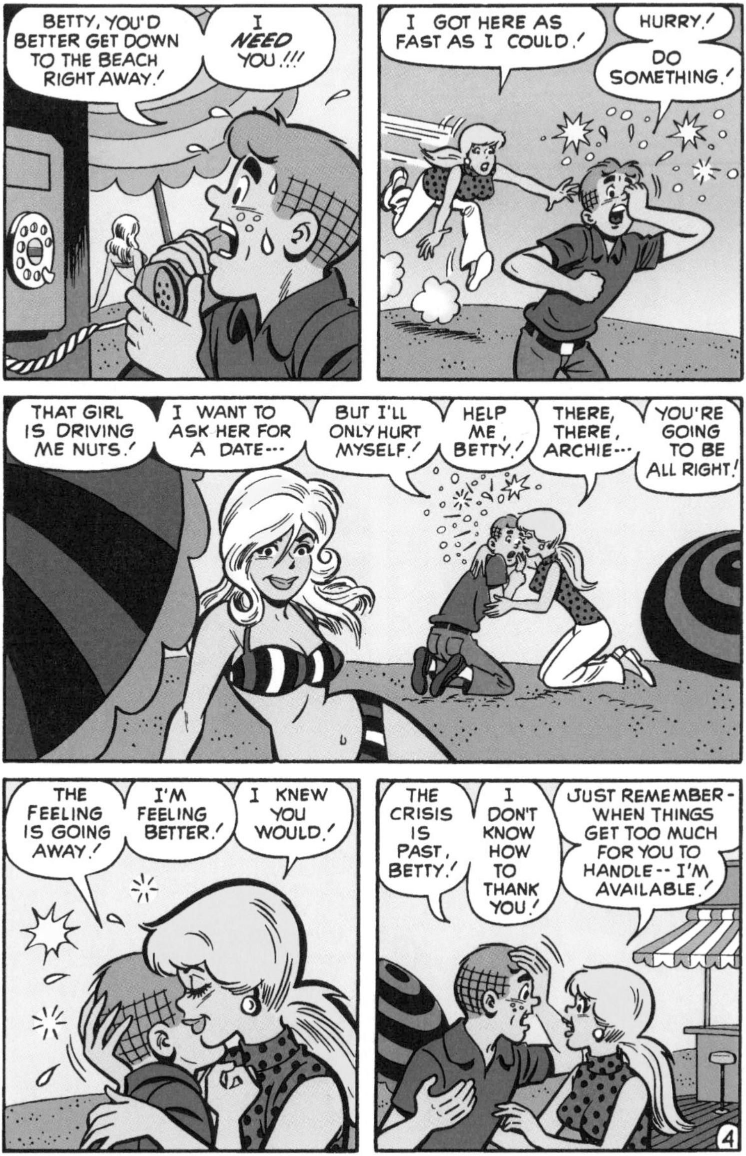

BETTY, YOU'D BETTER GET DOWN TO THE BEACH RIGHT AWAY!
I NEED YOU!!!
I GOT HERE AS FAST AS I COULD!
HURRY!
DO SOMETHING!
THAT GIRL IS DRIVING ME NUTS!
I WANT TO ASK HER FOR A DATE---
BUT I'LL ONLY HURT MYSELF!
HELP ME, BETTY!
THERE, THERE, ARCHIE---
YOU'RE GOING TO BE ALL RIGHT!
THE FEELING IS GOING AWAY!
I'M FEELING BETTER!
I KNEW YOU WOULD!
THE CRISIS IS PAST, BETTY!
I DON'T KNOW HOW TO THANK YOU!
JUST REMEMBER- WHEN THINGS GET TOO MUCH FOR YOU TO HANDLE-- I'M AVAILABLE!

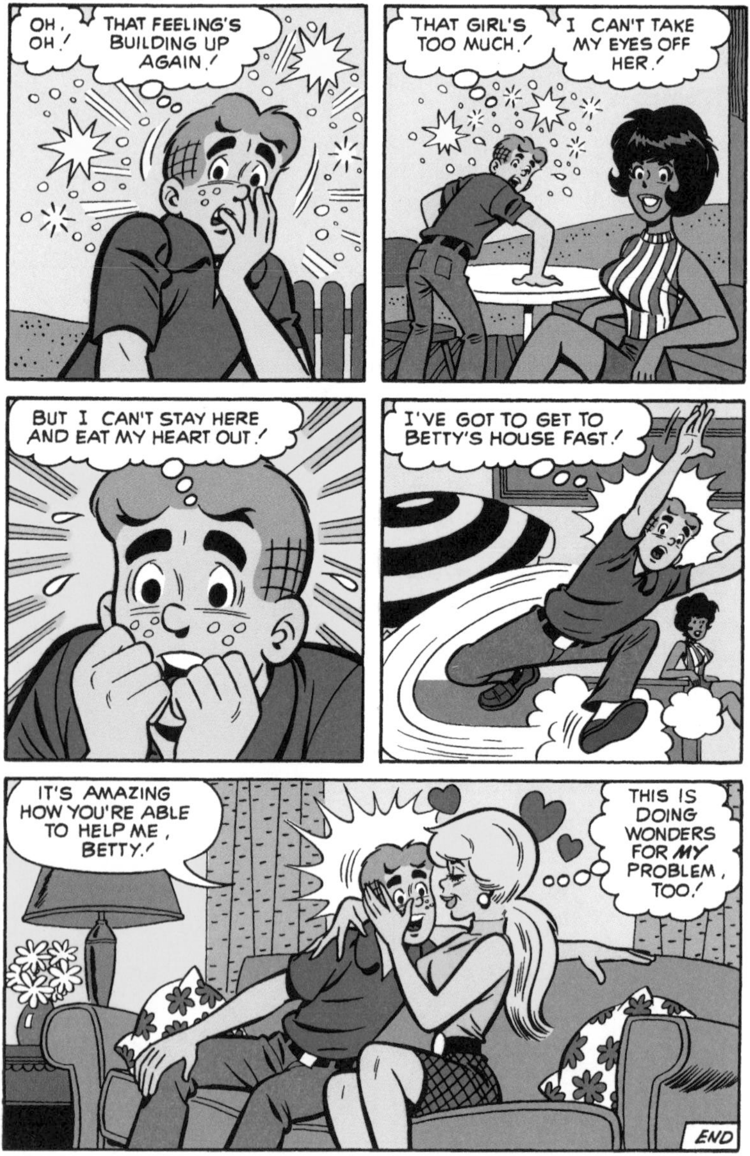
OH, OH!
THAT FEELING'S BUILDING UP AGAIN!
THAT GIRL'S TOO MUCH!
I CAN'T TAKE MY EYES OFF HER!
BUT I CAN'T STAY HERE AND EAT MY HEART OUT!
I'VE GOT TO GET TO BETTY'S HOUSE FAST!
IT'S AMAZING HOW YOU'RE ABLE TO HELP ME, BETTY!
THIS IS DOING WONDERS FOR MY PROBLEM, TOO!
END

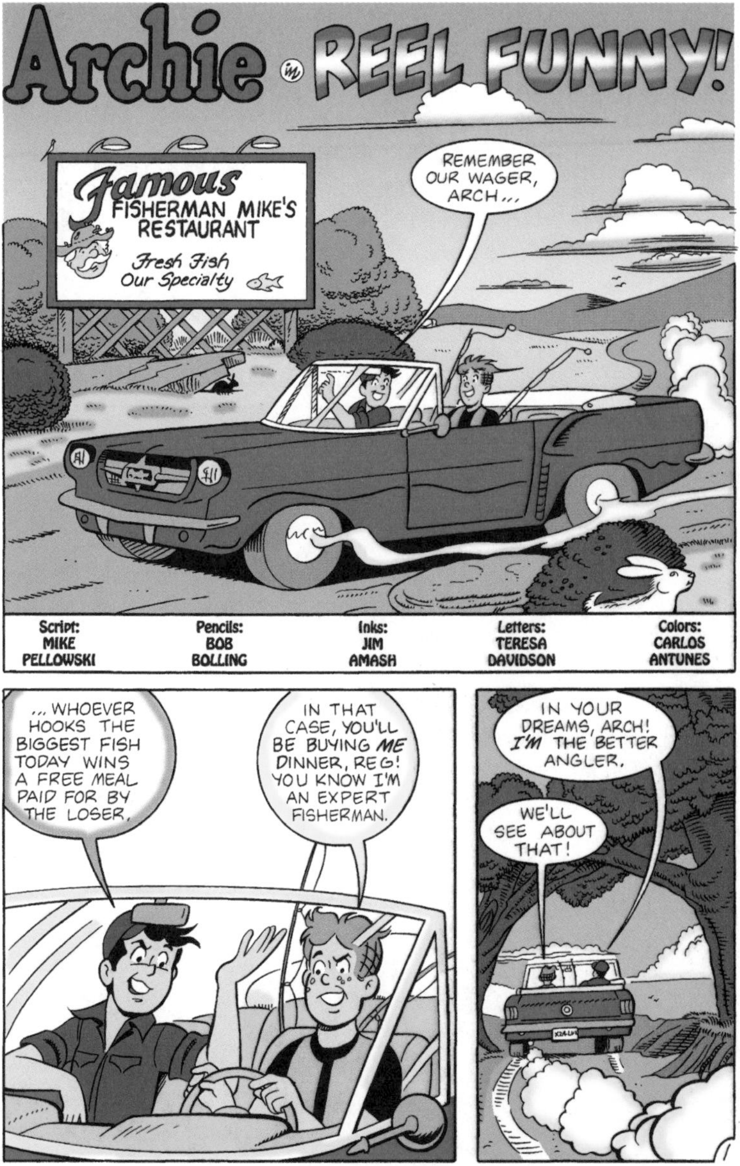
Archie in REEL FUNNY!
Famous FISHERMAN MIKE'S RESTAURANT
Fresh Fish Our Specialty
REMEMBER OUR WAGER, ARCH...
Script: MIKE PELLOWSKI
Pencils: BOB BOLLING
Inks: JIM AMASH
Letters: TERESA DAVIDSON
Colors: CARLOS ANTUNES
...WHOEVER HOOKS THE BIGGEST FISH TODAY WINS A FREE MEAL PAID FOR BY THE LOSER.
IN THAT CASE, YOU'LL BE BUYING *ME* DINNER, REG! YOU KNOW I'M AN EXPERT FISHERMAN.
IN YOUR DREAMS, ARCH! *I'M* THE BETTER ANGLER.
WE'LL SEE ABOUT THAT!

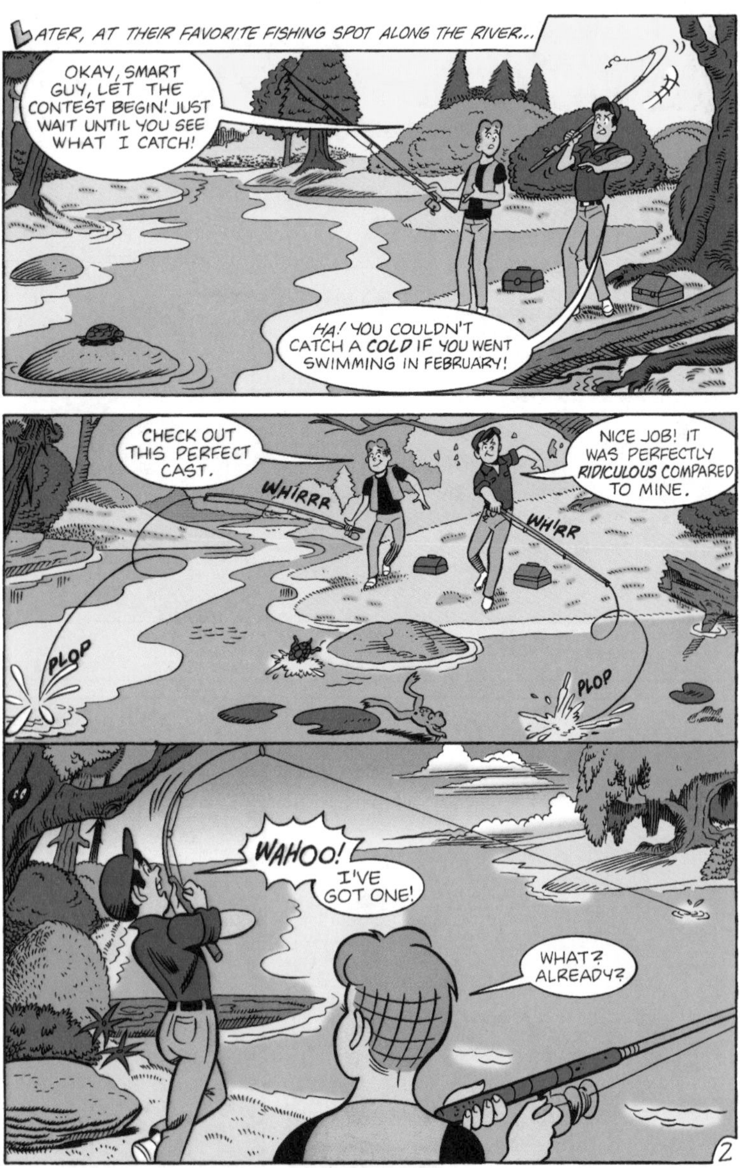
LATER, AT THEIR FAVORITE FISHING SPOT ALONG THE RIVER...
OKAY, SMART GUY, LET THE CONTEST BEGIN! JUST WAIT UNTIL YOU SEE WHAT I CATCH!
HA! YOU COULDN'T CATCH A COLD IF YOU WENT SWIMMING IN FEBRUARY!
CHECK OUT THIS PERFECT CAST.
NICE JOB! IT WAS PERFECTLY RIDICULOUS COMPARED TO MINE.
WHIRRR
WHIRR
PLOP
PLOP
WAHOO!
I'VE GOT ONE!
WHAT? ALREADY?

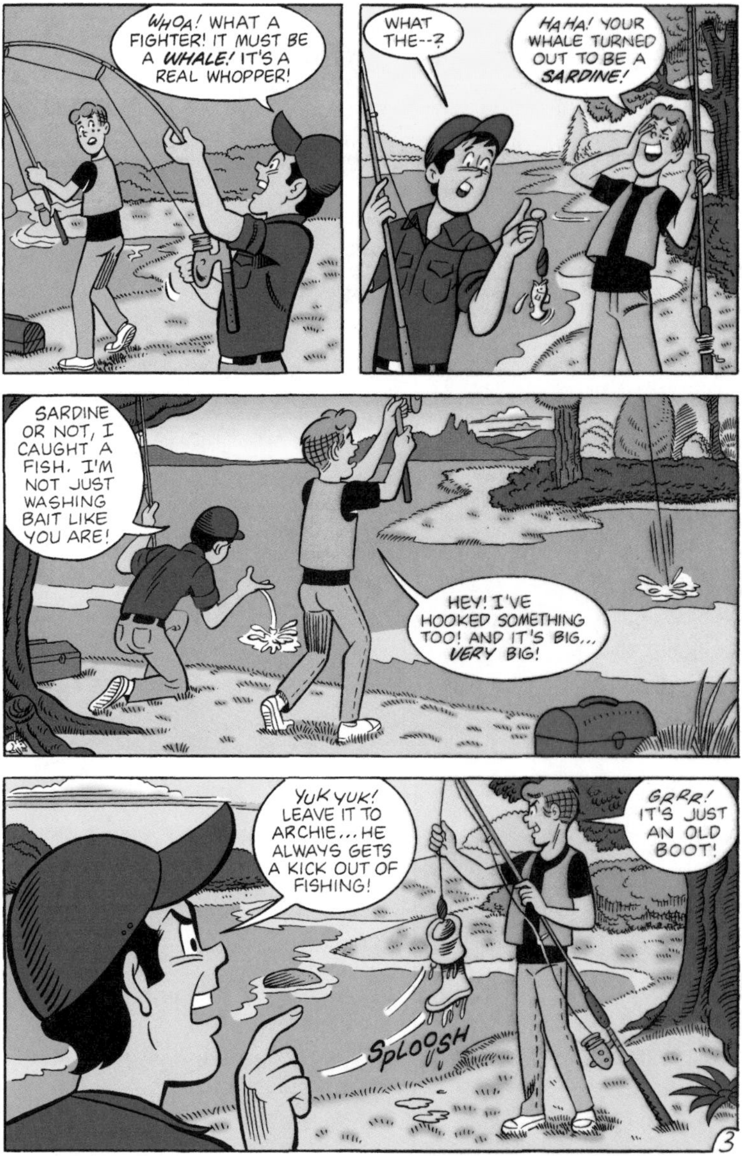
WHOA! WHAT A FIGHTER! IT MUST BE A WHALE! IT'S A REAL WHOPPER!
WHAT THE--?
HAHA! YOUR WHALE TURNED OUT TO BE A SARDINE!
SARDINE OR NOT, I CAUGHT A FISH. I'M NOT JUST WASHING BAIT LIKE YOU ARE!
HEY! I'VE HOOKED SOMETHING TOO! AND IT'S BIG... VERY BIG!
YUK YUK! LEAVE IT TO ARCHIE... HE ALWAYS GETS A KICK OUT OF FISHING!
GRRR! IT'S JUST AN OLD BOOT!
SPLOOSH
3

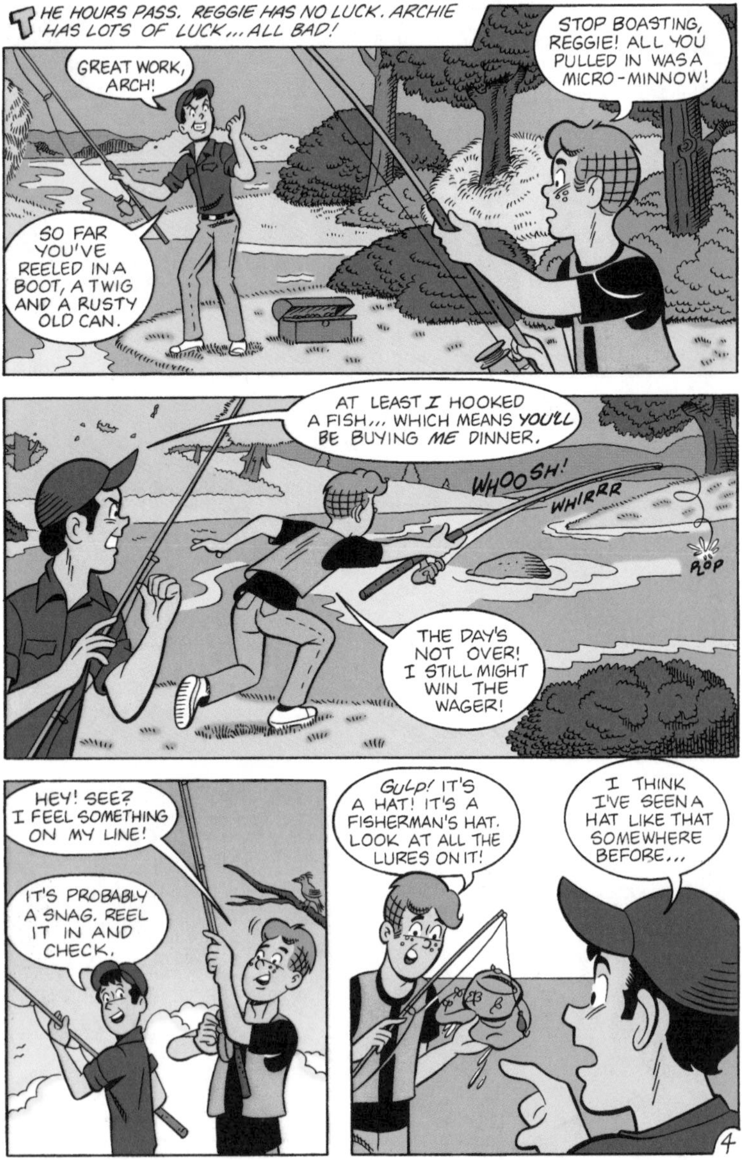
THE HOURS PASS. REGGIE HAS NO LUCK. ARCHIE HAS LOTS OF LUCK... ALL BAD!
GREAT WORK, ARCH!
SO FAR YOU'VE REELED IN A BOOT, A TWIG AND A RUSTY OLD CAN.
STOP BOASTING, REGGIE! ALL YOU PULLED IN WAS A MICRO-MINNOW!
AT LEAST I HOOKED A FISH... WHICH MEANS YOU'LL BE BUYING ME DINNER.
WHOOSH!
WHIRRR
PLOP
THE DAY'S NOT OVER! I STILL MIGHT WIN THE WAGER!
HEY! SEE? I FEEL SOMETHING ON MY LINE!
IT'S PROBABLY A SNAG. REEL IT IN AND CHECK.
GULP! IT'S A HAT! IT'S A FISHERMAN'S HAT. LOOK AT ALL THE LURES ON IT!
I THINK I'VE SEEN A HAT LIKE THAT SOMEWHERE BEFORE...
4

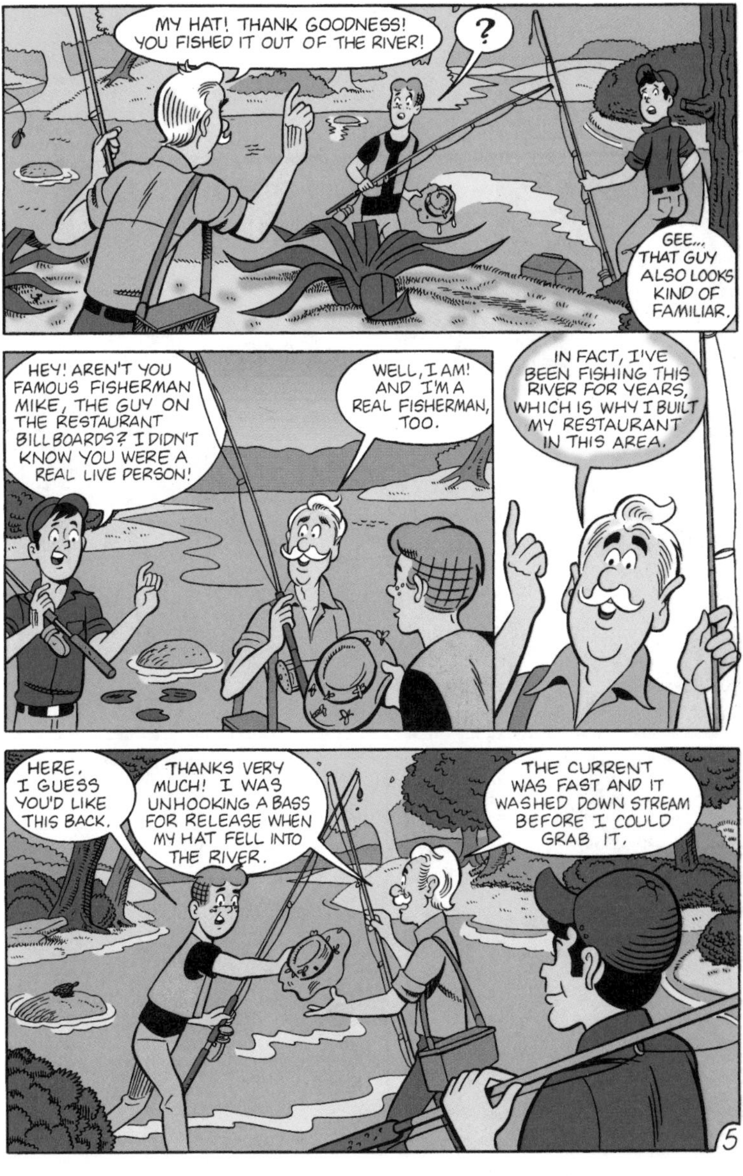
MY HAT! THANK GOODNESS! YOU FISHED IT OUT OF THE RIVER!
?
GEE... THAT GUY ALSO LOOKS KIND OF FAMILIAR.
HEY! AREN'T YOU FAMOUS FISHERMAN MIKE, THE GUY ON THE RESTAURANT BILLBOARDS? I DIDN'T KNOW YOU WERE A REAL LIVE PERSON!
WELL, I AM! AND I'M A REAL FISHERMAN, TOO.
IN FACT, I'VE BEEN FISHING THIS RIVER FOR YEARS, WHICH IS WHY I BUILT MY RESTAURANT IN THIS AREA.
HERE. I GUESS YOU'D LIKE THIS BACK.
THANKS VERY MUCH! I WAS UNHOOKING A BASS FOR RELEASE WHEN MY HAT FELL INTO THE RIVER.
THE CURRENT WAS FAST AND IT WASHED DOWN STREAM BEFORE I COULD GRAB IT.

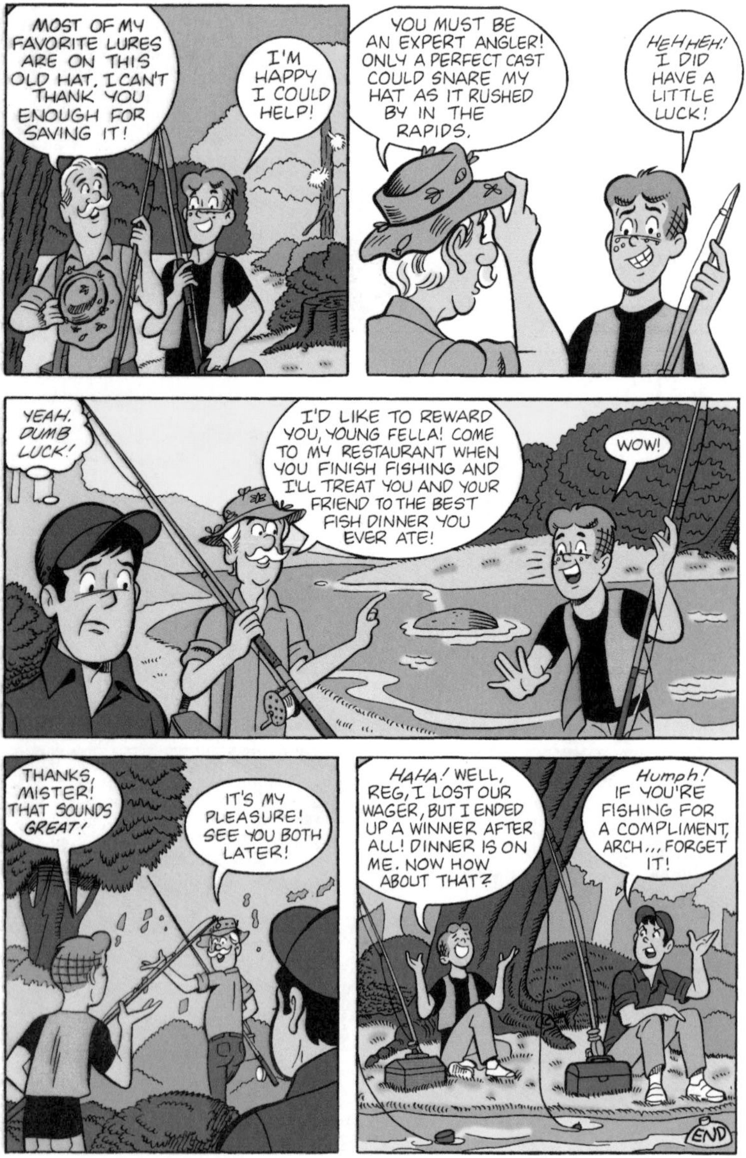

MOST OF MY FAVORITE LURES ARE ON THIS OLD HAT. I CAN'T THANK YOU ENOUGH FOR SAVING IT!
I'M HAPPY I COULD HELP!
YOU MUST BE AN EXPERT ANGLER! ONLY A PERFECT CAST COULD SNARE MY HAT AS IT RUSHED BY IN THE RAPIDS.
HEH HEH! I DID HAVE A LITTLE LUCK!
YEAH. DUMB LUCK!
I'D LIKE TO REWARD YOU, YOUNG FELLA! COME TO MY RESTAURANT WHEN YOU FINISH FISHING AND I'LL TREAT YOU AND YOUR FRIEND TO THE BEST FISH DINNER YOU EVER ATE!
WOW!
THANKS, MISTER! THAT SOUNDS GREAT!
IT'S MY PLEASURE! SEE YOU BOTH LATER!
HAHA! WELL, REG, I LOST OUR WAGER, BUT I ENDED UP A WINNER AFTER ALL! DINNER IS ON ME. NOW HOW ABOUT THAT?
Humph! IF YOU'RE FISHING FOR A COMPLIMENT, ARCH... FORGET IT!
END

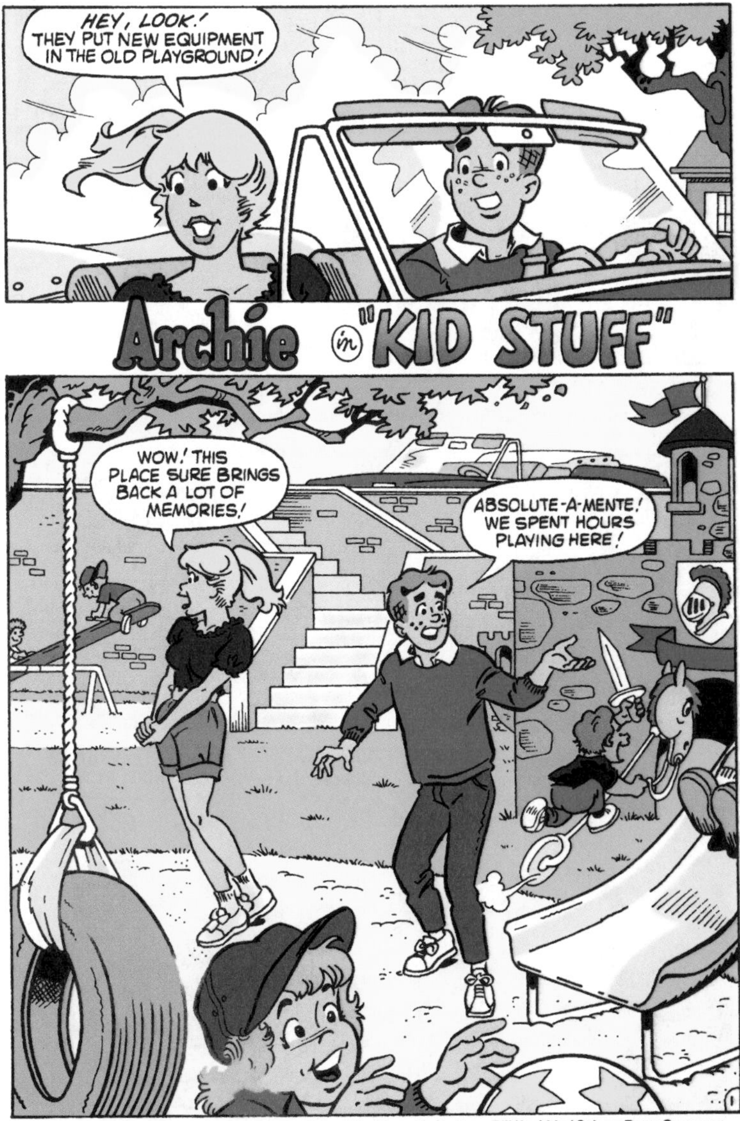

HEY, LOOK! THEY PUT NEW EQUIPMENT IN THE OLD PLAYGROUND!
Archie in "KID STUFF"
WOW! THIS PLACE SURE BRINGS BACK A LOT OF MEMORIES!
ABSOLUTE-A-MENTE! WE SPENT HOURS PLAYING HERE!
1


Script: Mike Pellowski / Pencils: Doug Crane / Inks: Mike Esposito / Letters: Bill Yoshida / Colors: Barry Grossman

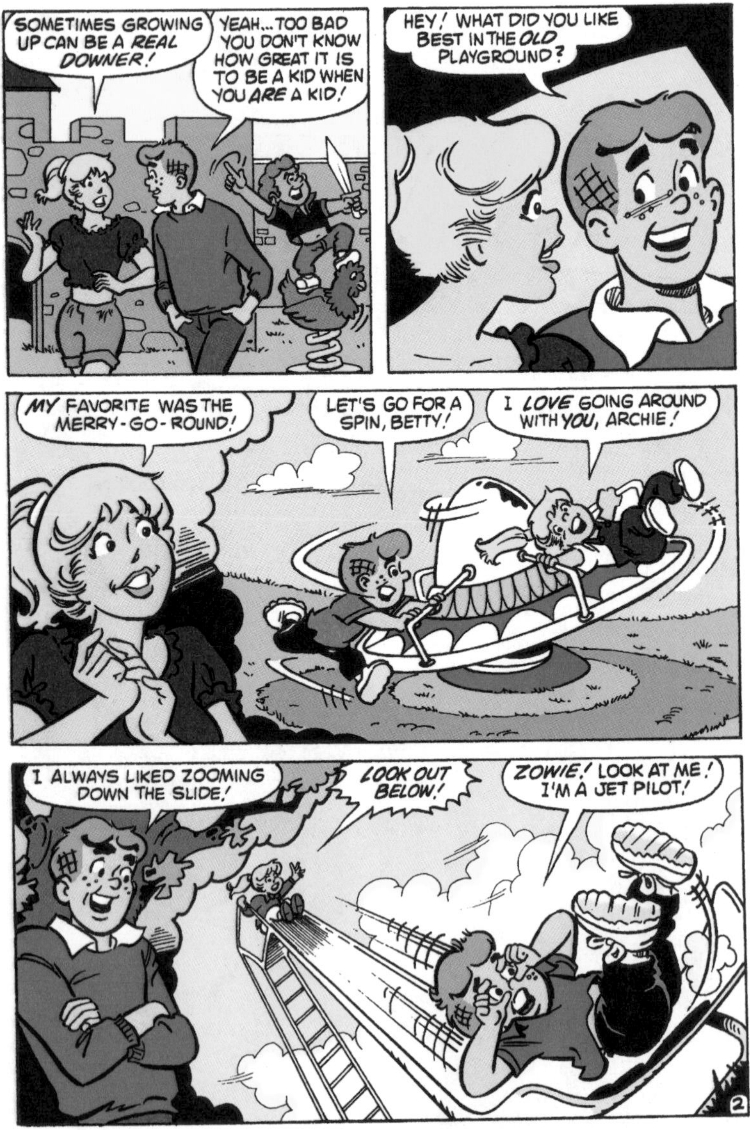

SOMETIMES GROWING UP CAN BE A REAL DOWNER!
YEAH...TOO BAD YOU DON'T KNOW HOW GREAT IT IS TO BE A KID WHEN YOU ARE A KID!
HEY! WHAT DID YOU LIKE BEST IN THE OLD PLAYGROUND?
MY FAVORITE WAS THE MERRY-GO-ROUND!
LET'S GO FOR A SPIN, BETTY!
I LOVE GOING AROUND WITH YOU, ARCHIE!
I ALWAYS LIKED ZOOMING DOWN THE SLIDE!
LOOK OUT BELOW!
ZOWIE! LOOK AT ME! I'M A JET PILOT!
2

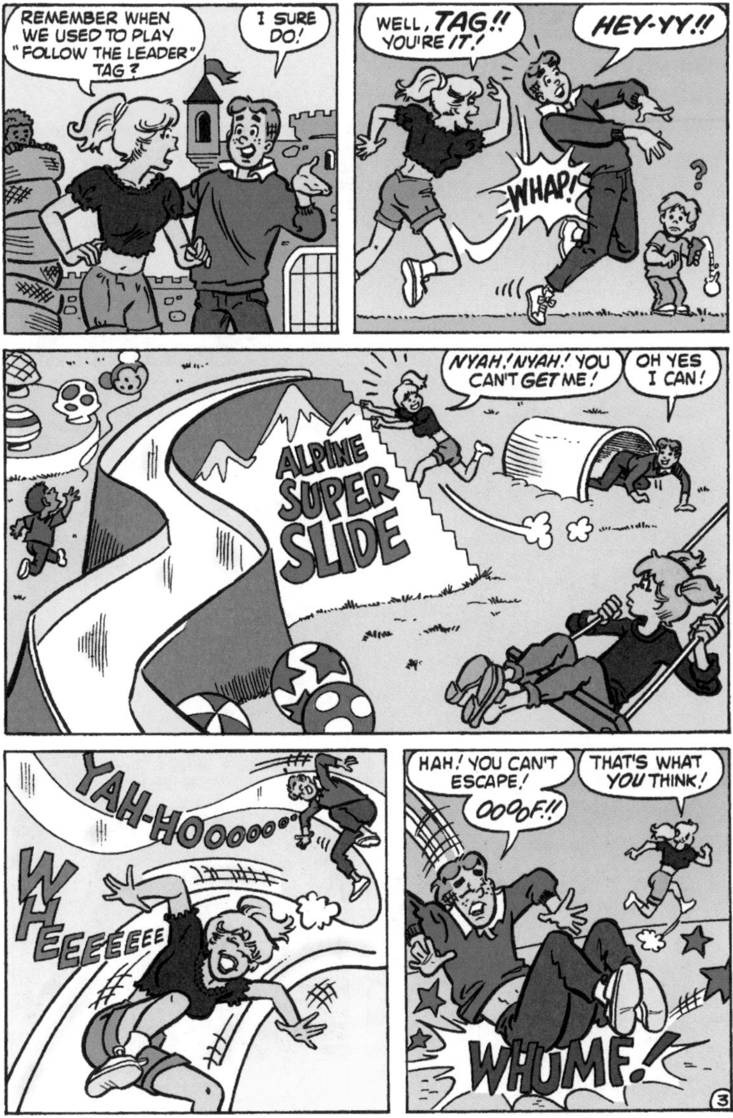
REMEMBER WHEN WE USED TO PLAY "FOLLOW THE LEADER" TAG?
I SURE DO!
WELL, TAG!! YOU'RE IT!
HEY-YY!!
WHAP!
?
ALPINE SUPER SLIDE
NYAH! NYAH! YOU CAN'T GET ME!
OH YES I CAN!
YAH-HOOOOOO
WHEEEEEEE
HAH! YOU CAN'T ESCAPE!
OOOOF!!
THAT'S WHAT YOU THINK!
WHUMF!
3

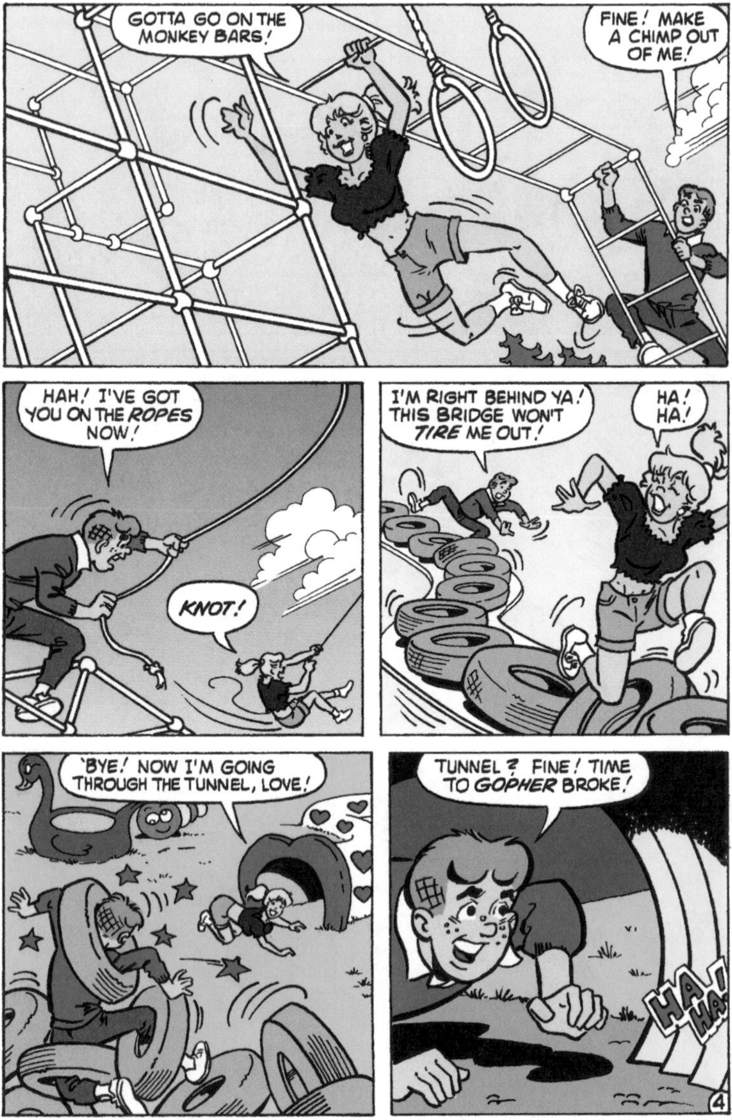

GOTTA GO ON THE MONKEY BARS!
FINE! MAKE A CHIMP OUT OF ME!
HAH! I'VE GOT YOU ON THE *ROPES* NOW!
KNOT!
I'M RIGHT BEHIND YA! THIS BRIDGE WON'T *TIRE* ME OUT!
HA! HA!
'BYE! NOW I'M GOING THROUGH THE TUNNEL, LOVE!
TUNNEL? FINE! TIME TO *GOPHER* BROKE!
HA! HA!
4

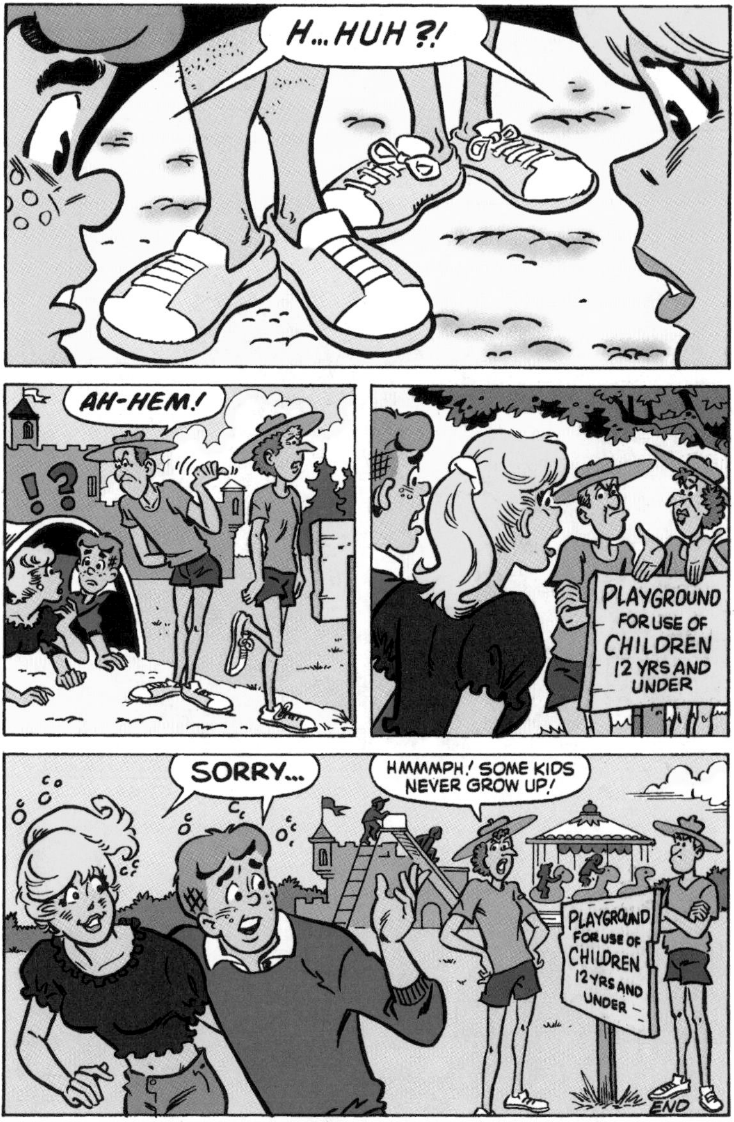
H...HUH ?!
AH-HEM!
PLAYGROUND FOR USE OF CHILDREN 12 YRS AND UNDER
SORRY...
HMMMPH! SOME KIDS NEVER GROW UP!
PLAYGROUND FOR USE OF CHILDREN 12 YRS AND UNDER
END

# Archie in "Bold Cold"

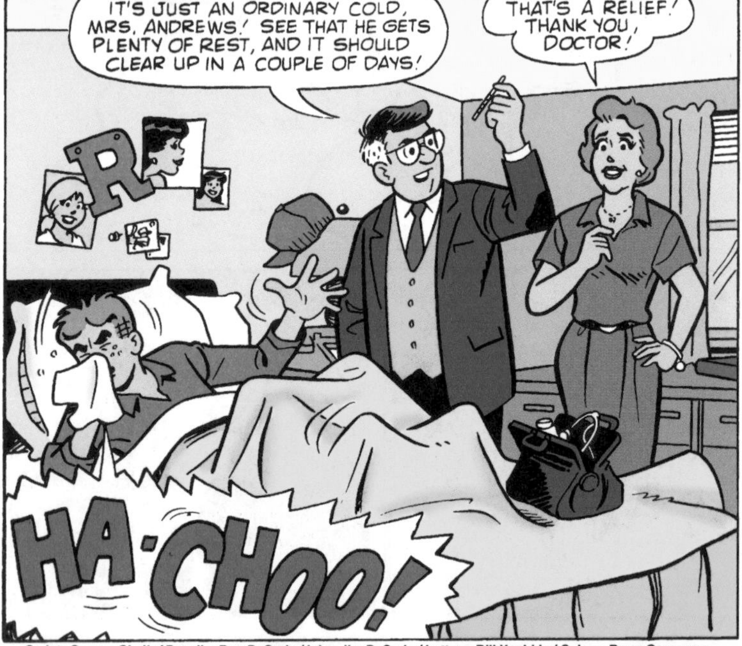
IT'S JUST AN ORDINARY COLD, MRS. ANDREWS! SEE THAT HE GETS PLENTY OF REST, AND IT SHOULD CLEAR UP IN A COUPLE OF DAYS!
THAT'S A RELIEF! THANK YOU, DOCTOR!
HA-CHOO!

Script: George Gladir / Pencils: Dan DeCarlo / Inks: Jim DeCarlo / Letters: Bill Yoshida / Colors: Barry Grossman

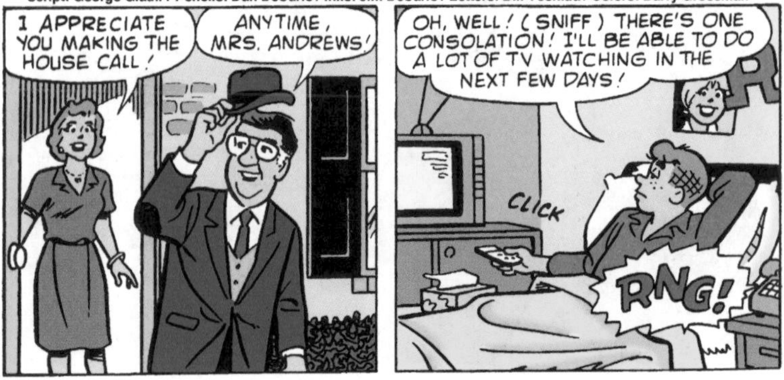
I APPRECIATE YOU MAKING THE HOUSE CALL!
ANYTIME, MRS. ANDREWS!
OH, WELL! (SNIFF) THERE'S ONE CONSOLATION! I'LL BE ABLE TO DO A LOT OF TV WATCHING IN THE NEXT FEW DAYS!
CLICK
RNG!

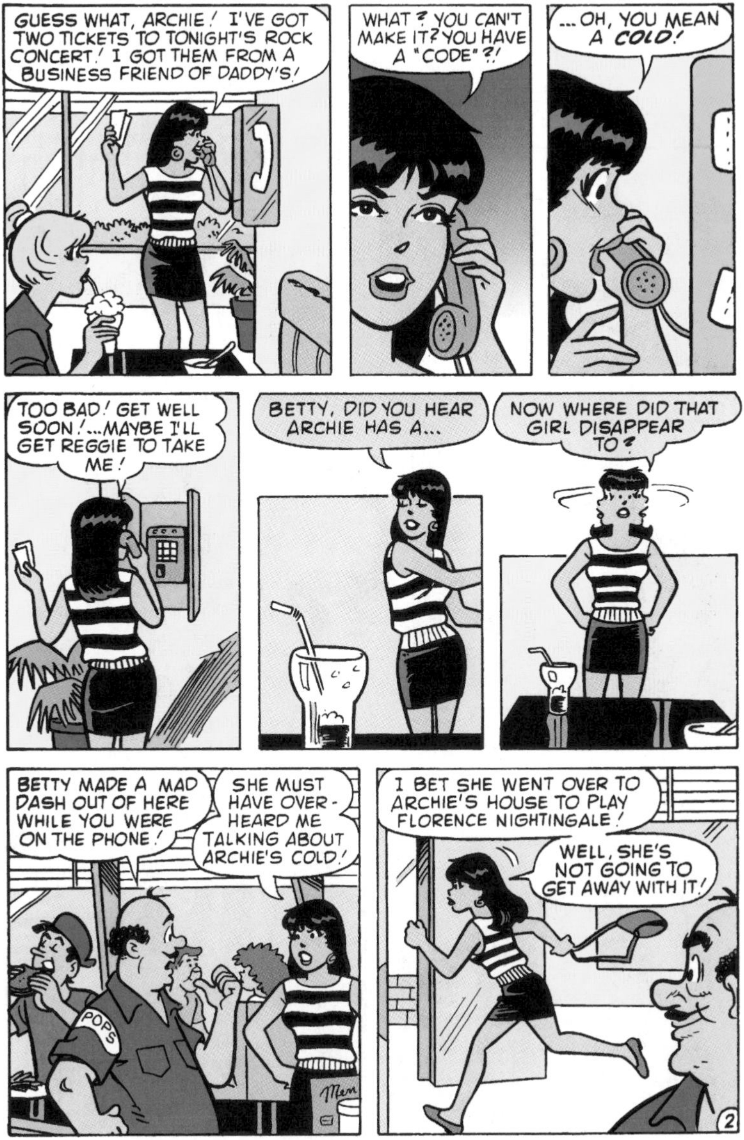
GUESS WHAT, ARCHIE! I'VE GOT TWO TICKETS TO TONIGHT'S ROCK CONCERT! I GOT THEM FROM A BUSINESS FRIEND OF DADDY'S!
WHAT? YOU CAN'T MAKE IT? YOU HAVE A "CODE"?!
...OH, YOU MEAN A COLD!
TOO BAD! GET WELL SOON!...MAYBE I'LL GET REGGIE TO TAKE ME!
BETTY, DID YOU HEAR ARCHIE HAS A...
NOW WHERE DID THAT GIRL DISAPPEAR TO?
BETTY MADE A MAD DASH OUT OF HERE WHILE YOU WERE ON THE PHONE!
SHE MUST HAVE OVER-HEARD ME TALKING ABOUT ARCHIE'S COLD!
POP'S
I BET SHE WENT OVER TO ARCHIE'S HOUSE TO PLAY FLORENCE NIGHTINGALE!
WELL, SHE'S NOT GOING TO GET AWAY WITH IT!
2

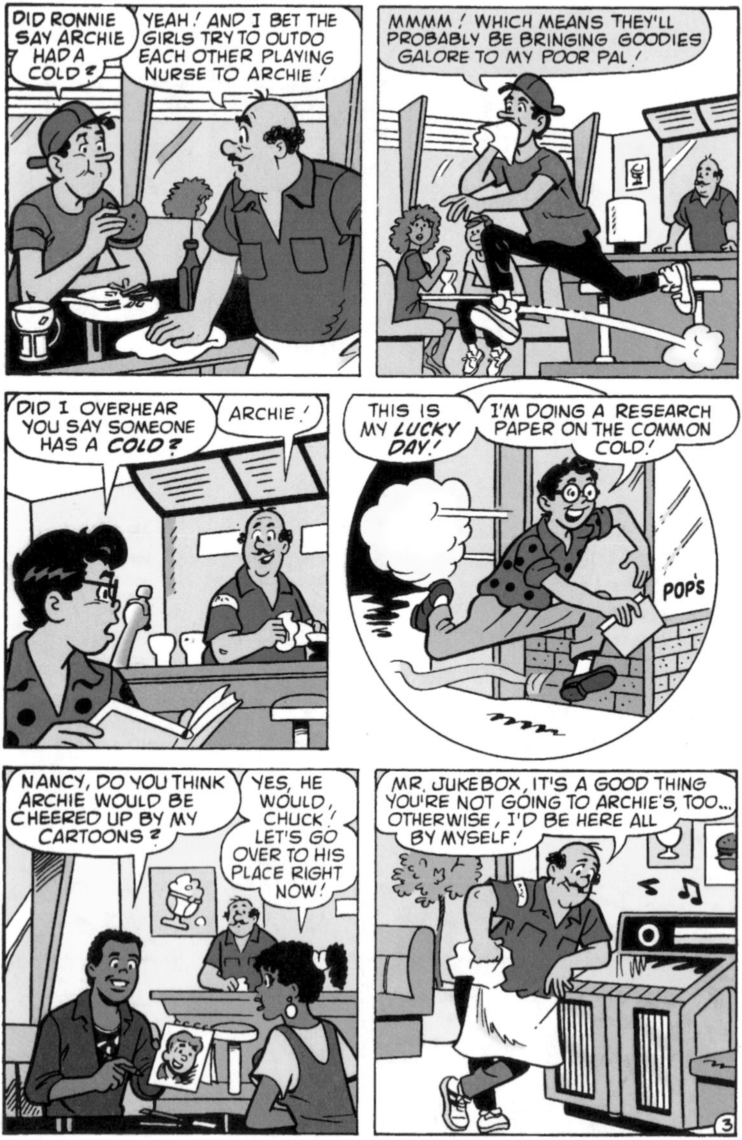
DID RONNIE SAY ARCHIE HAD A COLD?
YEAH! AND I BET THE GIRLS TRY TO OUTDO EACH OTHER PLAYING NURSE TO ARCHIE!
MMMM! WHICH MEANS THEY'LL PROBABLY BE BRINGING GOODIES GALORE TO MY POOR PAL!
DID I OVERHEAR YOU SAY SOMEONE HAS A COLD?
ARCHIE!
THIS IS MY LUCKY DAY!
I'M DOING A RESEARCH PAPER ON THE COMMON COLD!
POP'S
NANCY, DO YOU THINK ARCHIE WOULD BE CHEERED UP BY MY CARTOONS?
YES, HE WOULD, CHUCK! LET'S GO OVER TO HIS PLACE RIGHT NOW!
MR. JUKEBOX, IT'S A GOOD THING YOU'RE NOT GOING TO ARCHIE'S, TOO... OTHERWISE, I'D BE HERE ALL BY MYSELF!
3

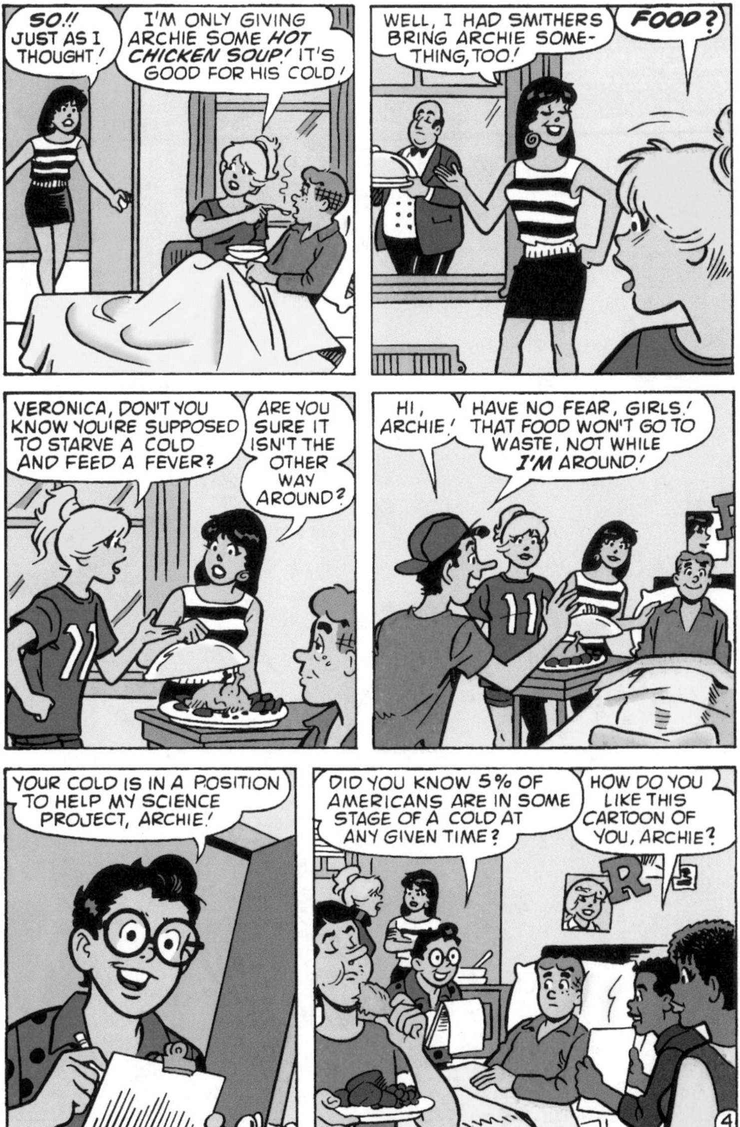
SO!! JUST AS I THOUGHT!
I'M ONLY GIVING ARCHIE SOME HOT CHICKEN SOUP! IT'S GOOD FOR HIS COLD!
WELL, I HAD SMITHERS BRING ARCHIE SOME-THING, TOO!
FOOD?
VERONICA, DON'T YOU KNOW YOU'RE SUPPOSED TO STARVE A COLD AND FEED A FEVER?
ARE YOU SURE IT ISN'T THE OTHER WAY AROUND?
HI, ARCHIE!
HAVE NO FEAR, GIRLS! THAT FOOD WON'T GO TO WASTE, NOT WHILE I'M AROUND!
YOUR COLD IS IN A POSITION TO HELP MY SCIENCE PROJECT, ARCHIE!
DID YOU KNOW 5% OF AMERICANS ARE IN SOME STAGE OF A COLD AT ANY GIVEN TIME?
HOW DO YOU LIKE THIS CARTOON OF YOU, ARCHIE?
4

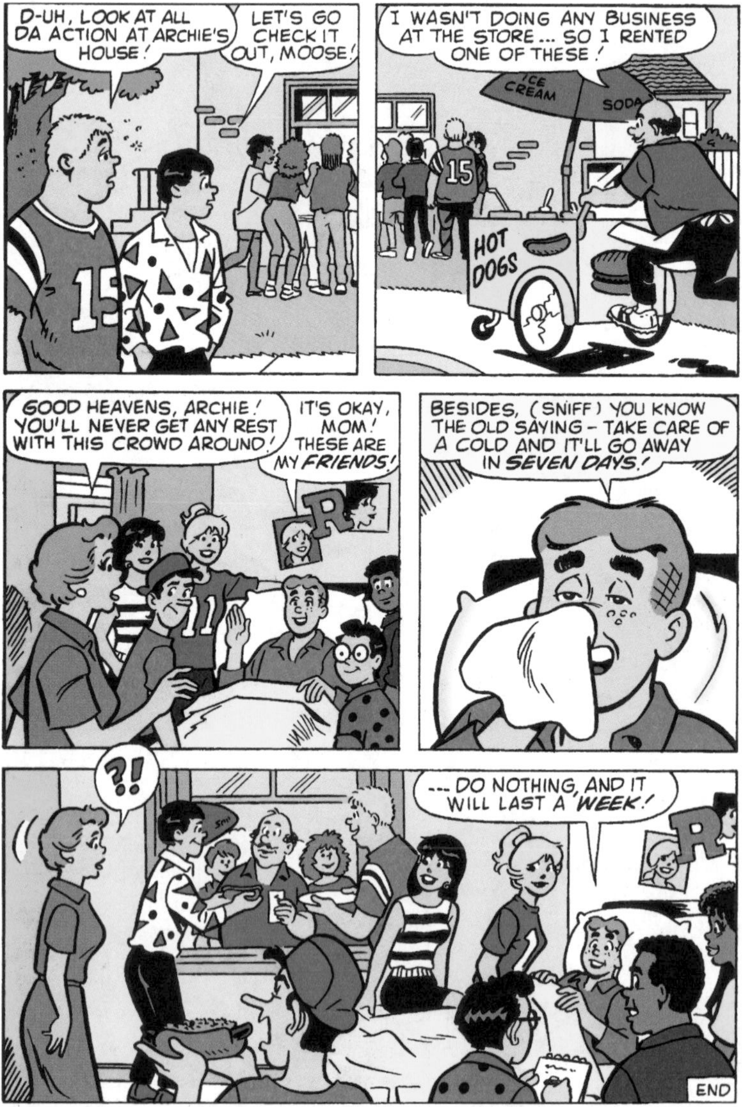

D-UH, LOOK AT ALL DA ACTION AT ARCHIE'S HOUSE!
LET'S GO CHECK IT OUT, MOOSE!
I WASN'T DOING ANY BUSINESS AT THE STORE... SO I RENTED ONE OF THESE!
ICE CREAM
SODA
HOT DOGS
15
GOOD HEAVENS, ARCHIE! YOU'LL NEVER GET ANY REST WITH THIS CROWD AROUND!
IT'S OKAY, MOM! THESE ARE MY FRIENDS!
BESIDES, (SNIFF) YOU KNOW THE OLD SAYING - TAKE CARE OF A COLD AND IT'LL GO AWAY IN SEVEN DAYS!
?!
--- DO NOTHING, AND IT WILL LAST A WEEK!
END

# Betty and Veronica in "Instant Fun!"

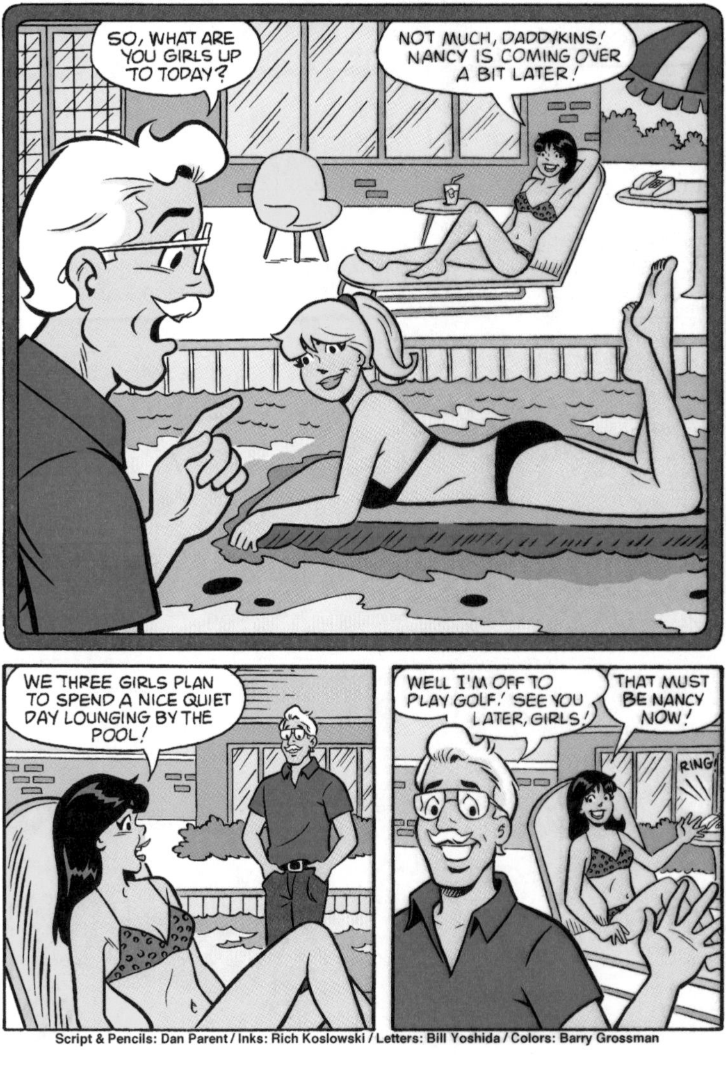

SO, WHAT ARE YOU GIRLS UP TO TODAY?
NOT MUCH, DADDYKINS! NANCY IS COMING OVER A BIT LATER!
WE THREE GIRLS PLAN TO SPEND A NICE QUIET DAY LOUNGING BY THE POOL!
WELL I'M OFF TO PLAY GOLF! SEE YOU LATER, GIRLS!
THAT MUST BE NANCY NOW!
RING


Script & Pencils: Dan Parent / Inks: Rich Koslowski / Letters: Bill Yoshida / Colors: Barry Grossman

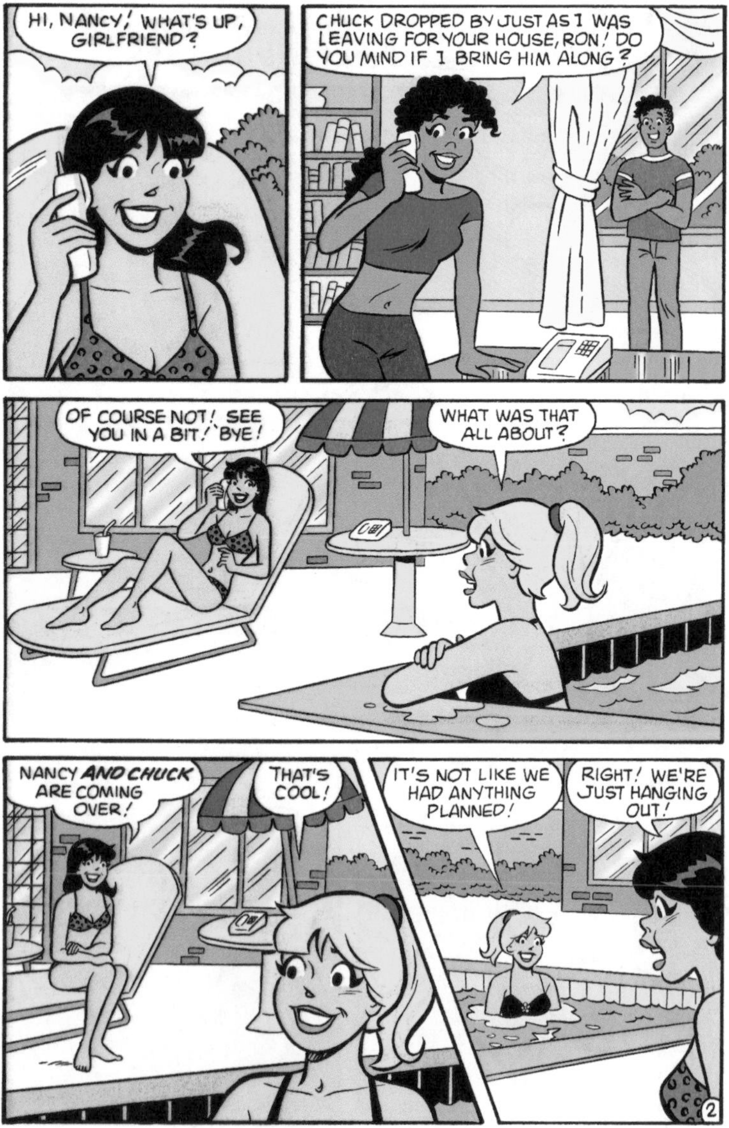
HI, NANCY! WHAT'S UP, GIRLFRIEND?
CHUCK DROPPED BY JUST AS I WAS LEAVING FOR YOUR HOUSE, RON! DO YOU MIND IF I BRING HIM ALONG?
OF COURSE NOT! SEE YOU IN A BIT! BYE!
WHAT WAS THAT ALL ABOUT?
NANCY AND CHUCK ARE COMING OVER!
THAT'S COOL!
IT'S NOT LIKE WE HAD ANYTHING PLANNED!
RIGHT! WE'RE JUST HANGING OUT!
2

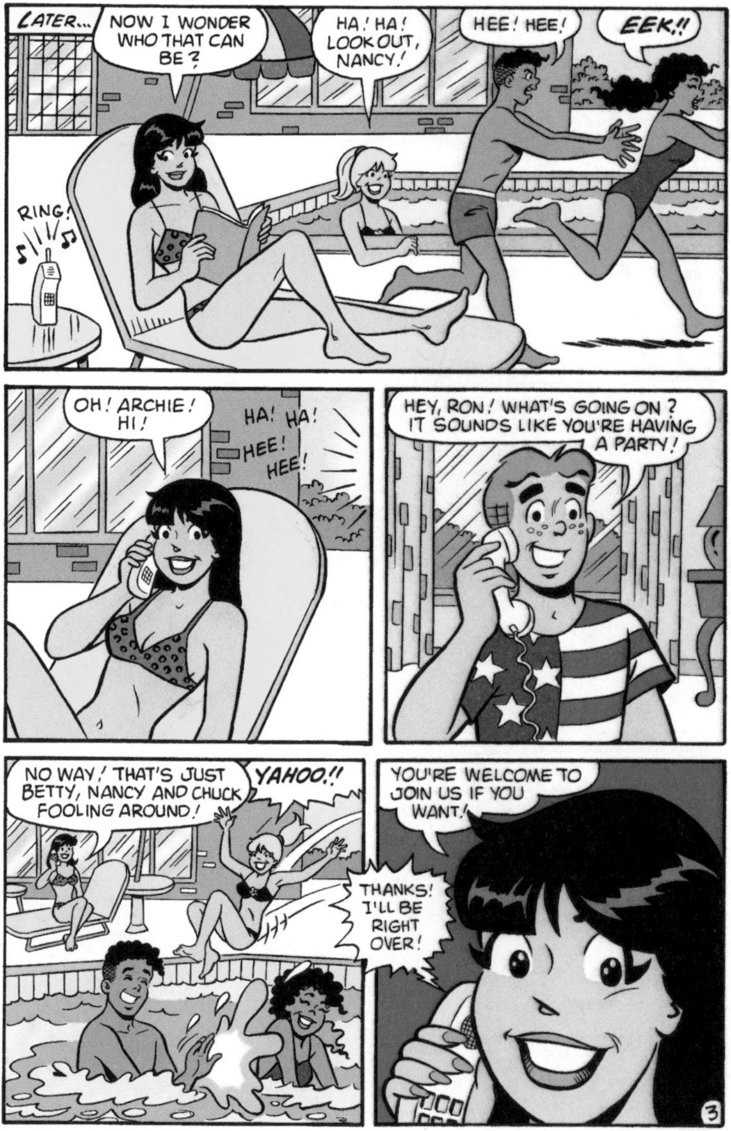
LATER...
NOW I WONDER WHO THAT CAN BE ?
HA! HA! LOOK OUT, NANCY!
HEE! HEE!
EEK!!
RING!
OH! ARCHIE! HI!
HA! HA!
HEE! HEE!
HEY, RON! WHAT'S GOING ON? IT SOUNDS LIKE YOU'RE HAVING A PARTY!
NO WAY! THAT'S JUST BETTY, NANCY AND CHUCK FOOLING AROUND!
YAHOO!!
YOU'RE WELCOME TO JOIN US IF YOU WANT!
THANKS! I'LL BE RIGHT OVER!
3

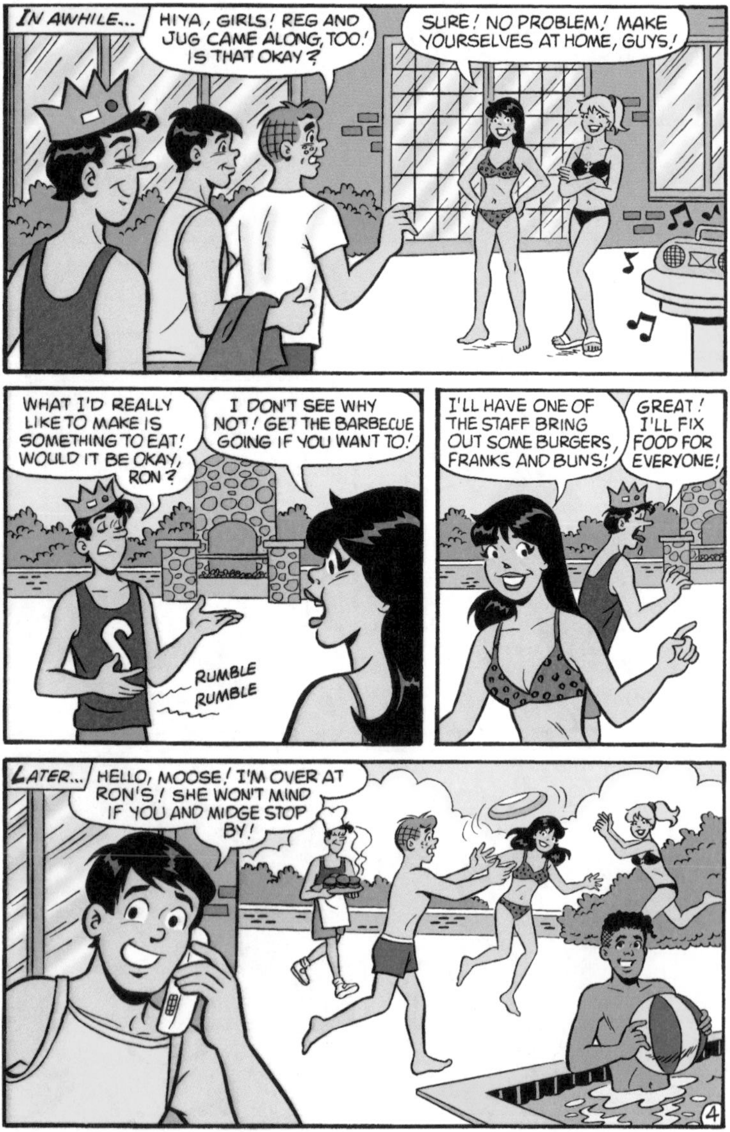
IN AWHILE...
HIYA, GIRLS! REG AND JUG CAME ALONG, TOO! IS THAT OKAY?
SURE! NO PROBLEM! MAKE YOURSELVES AT HOME, GUYS!
WHAT I'D REALLY LIKE TO MAKE IS SOMETHING TO EAT! WOULD IT BE OKAY, RON?
I DON'T SEE WHY NOT! GET THE BARBECUE GOING IF YOU WANT TO!
RUMBLE
RUMBLE
I'LL HAVE ONE OF THE STAFF BRING OUT SOME BURGERS, FRANKS AND BUNS!
GREAT! I'LL FIX FOOD FOR EVERYONE!
LATER...
HELLO, MOOSE! I'M OVER AT RON'S! SHE WON'T MIND IF YOU AND MIDGE STOP BY!
4

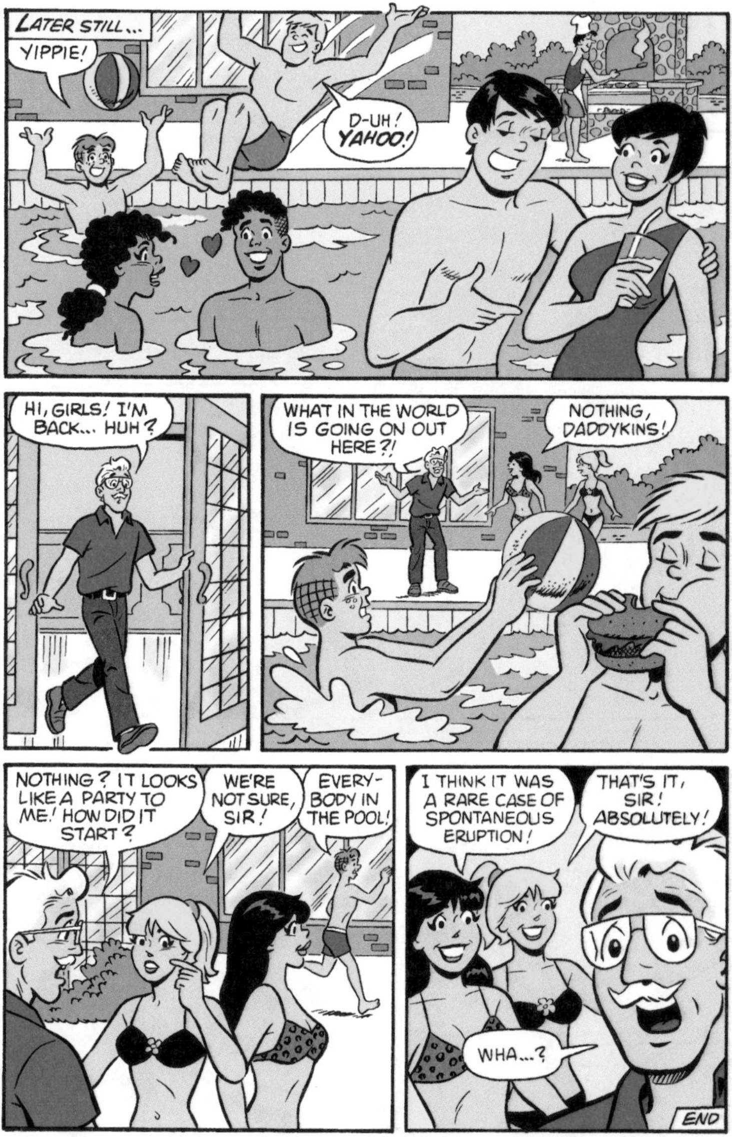
LATER STILL...
YIPPIE!
D-UH! YAHOO!
HI, GIRLS! I'M BACK... HUH?
WHAT IN THE WORLD IS GOING ON OUT HERE?!
NOTHING, DADDYKINS!
NOTHING? IT LOOKS LIKE A PARTY TO ME! HOW DID IT START?
WE'RE NOT SURE, SIR!
EVERY-BODY IN THE POOL!
I THINK IT WAS A RARE CASE OF SPONTANEOUS ERUPTION!
THAT'S IT, SIR! ABSOLUTELY!
WHA...?
END

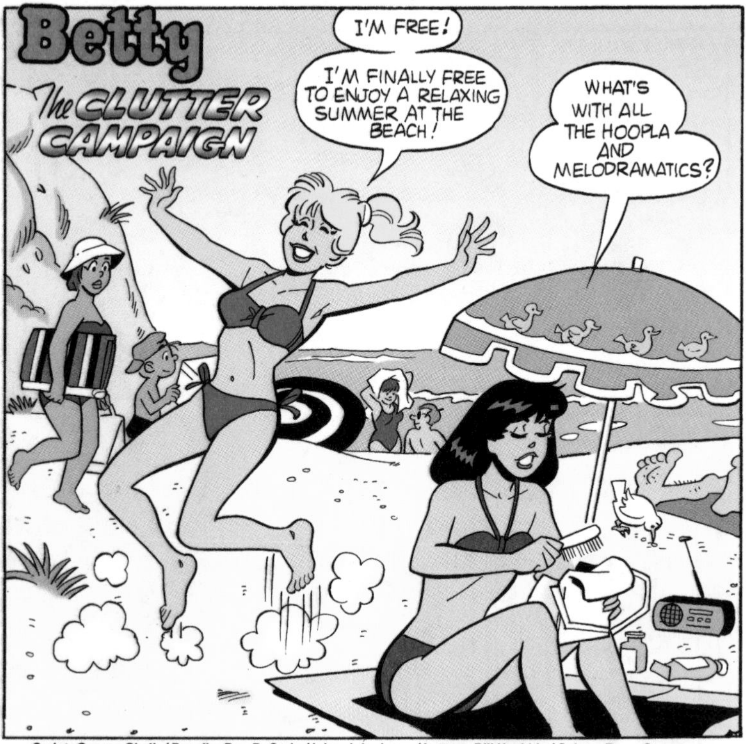
Betty
The CLUTTER CAMPAIGN
I'M FREE!
I'M FINALLY FREE TO ENJOY A RELAXING SUMMER AT THE BEACH!
WHAT'S WITH ALL THE HOOPLA AND MELODRAMATICS?

Script: George Gladir / Pencils: Dan DeCarlo / Inks: John Lowe / Letters: Bill Yoshida / Colors: Barry Grossman

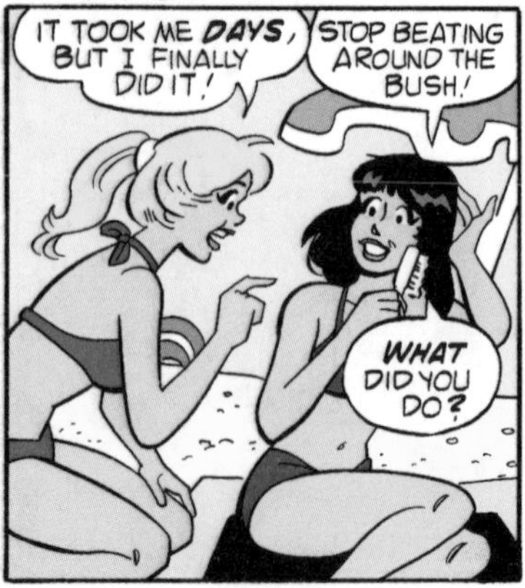
IT TOOK ME DAYS, BUT I FINALLY DID IT!
STOP BEATING AROUND THE BUSH!
WHAT DID YOU DO?

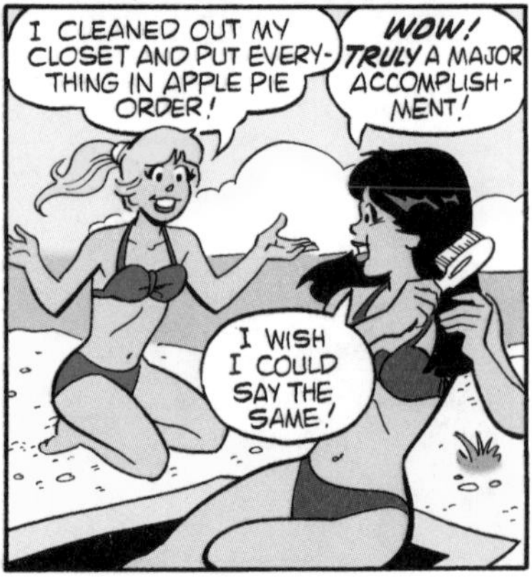
I CLEANED OUT MY CLOSET AND PUT EVERY-THING IN APPLE PIE ORDER!
WOW! TRULY A MAJOR ACCOMPLISH-MENT!
I WISH I COULD SAY THE SAME!

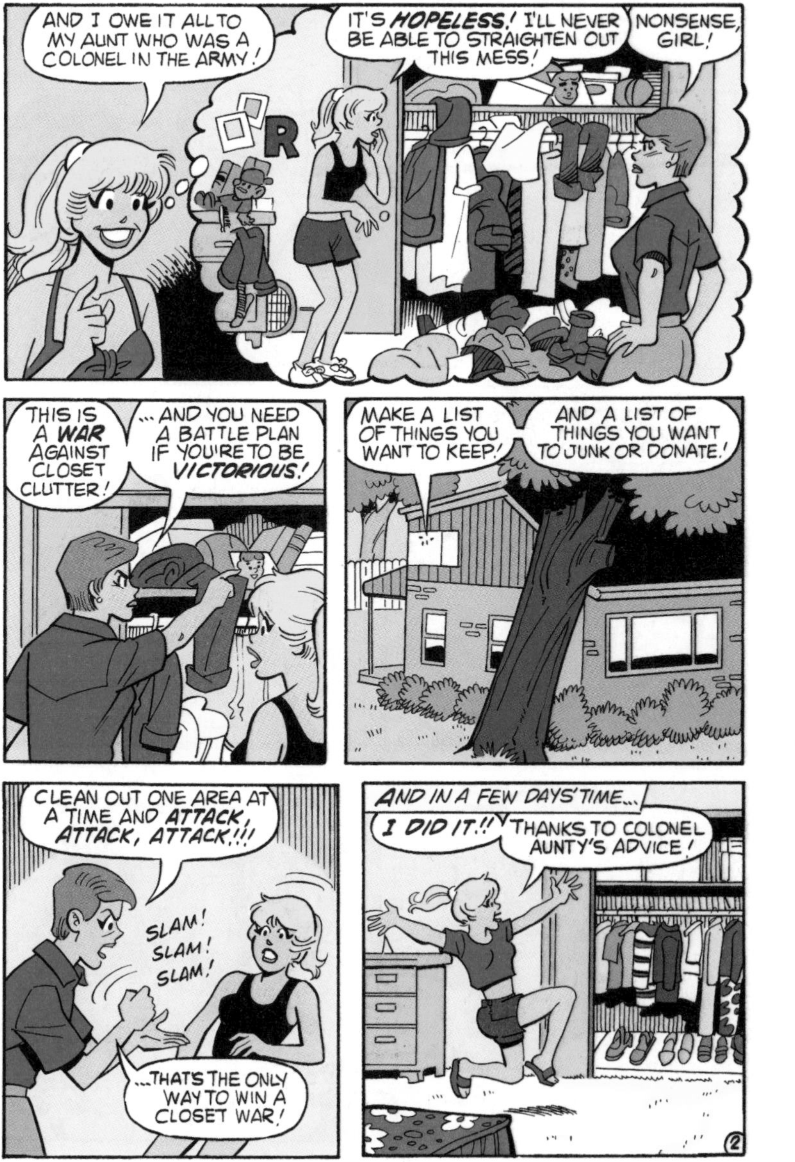
AND I OWE IT ALL TO MY AUNT WHO WAS A COLONEL IN THE ARMY!
IT'S HOPELESS! I'LL NEVER BE ABLE TO STRAIGHTEN OUT THIS MESS!
NONSENSE, GIRL!
THIS IS A WAR AGAINST CLOSET CLUTTER!
...AND YOU NEED A BATTLE PLAN IF YOU'RE TO BE VICTORIOUS!
MAKE A LIST OF THINGS YOU WANT TO KEEP!
AND A LIST OF THINGS YOU WANT TO JUNK OR DONATE!
CLEAN OUT ONE AREA AT A TIME AND ATTACK, ATTACK, ATTACK!!!
SLAM! SLAM! SLAM!
...THAT'S THE ONLY WAY TO WIN A CLOSET WAR!
AND IN A FEW DAYS' TIME...
I DID IT!!
THANKS TO COLONEL AUNTY'S ADVICE!
2

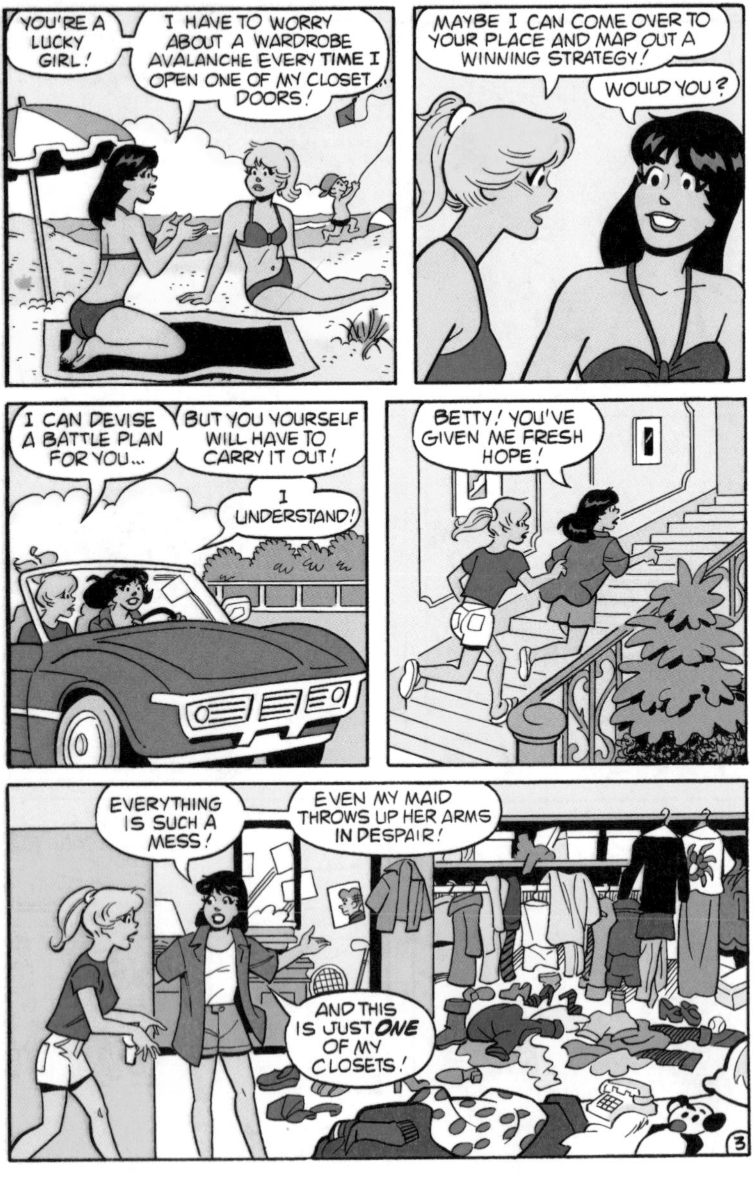
YOU'RE A LUCKY GIRL!
I HAVE TO WORRY ABOUT A WARDROBE AVALANCHE EVERY TIME I OPEN ONE OF MY CLOSET DOORS!
MAYBE I CAN COME OVER TO YOUR PLACE AND MAP OUT A WINNING STRATEGY!
WOULD YOU?
I CAN DEVISE A BATTLE PLAN FOR YOU...
BUT YOU YOURSELF WILL HAVE TO CARRY IT OUT!
I UNDERSTAND!
BETTY! YOU'VE GIVEN ME FRESH HOPE!
EVERYTHING IS SUCH A MESS!
EVEN MY MAID THROWS UP HER ARMS IN DESPAIR!
AND THIS IS JUST ONE OF MY CLOSETS!
3

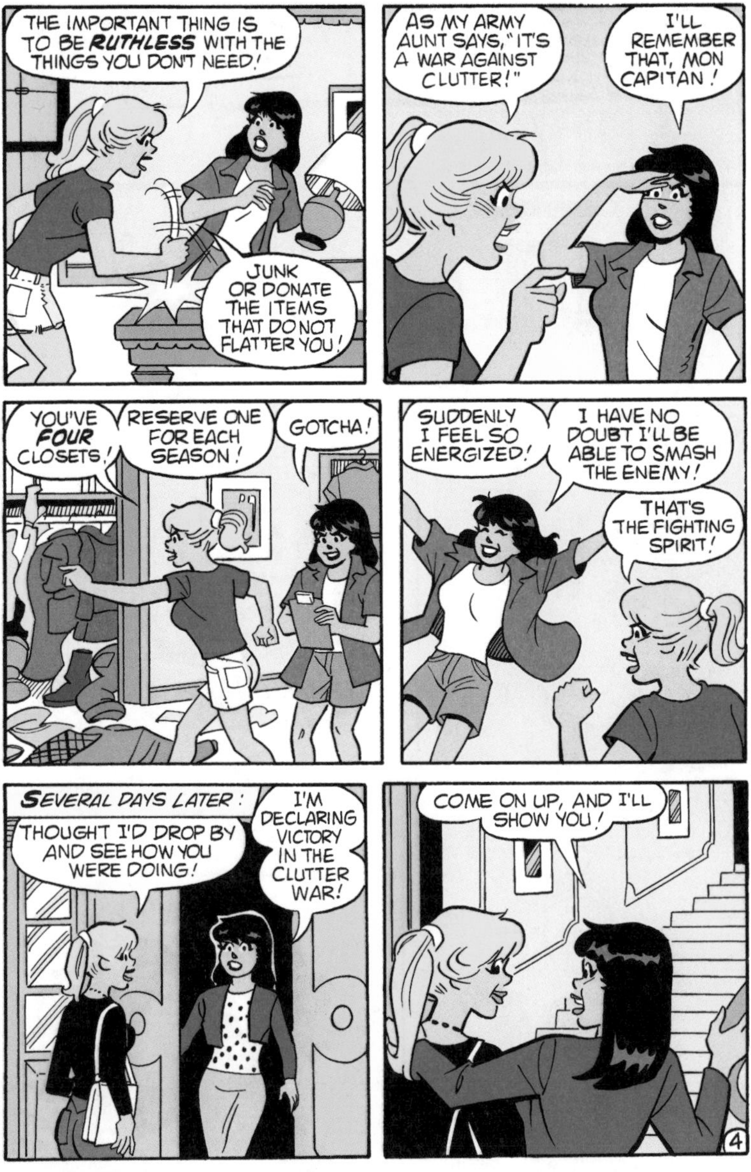
THE IMPORTANT THING IS TO BE RUTHLESS WITH THE THINGS YOU DON'T NEED!
JUNK OR DONATE THE ITEMS THAT DO NOT FLATTER YOU!
AS MY ARMY AUNT SAYS, "IT'S A WAR AGAINST CLUTTER!"
I'LL REMEMBER THAT, MON CAPITAN!
YOU'VE FOUR CLOSETS!
RESERVE ONE FOR EACH SEASON!
GOTCHA!
SUDDENLY I FEEL SO ENERGIZED!
I HAVE NO DOUBT I'LL BE ABLE TO SMASH THE ENEMY!
THAT'S THE FIGHTING SPIRIT!
SEVERAL DAYS LATER:
THOUGHT I'D DROP BY AND SEE HOW YOU WERE DOING!
I'M DECLARING VICTORY IN THE CLUTTER WAR!
COME ON UP, AND I'LL SHOW YOU!
4

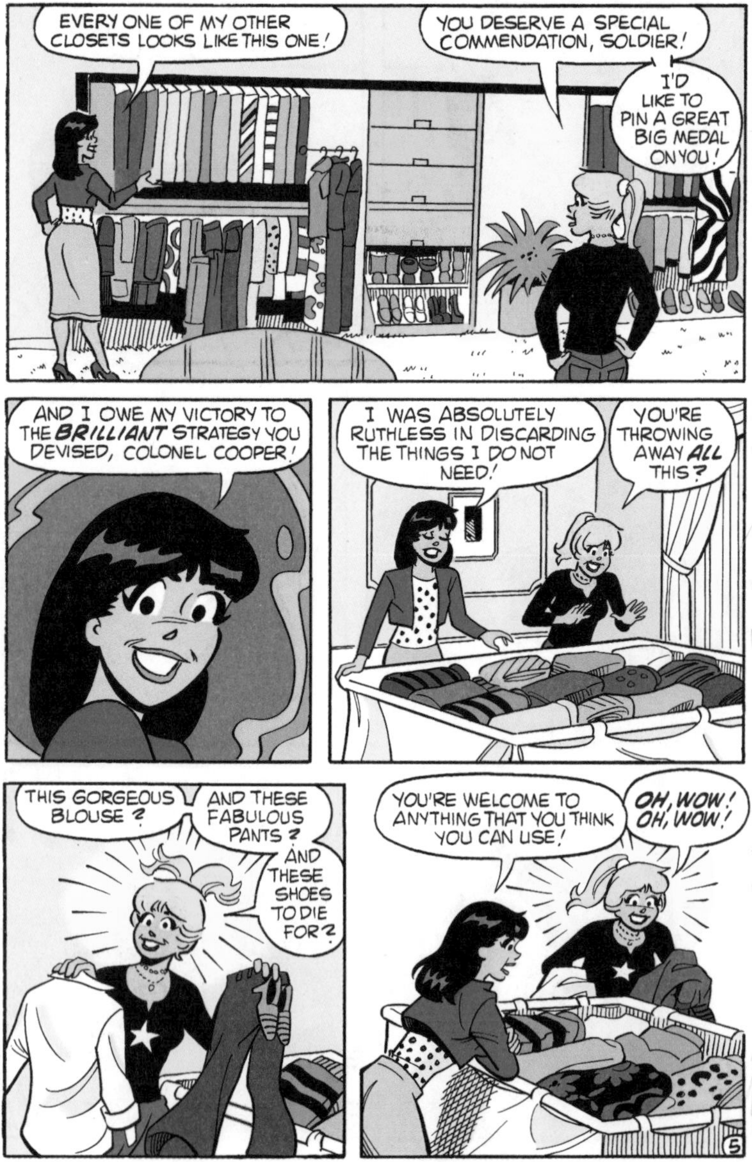

EVERY ONE OF MY OTHER CLOSETS LOOKS LIKE THIS ONE!
YOU DESERVE A SPECIAL COMMENDATION, SOLDIER!
I'D LIKE TO PIN A GREAT BIG MEDAL ON YOU!
AND I OWE MY VICTORY TO THE **BRILLIANT** STRATEGY YOU DEVISED, COLONEL COOPER!
I WAS ABSOLUTELY RUTHLESS IN DISCARDING THE THINGS I DO NOT NEED!
YOU'RE THROWING AWAY **ALL** THIS?
THIS GORGEOUS BLOUSE?
AND THESE FABULOUS PANTS?
AND THESE SHOES TO DIE FOR?
YOU'RE WELCOME TO ANYTHING THAT YOU THINK YOU CAN USE!
**OH, WOW! OH, WOW!**
5

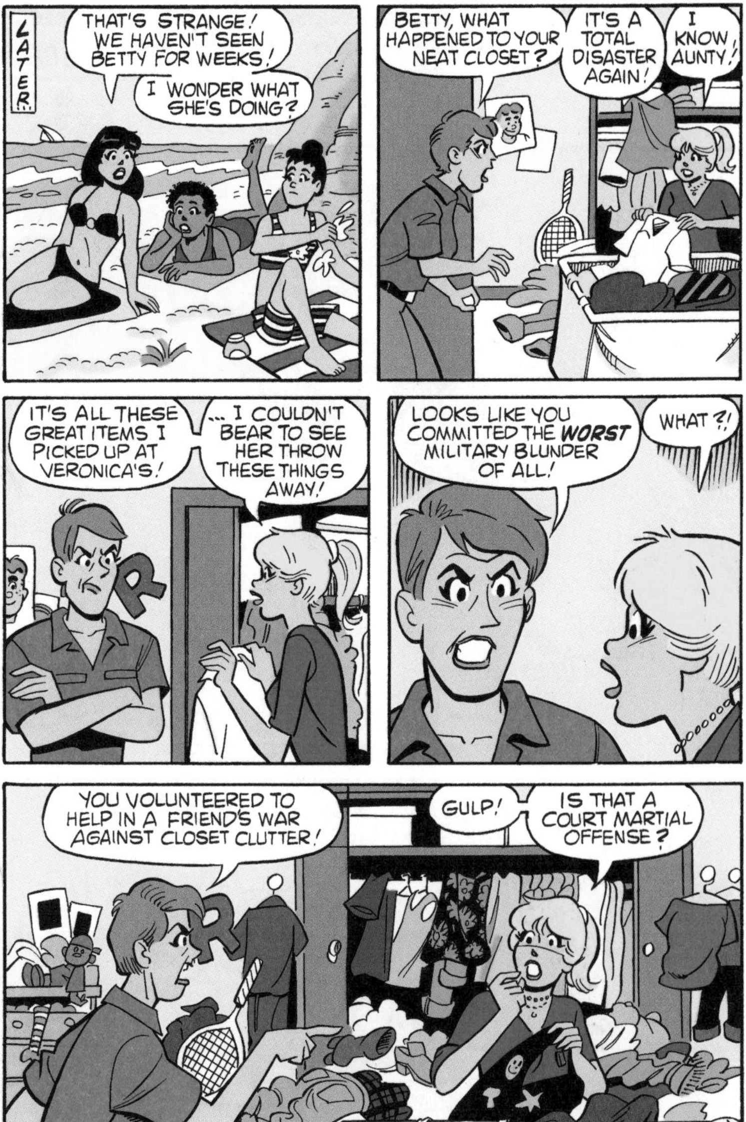
LATER...
THAT'S STRANGE! WE HAVEN'T SEEN BETTY FOR WEEKS!
I WONDER WHAT SHE'S DOING?
BETTY, WHAT HAPPENED TO YOUR NEAT CLOSET?
IT'S A TOTAL DISASTER AGAIN!
I KNOW, AUNTY!
IT'S ALL THESE GREAT ITEMS I PICKED UP AT VERONICA'S!
... I COULDN'T BEAR TO SEE HER THROW THESE THINGS AWAY!
LOOKS LIKE YOU COMMITTED THE WORST MILITARY BLUNDER OF ALL!
WHAT?!
YOU VOLUNTEERED TO HELP IN A FRIEND'S WAR AGAINST CLOSET CLUTTER!
GULP!
IS THAT A COURT MARTIAL OFFENSE?
End

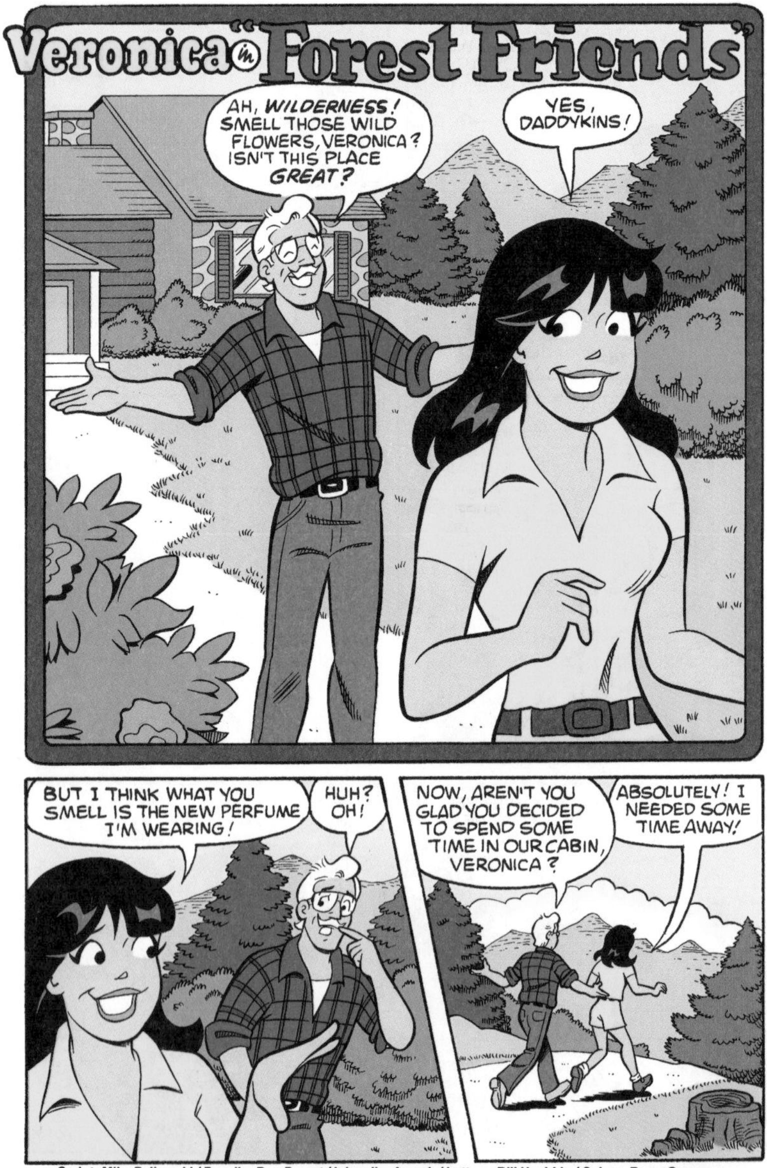
Veronica in "Forest Friends"
AH, WILDERNESS! SMELL THOSE WILD FLOWERS, VERONICA? ISN'T THIS PLACE GREAT?
YES, DADDYKINS!
BUT I THINK WHAT YOU SMELL IS THE NEW PERFUME I'M WEARING!
HUH? OH!
NOW, AREN'T YOU GLAD YOU DECIDED TO SPEND SOME TIME IN OUR CABIN, VERONICA?
ABSOLUTELY! I NEEDED SOME TIME AWAY!

Script: Mike Pellowski / Pencils: Dan Parent / Inks: Jim Amash / Letters: Bill Yoshida / Colors: Barry Grossman

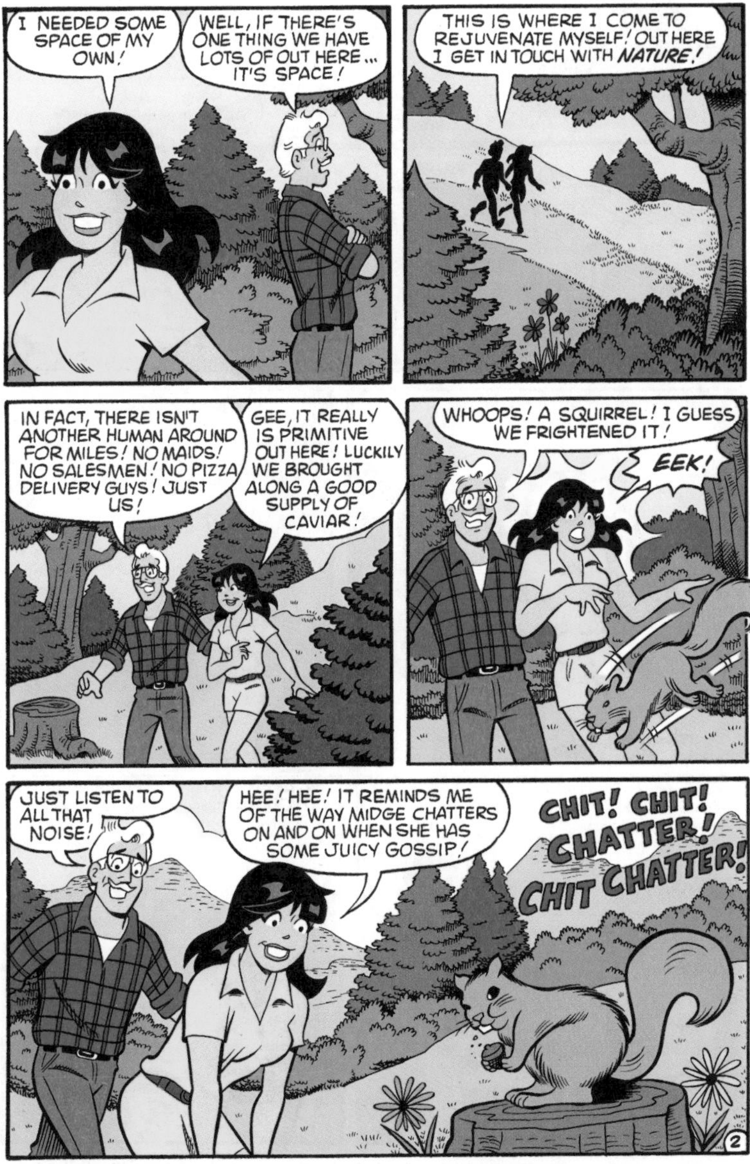

I NEEDED SOME SPACE OF MY OWN!
WELL, IF THERE'S ONE THING WE HAVE LOTS OF OUT HERE... IT'S SPACE!
THIS IS WHERE I COME TO REJUVENATE MYSELF! OUT HERE I GET IN TOUCH WITH NATURE!
IN FACT, THERE ISN'T ANOTHER HUMAN AROUND FOR MILES! NO MAIDS! NO SALESMEN! NO PIZZA DELIVERY GUYS! JUST US!
GEE, IT REALLY IS PRIMITIVE OUT HERE! LUCKILY WE BROUGHT ALONG A GOOD SUPPLY OF CAVIAR!
WHOOPS! A SQUIRREL! I GUESS WE FRIGHTENED IT!
EEK!
JUST LISTEN TO ALL THAT NOISE!
HEE! HEE! IT REMINDS ME OF THE WAY MIDGE CHATTERS ON AND ON WHEN SHE HAS SOME JUICY GOSSIP!
CHIT! CHIT! CHATTER! CHIT CHATTER!
2

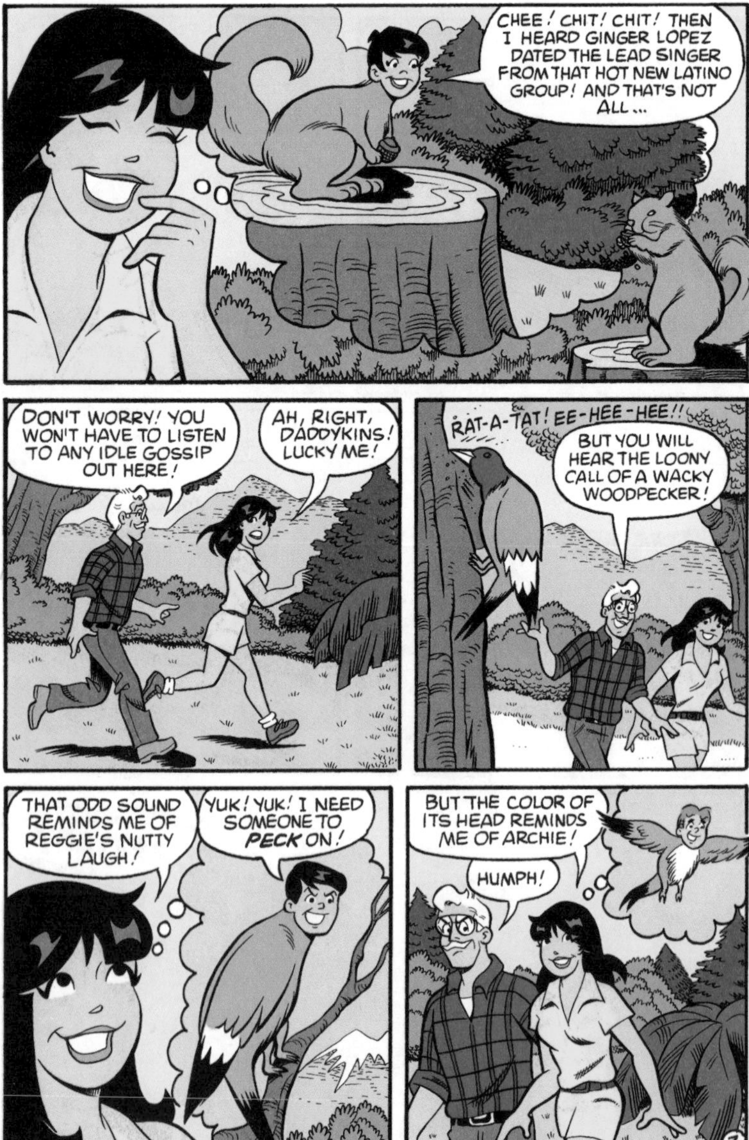
CHEE! CHIT! CHIT! THEN I HEARD GINGER LOPEZ DATED THE LEAD SINGER FROM THAT HOT NEW LATINO GROUP! AND THAT'S NOT ALL...
DON'T WORRY! YOU WON'T HAVE TO LISTEN TO ANY IDLE GOSSIP OUT HERE!
AH, RIGHT, DADDYKINS! LUCKY ME!
RAT-A-TAT! EE-HEE-HEE!!
BUT YOU WILL HEAR THE LOONY CALL OF A WACKY WOODPECKER!
THAT ODD SOUND REMINDS ME OF REGGIE'S NUTTY LAUGH!
YUK! YUK! I NEED SOMEONE TO PECK ON!
BUT THE COLOR OF ITS HEAD REMINDS ME OF ARCHIE!
HUMPH!

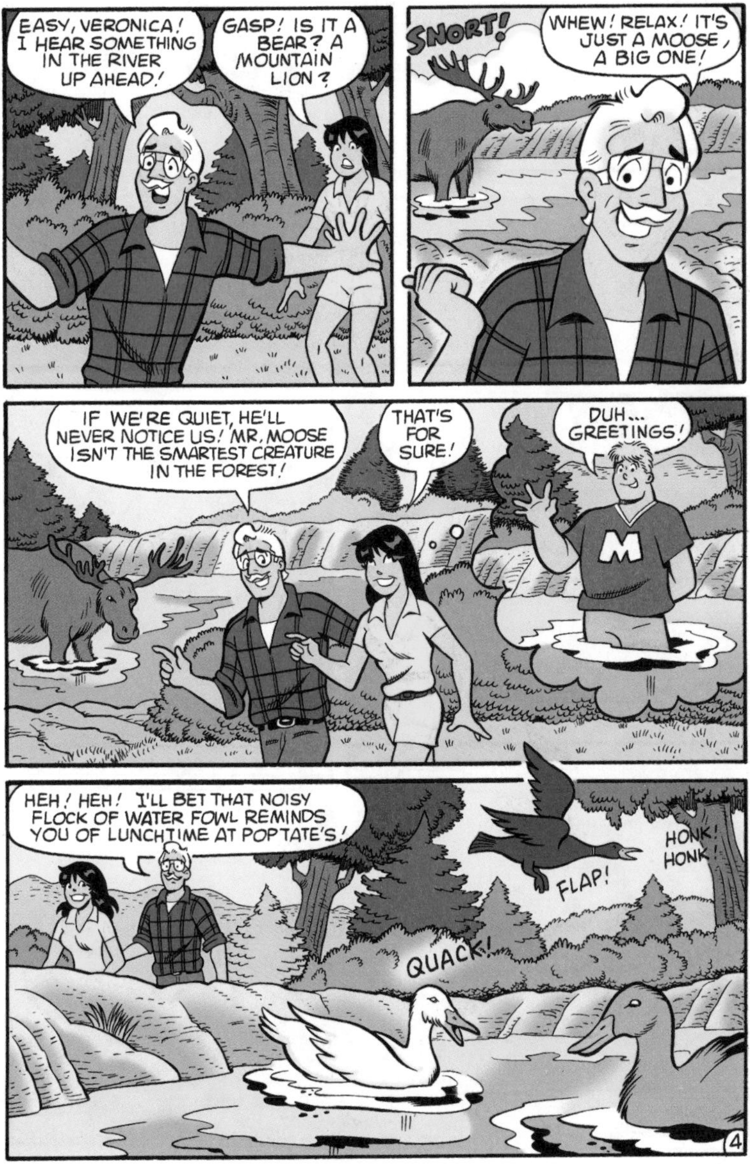
EASY, VERONICA! I HEAR SOMETHING IN THE RIVER UP AHEAD!
GASP! IS IT A BEAR? A MOUNTAIN LION?
SNORT!
WHEW! RELAX! IT'S JUST A MOOSE, A BIG ONE!
IF WE'RE QUIET, HE'LL NEVER NOTICE US! MR. MOOSE ISN'T THE SMARTEST CREATURE IN THE FOREST!
THAT'S FOR SURE!
DUH... GREETINGS!
M
HEH! HEH! I'LL BET THAT NOISY FLOCK OF WATER FOWL REMINDS YOU OF LUNCHTIME AT POPTATE'S!
HONK! HONK!
FLAP!
QUACK!
4

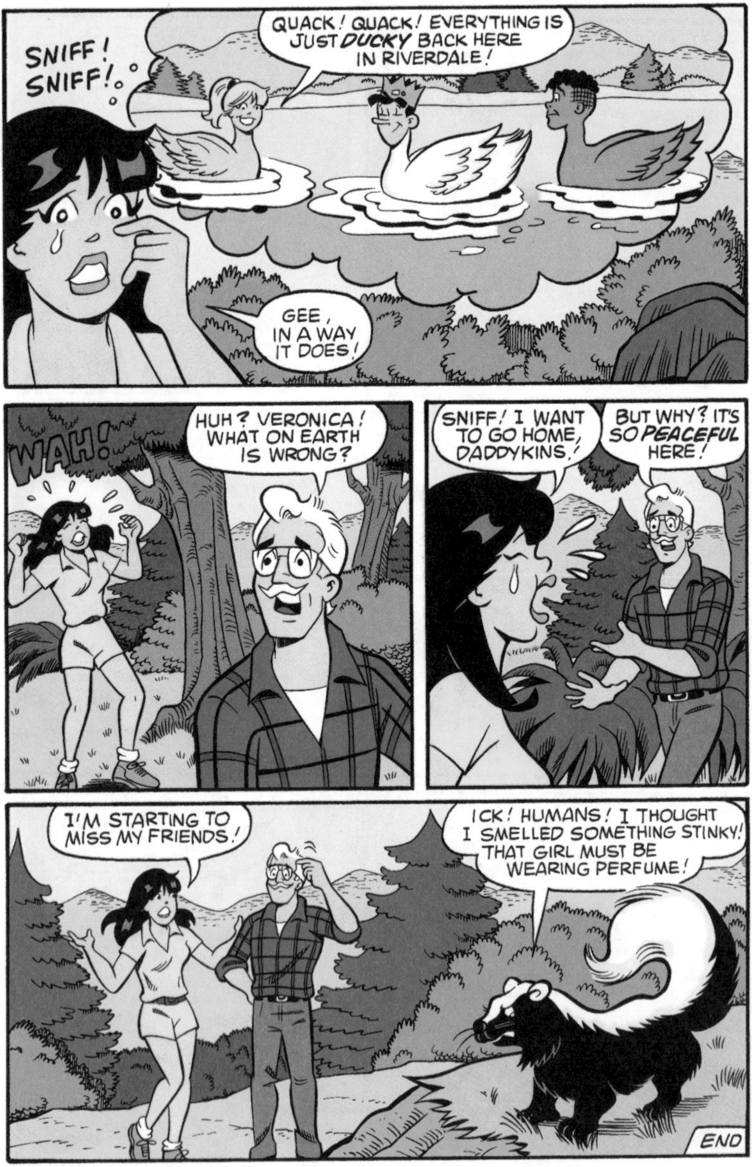
SNIFF! SNIFF!
QUACK! QUACK! EVERYTHING IS JUST DUCKY BACK HERE IN RIVERDALE!
GEE, IN A WAY IT DOES!
WAH!
HUH? VERONICA! WHAT ON EARTH IS WRONG?
SNIFF! I WANT TO GO HOME, DADDYKINS!
BUT WHY? IT'S SO PEACEFUL HERE!
I'M STARTING TO MISS MY FRIENDS!
ICK! HUMANS! I THOUGHT I SMELLED SOMETHING STINKY! THAT GIRL MUST BE WEARING PERFUME!
END

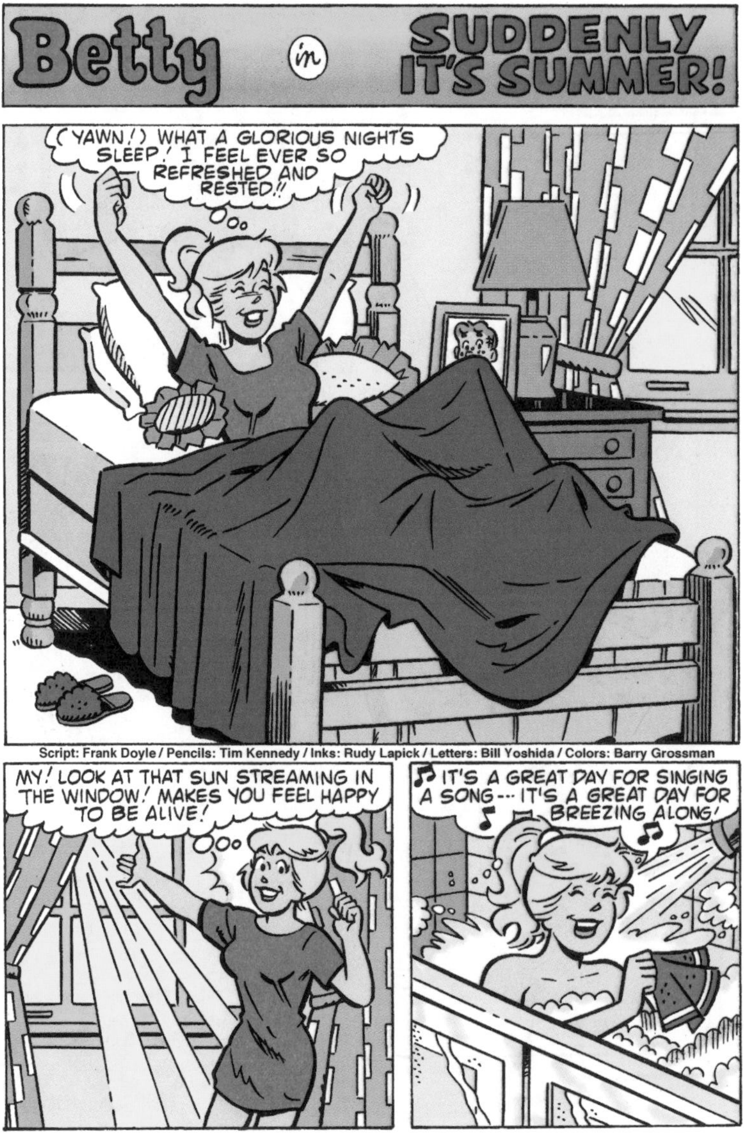
Betty in SUDDENLY IT'S SUMMER!
(YAWN!) WHAT A GLORIOUS NIGHT'S SLEEP! I FEEL EVER SO REFRESHED AND RESTED!!
Script: Frank Doyle / Pencils: Tim Kennedy / Inks: Rudy Lapick / Letters: Bill Yoshida / Colors: Barry Grossman
MY! LOOK AT THAT SUN STREAMING IN THE WINDOW! MAKES YOU FEEL HAPPY TO BE ALIVE!
IT'S A GREAT DAY FOR SINGING A SONG--- IT'S A GREAT DAY FOR BREEZING ALONG!

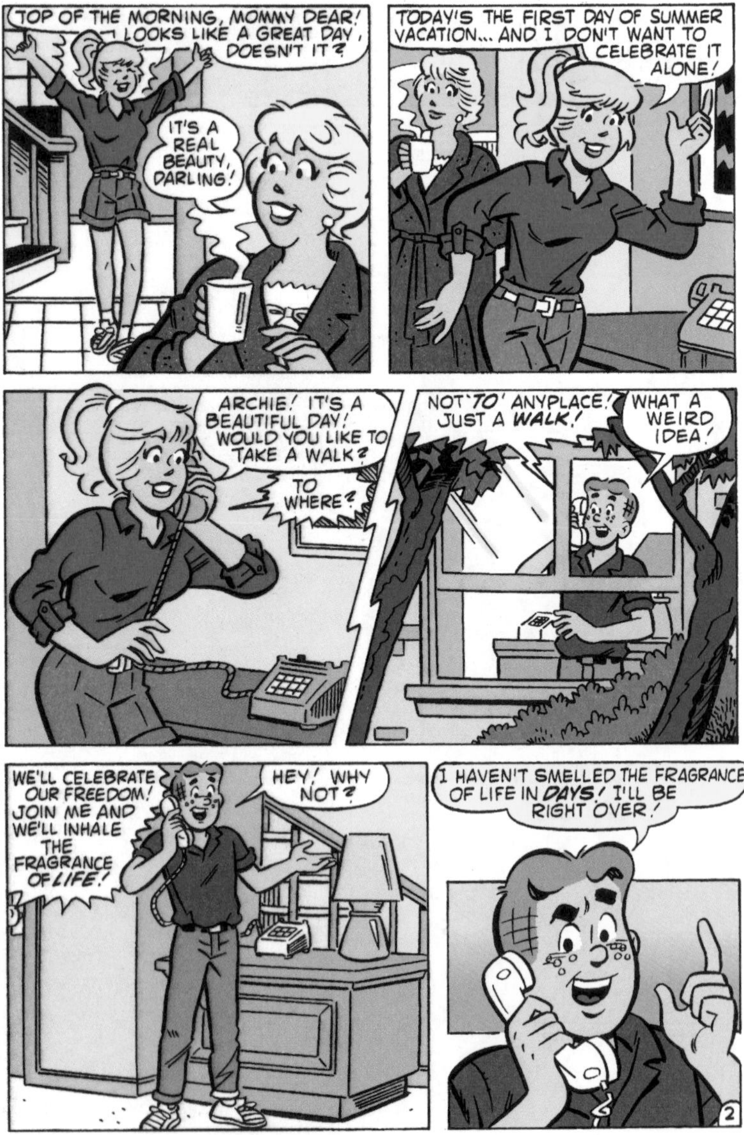
TOP OF THE MORNING, MOMMY DEAR! LOOKS LIKE A GREAT DAY, DOESN'T IT?
IT'S A REAL BEAUTY, DARLING!
TODAY'S THE FIRST DAY OF SUMMER VACATION... AND I DON'T WANT TO CELEBRATE IT ALONE!
ARCHIE! IT'S A BEAUTIFUL DAY! WOULD YOU LIKE TO TAKE A WALK?
TO WHERE?
NOT 'TO' ANYPLACE! JUST A WALK!
WHAT A WEIRD IDEA!
WE'LL CELEBRATE OUR FREEDOM! JOIN ME AND WE'LL INHALE THE FRAGRANCE OF LIFE!
HEY! WHY NOT?
I HAVEN'T SMELLED THE FRAGRANCE OF LIFE IN DAYS! I'LL BE RIGHT OVER!
2

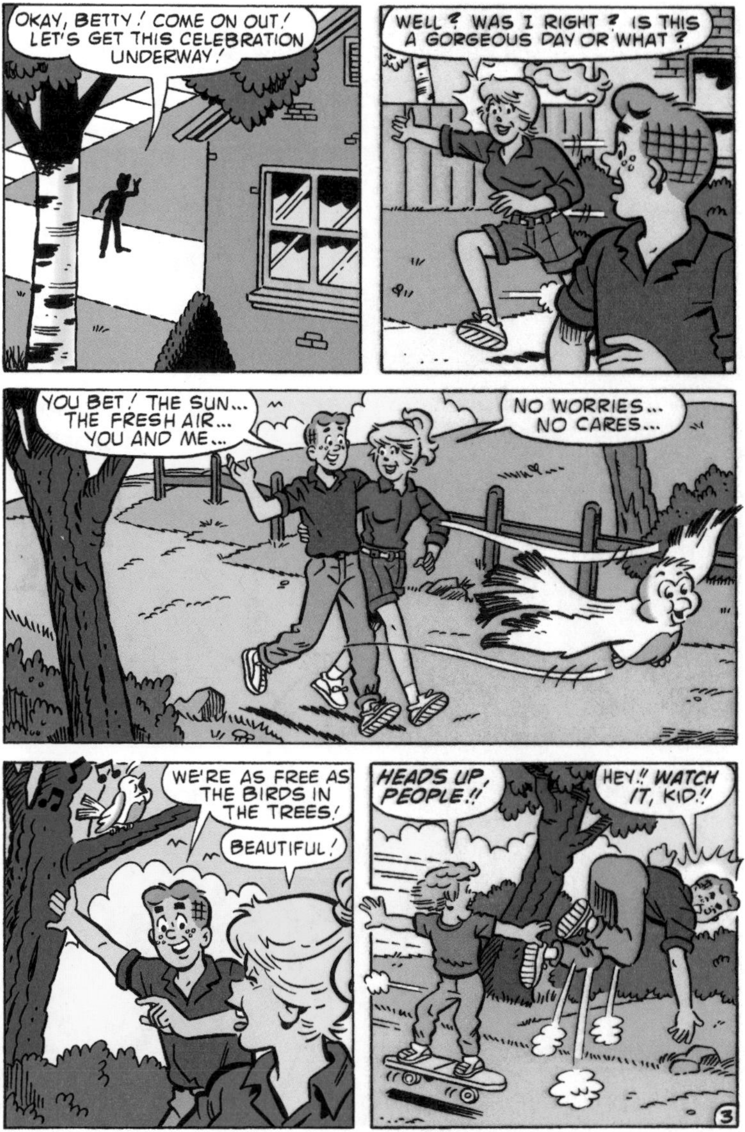
OKAY, BETTY! COME ON OUT! LET'S GET THIS CELEBRATION UNDERWAY!
WELL? WAS I RIGHT? IS THIS A GORGEOUS DAY OR WHAT?
YOU BET! THE SUN... THE FRESH AIR... YOU AND ME...
NO WORRIES... NO CARES...
WE'RE AS FREE AS THE BIRDS IN THE TREES!
BEAUTIFUL!
HEADS UP, PEOPLE!!
HEY!! WATCH IT, KID!!
3

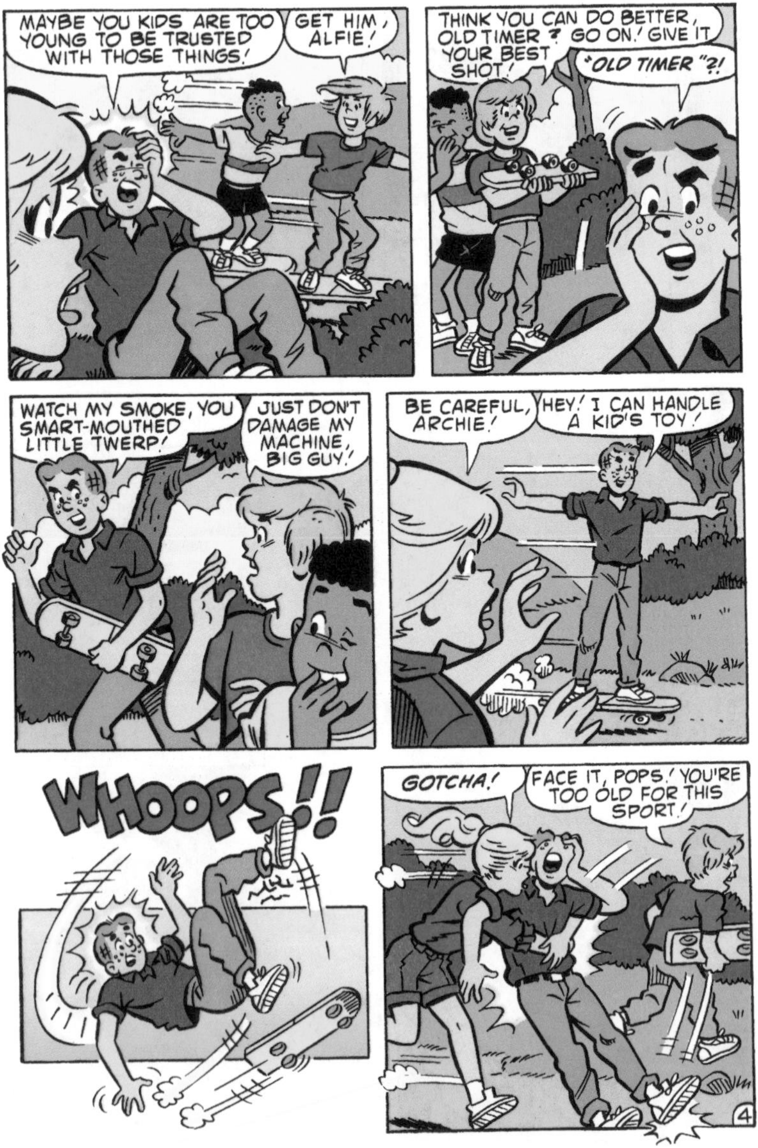
MAYBE YOU KIDS ARE TOO YOUNG TO BE TRUSTED WITH THOSE THINGS!
GET HIM, ALFIE!
THINK YOU CAN DO BETTER, OLD TIMER? GO ON! GIVE IT YOUR BEST SHOT!
"OLD TIMER"?!
WATCH MY SMOKE, YOU SMART-MOUTHED LITTLE TWERP!
JUST DON'T DAMAGE MY MACHINE, BIG GUY!
BE CAREFUL, ARCHIE!
HEY! I CAN HANDLE A KID'S TOY!
WHOOPS!!
GOTCHA!
FACE IT, POPS! YOU'RE TOO OLD FOR THIS SPORT!
4

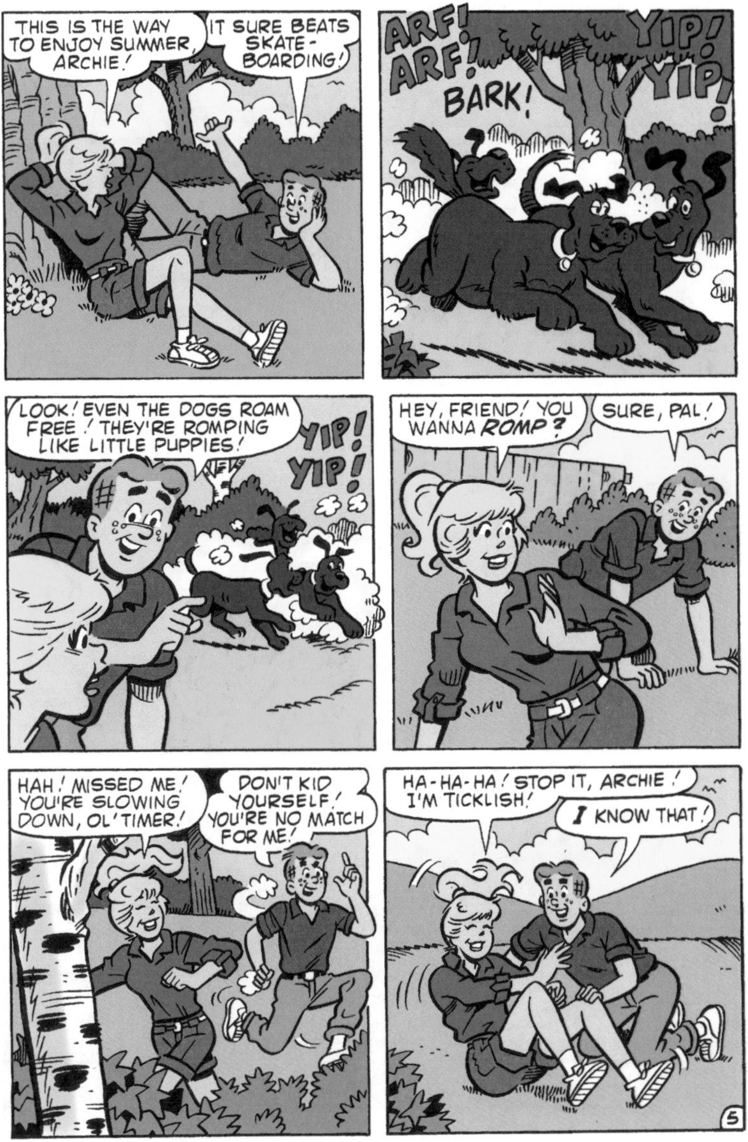
THIS IS THE WAY TO ENJOY SUMMER, ARCHIE!
IT SURE BEATS SKATE-BOARDING!
ARF! ARF!
BARK!
YIP! YIP!
LOOK! EVEN THE DOGS ROAM FREE! THEY'RE ROMPING LIKE LITTLE PUPPIES!
YIP! YIP!
HEY, FRIEND! YOU WANNA ROMP?
SURE, PAL!
HAH! MISSED ME! YOU'RE SLOWING DOWN, OL' TIMER!
DON'T KID YOURSELF! YOU'RE NO MATCH FOR ME!
HA-HA-HA! STOP IT, ARCHIE! I'M TICKLISH!
I KNOW THAT!
5

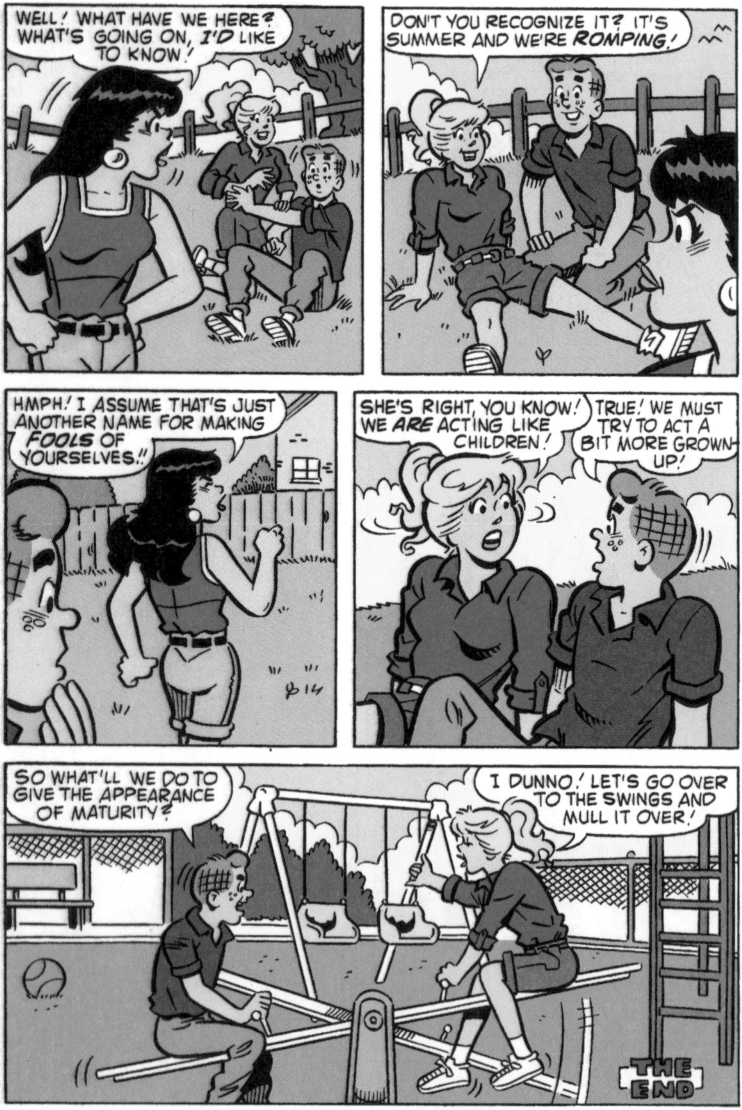
WELL! WHAT HAVE WE HERE? WHAT'S GOING ON, I'D LIKE TO KNOW!
DON'T YOU RECOGNIZE IT? IT'S SUMMER AND WE'RE ROMPING!
HMPH! I ASSUME THAT'S JUST ANOTHER NAME FOR MAKING FOOLS OF YOURSELVES!!
SHE'S RIGHT, YOU KNOW! WE ARE ACTING LIKE CHILDREN!
TRUE! WE MUST TRY TO ACT A BIT MORE GROWN-UP!
SO WHAT'LL WE DO TO GIVE THE APPEARANCE OF MATURITY?
I DUNNO! LET'S GO OVER TO THE SWINGS AND MULL IT OVER!
THE END

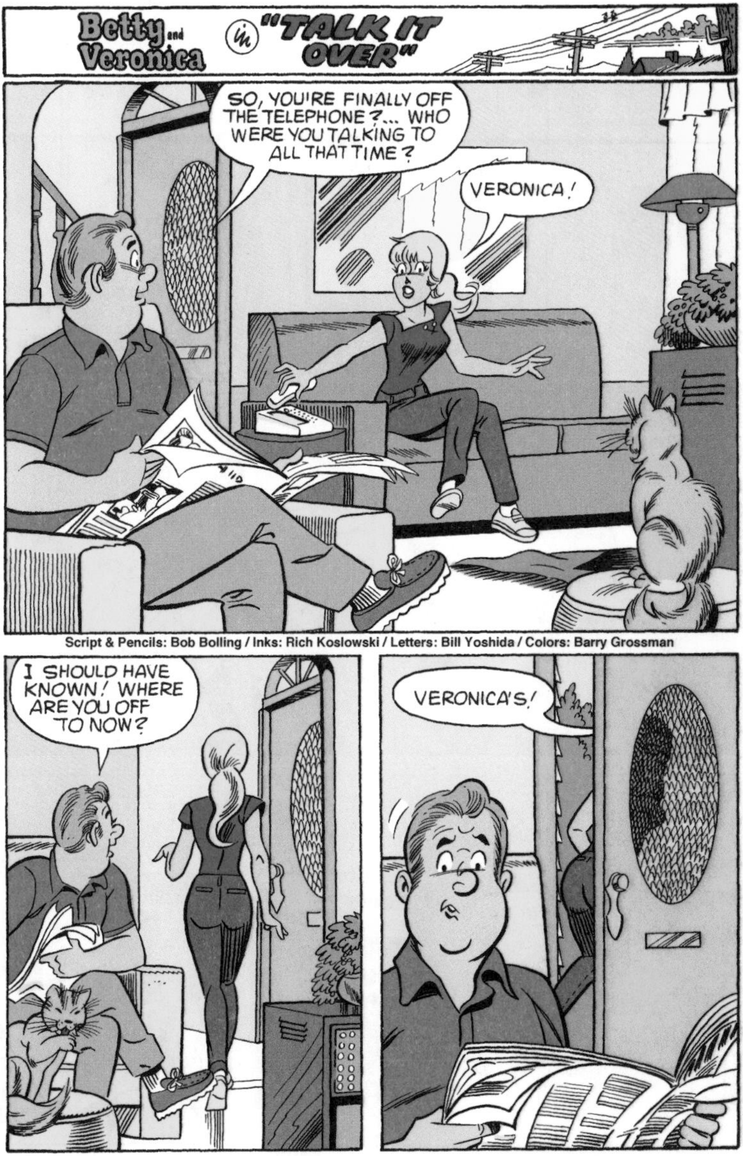
Betty and Veronica
in "TALK IT OVER"
SO, YOU'RE FINALLY OFF THE TELEPHONE?... WHO WERE YOU TALKING TO ALL THAT TIME?
VERONICA!
I SHOULD HAVE KNOWN! WHERE ARE YOU OFF TO NOW?
VERONICA'S!

Script & Pencils: Bob Bolling / Inks: Rich Koslowski / Letters: Bill Yoshida / Colors: Barry Grossman

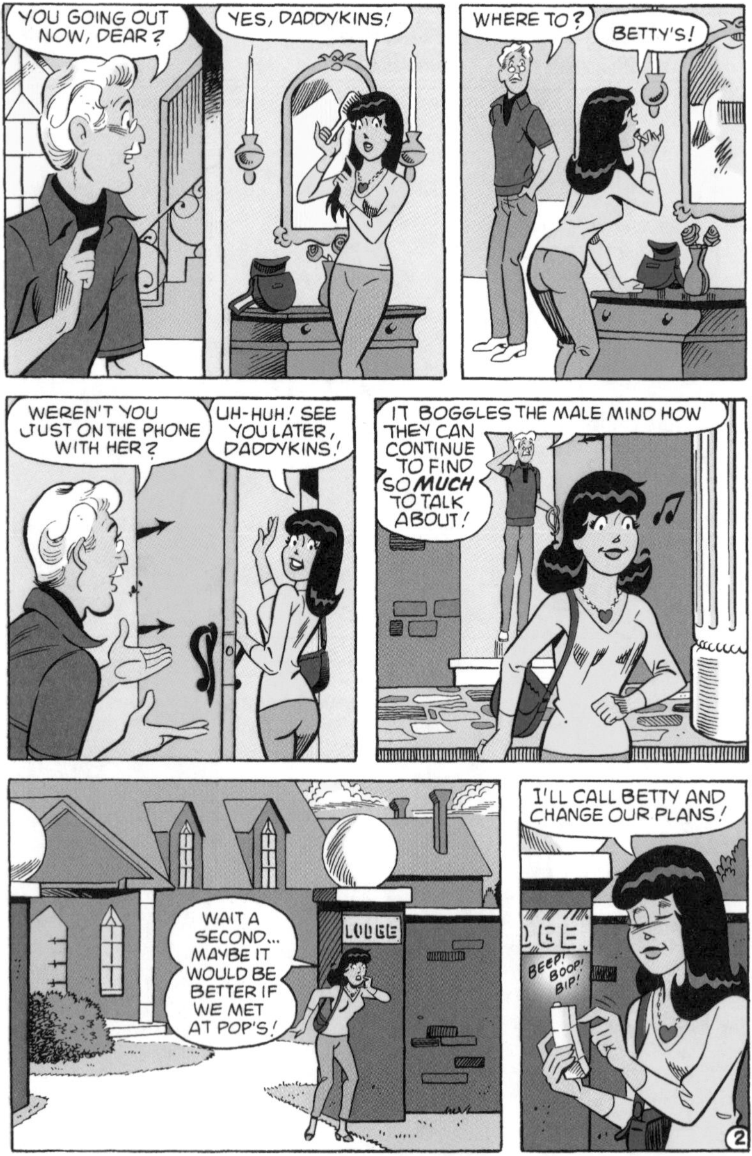
YOU GOING OUT NOW, DEAR?
YES, DADDYKINS!
WHERE TO?
BETTY'S!
WEREN'T YOU JUST ON THE PHONE WITH HER?
UH-HUH! SEE YOU LATER, DADDYKINS!
IT BOGGLES THE MALE MIND HOW THEY CAN CONTINUE TO FIND SO MUCH TO TALK ABOUT!
LODGE
WAIT A SECOND... MAYBE IT WOULD BE BETTER IF WE MET AT POP'S!
I'LL CALL BETTY AND CHANGE OUR PLANS!
BEEP! BOOP! BIP!
2

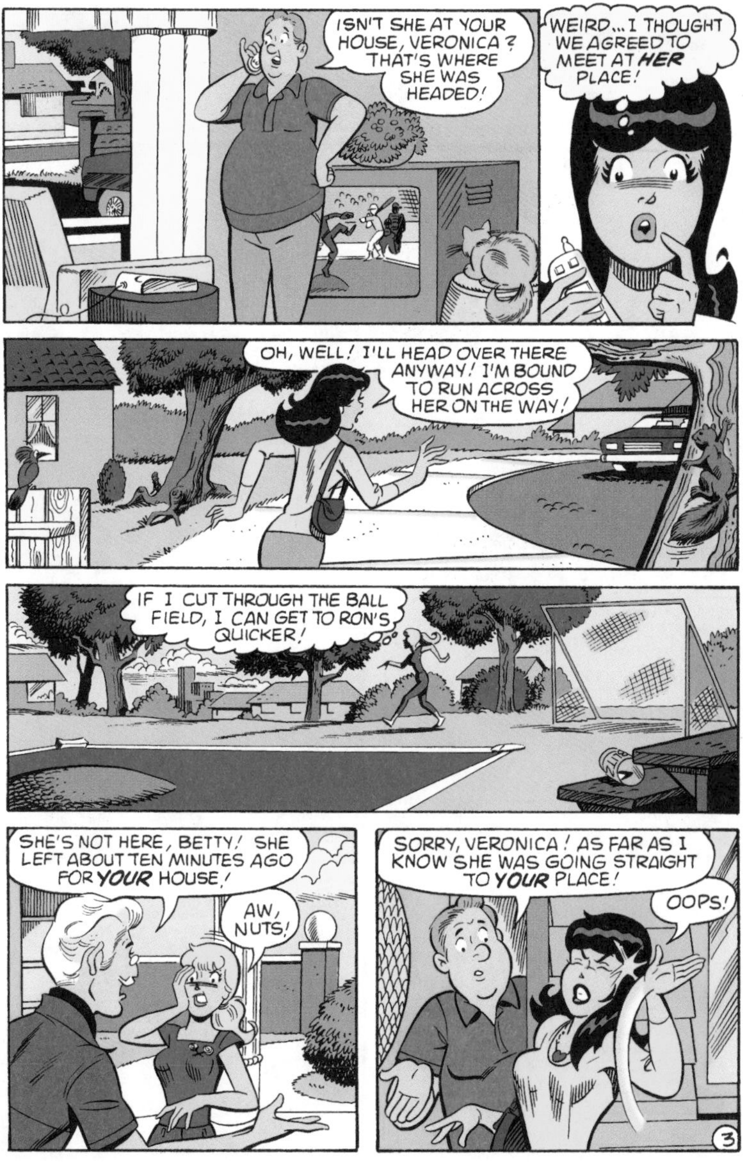
ISN'T SHE AT YOUR HOUSE, VERONICA? THAT'S WHERE SHE WAS HEADED!
WEIRD... I THOUGHT WE AGREED TO MEET AT HER PLACE!
OH, WELL! I'LL HEAD OVER THERE ANYWAY! I'M BOUND TO RUN ACROSS HER ON THE WAY!
IF I CUT THROUGH THE BALL FIELD, I CAN GET TO RON'S QUICKER!
SHE'S NOT HERE, BETTY! SHE LEFT ABOUT TEN MINUTES AGO FOR YOUR HOUSE!
AW, NUTS!
SORRY, VERONICA! AS FAR AS I KNOW SHE WAS GOING STRAIGHT TO YOUR PLACE!
OOPS!
3

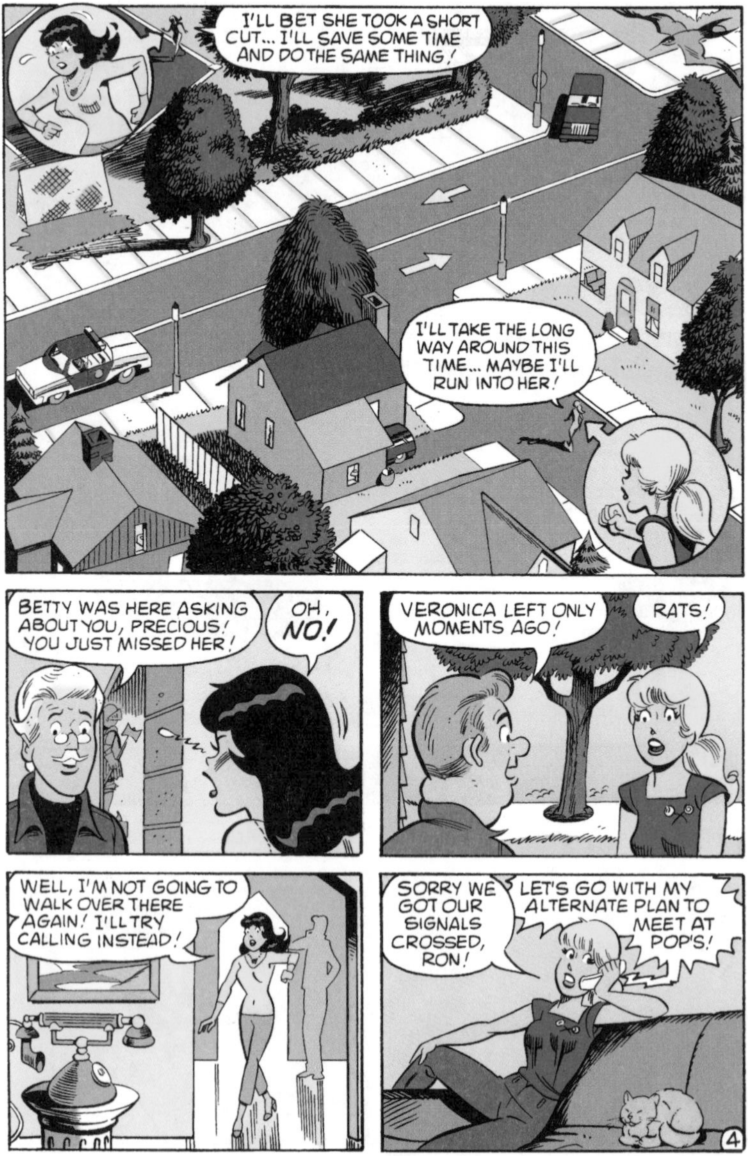
I'LL BET SHE TOOK A SHORT CUT... I'LL SAVE SOME TIME AND DO THE SAME THING!
I'LL TAKE THE LONG WAY AROUND THIS TIME... MAYBE I'LL RUN INTO HER!
BETTY WAS HERE ASKING ABOUT YOU, PRECIOUS! YOU JUST MISSED HER!
OH, NO!
VERONICA LEFT ONLY MOMENTS AGO!
RATS!
WELL, I'M NOT GOING TO WALK OVER THERE AGAIN! I'LL TRY CALLING INSTEAD!
SORRY WE GOT OUR SIGNALS CROSSED, RON!
LET'S GO WITH MY ALTERNATE PLAN TO MEET AT POP'S!
4

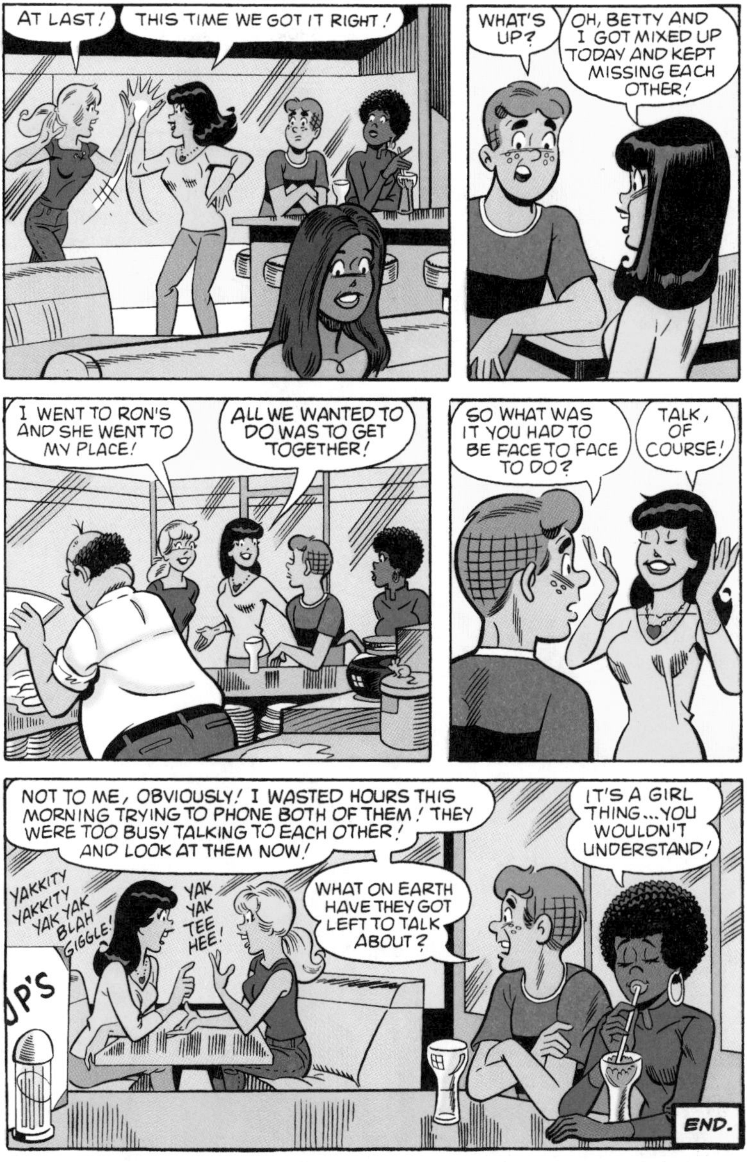
AT LAST!
THIS TIME WE GOT IT RIGHT!
WHAT'S UP?
OH, BETTY AND I GOT MIXED UP TODAY AND KEPT MISSING EACH OTHER!
I WENT TO RON'S AND SHE WENT TO MY PLACE!
ALL WE WANTED TO DO WAS TO GET TOGETHER!
SO WHAT WAS IT YOU HAD TO BE FACE TO FACE TO DO?
TALK, OF COURSE!
NOT TO ME, OBVIOUSLY! I WASTED HOURS THIS MORNING TRYING TO PHONE BOTH OF THEM! THEY WERE TOO BUSY TALKING TO EACH OTHER! AND LOOK AT THEM NOW!
IT'S A GIRL THING...YOU WOULDN'T UNDERSTAND!
YAKKITY YAKKITY YAK YAK BLAH GIGGLE!
YAK YAK TEE HEE!
WHAT ON EARTH HAVE THEY GOT LEFT TO TALK ABOUT?
END.

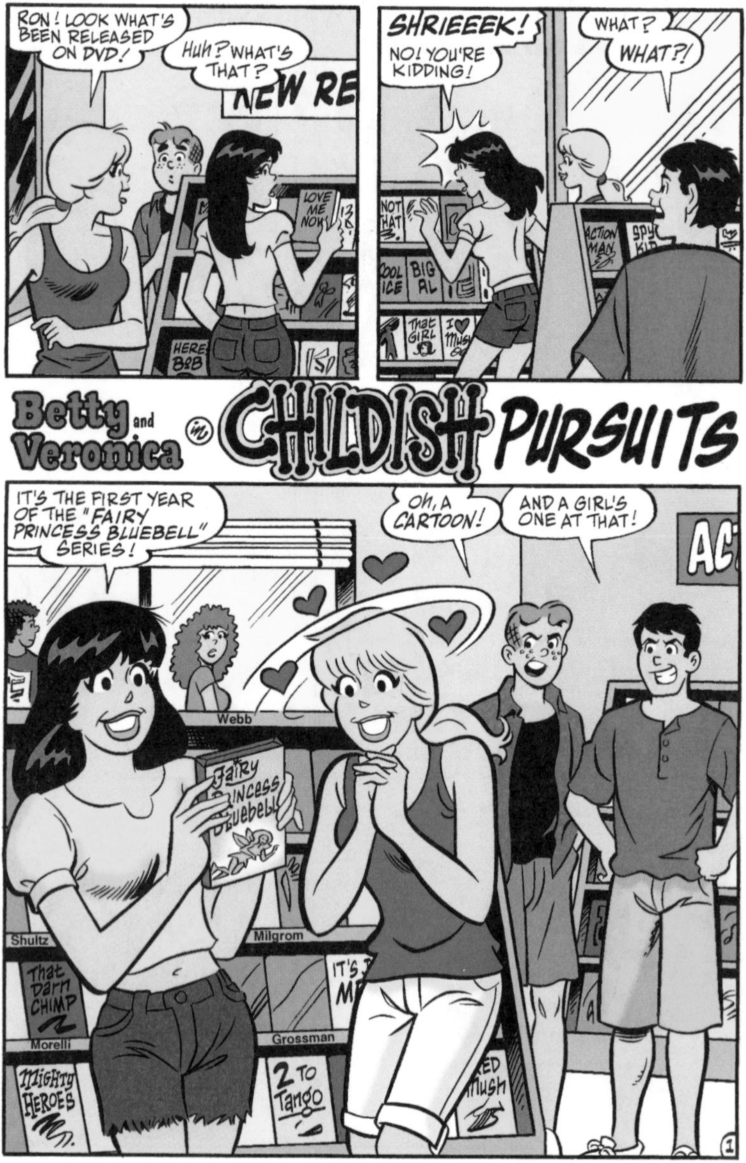
RON! LOOK WHAT'S BEEN RELEASED ON DVD!
Huh? WHAT'S THAT?
NEW RE
LOVE ME NOW
HERE B&B
SHRIEEEK!
NO! YOU'RE KIDDING!
WHAT? WHAT?!
NOT THAT
COOL ICE
BIG AL
That GIRL
ACTION MAN
SPY KID
Betty and Veronica in CHILDISH PURSUITS
IT'S THE FIRST YEAR OF THE "FAIRY PRINCESS BLUEBELL" SERIES!
Oh, A CARTOON!
AND A GIRL'S ONE AT THAT!
Webb
Shultz
Milgrom
That Darn CHIMP
Morelli
Grossman
Mighty HEROES
2 TO Tango
1

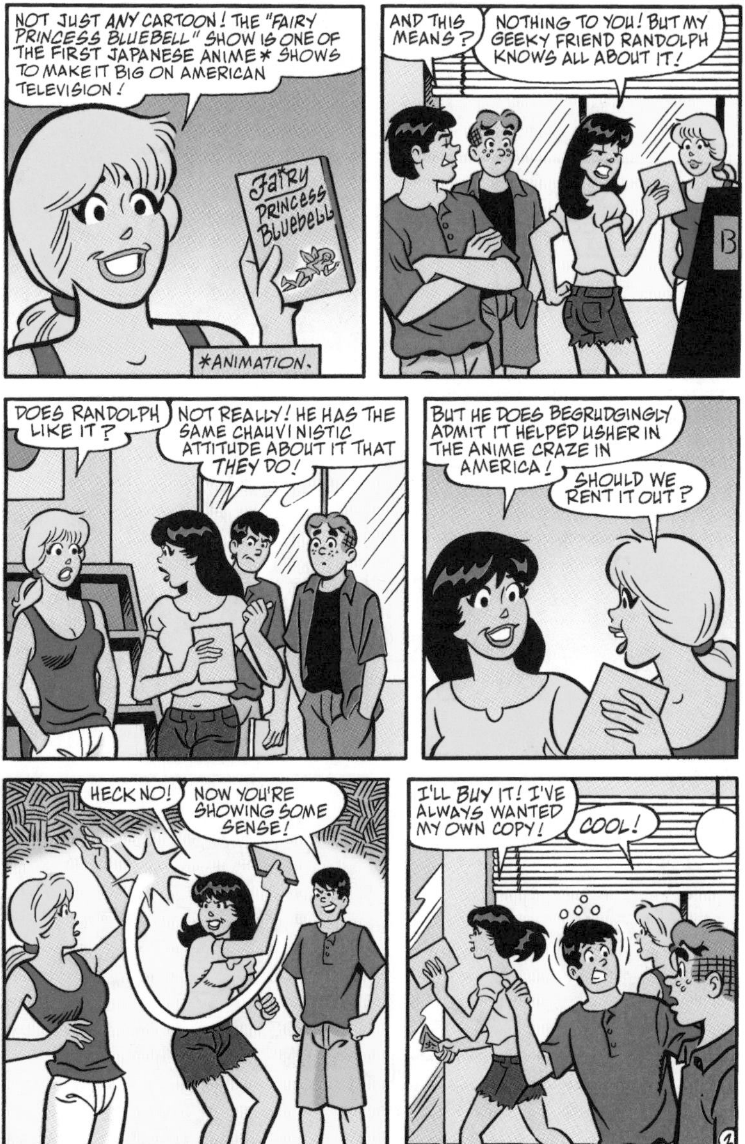
NOT JUST ANY CARTOON! THE "FAIRY PRINCESS BLUEBELL" SHOW IS ONE OF THE FIRST JAPANESE ANIME* SHOWS TO MAKE IT BIG ON AMERICAN TELEVISION!
FAIRY PRINCESS BLUEBELL
*ANIMATION.
AND THIS MEANS?
NOTHING TO YOU! BUT MY GEEKY FRIEND RANDOLPH KNOWS ALL ABOUT IT!
B
DOES RANDOLPH LIKE IT?
NOT REALLY! HE HAS THE SAME CHAUVINISTIC ATTITUDE ABOUT IT THAT THEY DO!
BUT HE DOES BEGRUDGINGLY ADMIT IT HELPED USHER IN THE ANIME CRAZE IN AMERICA!
SHOULD WE RENT IT OUT?
HECK NO!
NOW YOU'RE SHOWING SOME SENSE!
I'LL BUY IT! I'VE ALWAYS WANTED MY OWN COPY!
COOL!
2

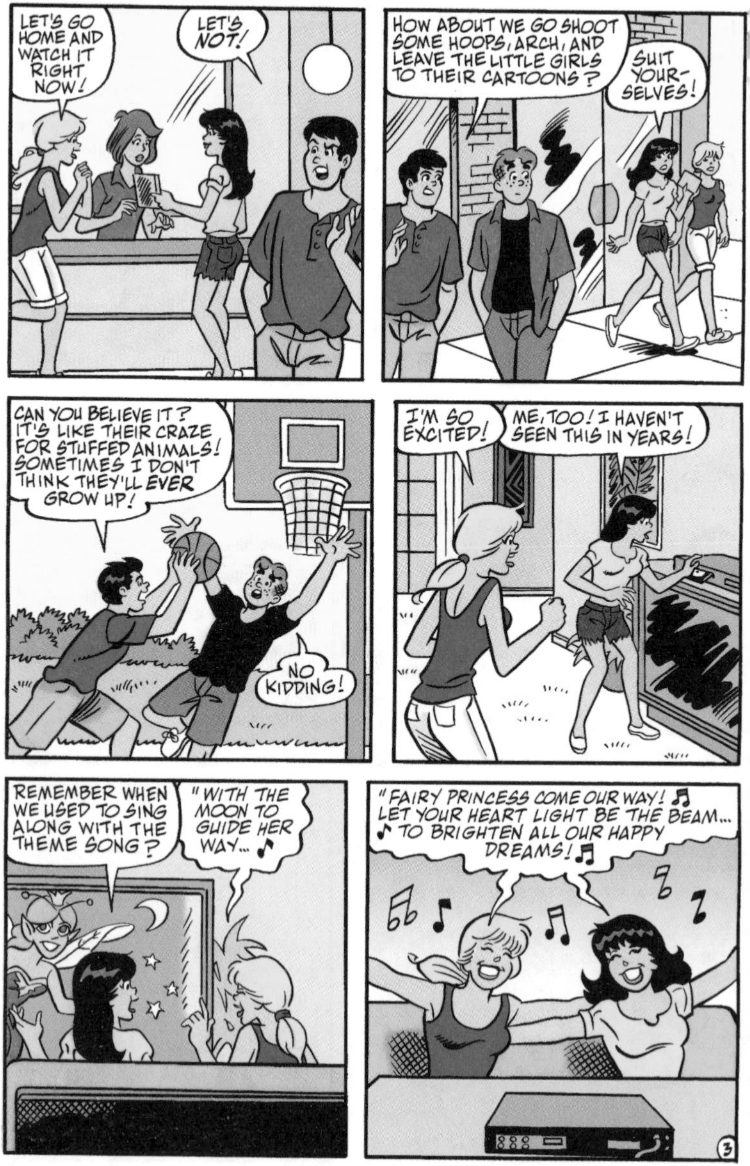
LET'S GO HOME AND WATCH IT RIGHT NOW!
LET'S NOT!
HOW ABOUT WE GO SHOOT SOME HOOPS, ARCH, AND LEAVE THE LITTLE GIRLS TO THEIR CARTOONS?
SUIT YOUR-SELVES!
CAN YOU BELIEVE IT? IT'S LIKE THEIR CRAZE FOR STUFFED ANIMALS! SOMETIMES I DON'T THINK THEY'LL EVER GROW UP!
NO KIDDING!
I'M SO EXCITED!
ME, TOO! I HAVEN'T SEEN THIS IN YEARS!
REMEMBER WHEN WE USED TO SING ALONG WITH THE THEME SONG?
"WITH THE MOON TO GUIDE HER WAY...
"FAIRY PRINCESS COME OUR WAY! LET YOUR HEART LIGHT BE THE BEAM... TO BRIGHTEN ALL OUR HAPPY DREAMS!
3

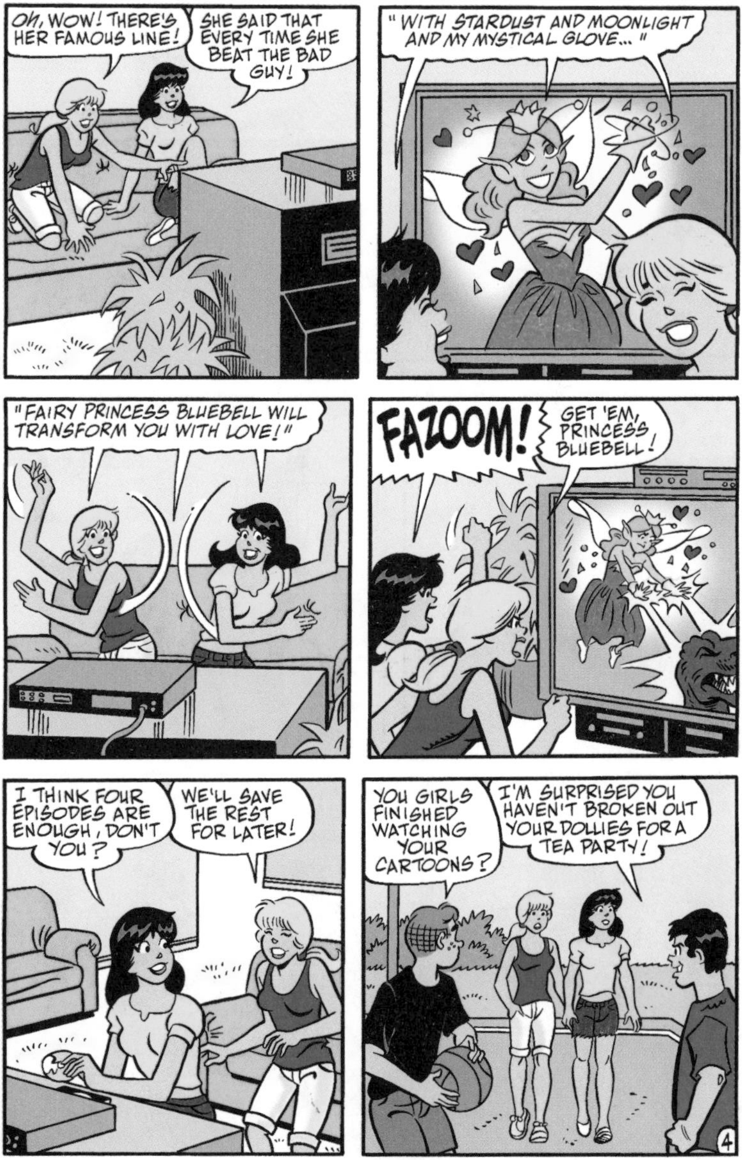
OH, WOW! THERE'S HER FAMOUS LINE!
SHE SAID THAT EVERY TIME SHE BEAT THE BAD GUY!
" WITH STARDUST AND MOONLIGHT AND MY MYSTICAL GLOVE... "
"FAIRY PRINCESS BLUEBELL WILL TRANSFORM YOU WITH LOVE!"
FAZOOM!
GET 'EM, PRINCESS BLUEBELL!
I THINK FOUR EPISODES ARE ENOUGH, DON'T YOU?
WE'LL SAVE THE REST FOR LATER!
YOU GIRLS FINISHED WATCHING YOUR CARTOONS?
I'M SURPRISED YOU HAVEN'T BROKEN OUT YOUR DOLLIES FOR A TEA PARTY!

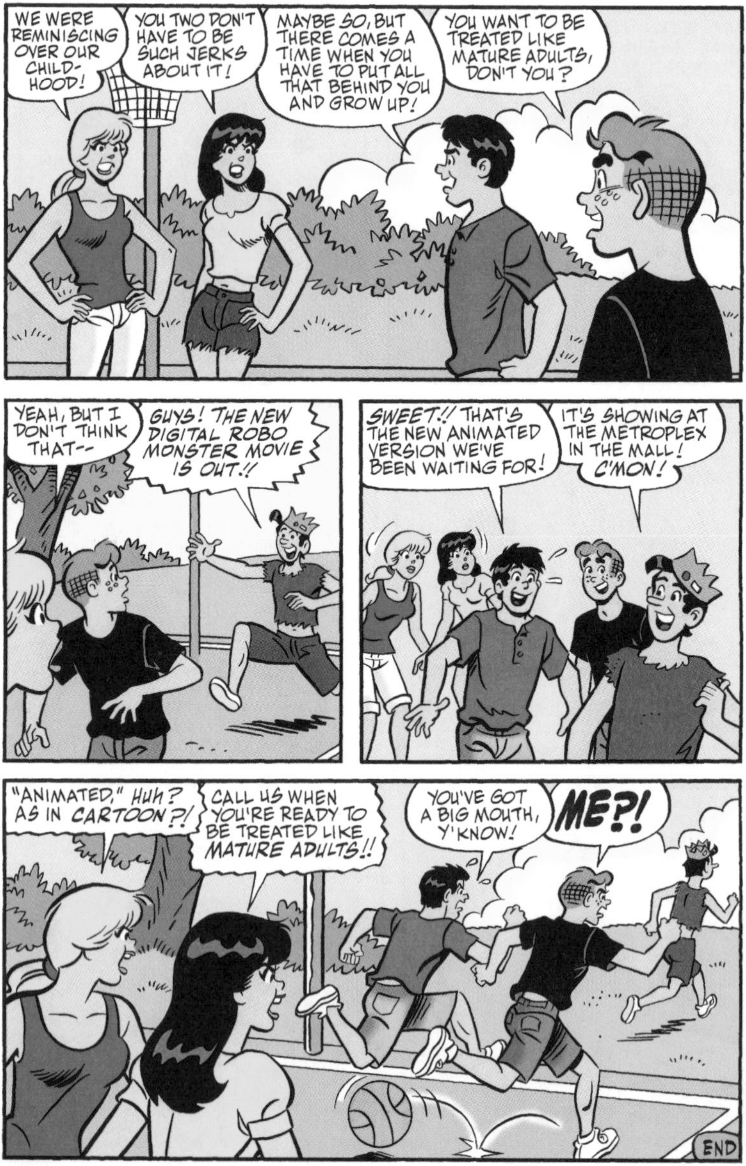
WE WERE REMINISCING OVER OUR CHILD-HOOD!
YOU TWO DON'T HAVE TO BE SUCH JERKS ABOUT IT!
MAYBE SO, BUT THERE COMES A TIME WHEN YOU HAVE TO PUT ALL THAT BEHIND YOU AND GROW UP!
YOU WANT TO BE TREATED LIKE MATURE ADULTS, DON'T YOU?
YEAH, BUT I DON'T THINK THAT--
GUYS! THE NEW DIGITAL ROBO MONSTER MOVIE IS OUT!!
SWEET!! THAT'S THE NEW ANIMATED VERSION WE'VE BEEN WAITING FOR!
IT'S SHOWING AT THE METROPLEX IN THE MALL! C'MON!
"ANIMATED," HUH? AS IN CARTOON?!
CALL US WHEN YOU'RE READY TO BE TREATED LIKE MATURE ADULTS!!
YOU'VE GOT A BIG MOUTH, Y'KNOW!
ME?!
END

## Pick Me Up
## *Betty & Veronica* #151, 2000
## by Kathleen Webb, Dan DeCarlo and Henry Scarpelli
## &
## Verve to Conserve
## *Archie* #292, 1980
## by George Gladir, Dan DeCarlo Jr., Rudy Lapick and Bill Yoshida

Archie and his friends brought me out of my shell. They showed me that I could speak to girls. I could be myself. Many would say that they created a monster, but to me they created a door, one that led out of the shell I'd made for myself and into the light.

**Tony Lee**
***New York Times*** *Bestselling Author*

## Melvin's Angels
## *Betty & Veronica* #277, 1979
## by Frank Doyle, Dan DeCarlo, Jim DeCarlo, Bill Yoshida, and Barry Grossman

Betty and Veronica play two glamorous detectives in a story that was undoubtedly influenced by an episode of Charlie's Angels. This story pays homage to pop culture and pokes fun at aspects of the decade—Archie gives an introspective view of society as a whole.

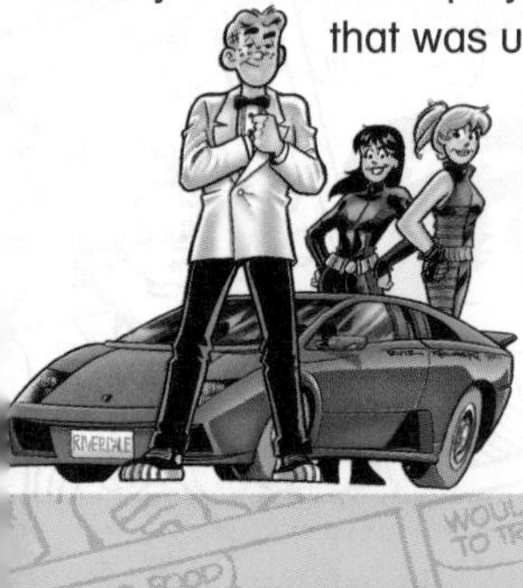
RIVERDALE

**Jamie Rotante**
*Proofreader, Archie Comics*

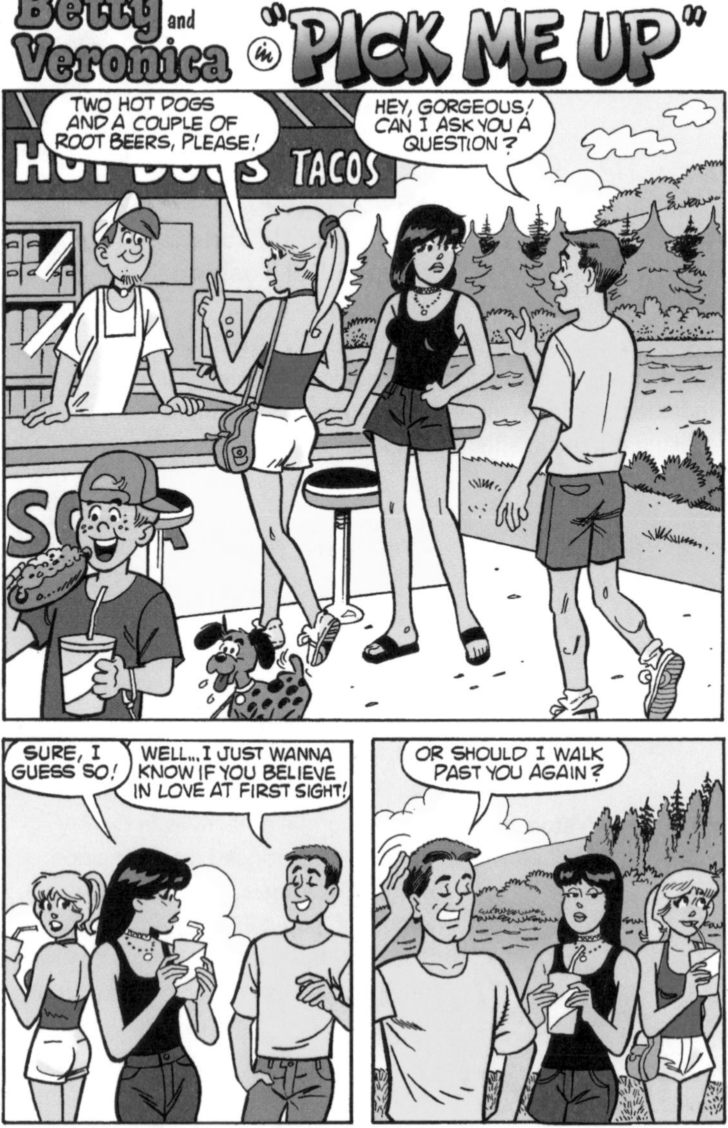
Betty and Veronica in "PICK ME UP"
TWO HOT DOGS AND A COUPLE OF ROOT BEERS, PLEASE!
HEY, GORGEOUS! CAN I ASK YOU A QUESTION?
TACOS
SURE, I GUESS SO!
WELL... I JUST WANNA KNOW IF YOU BELIEVE IN LOVE AT FIRST SIGHT!
OR SHOULD I WALK PAST YOU AGAIN?

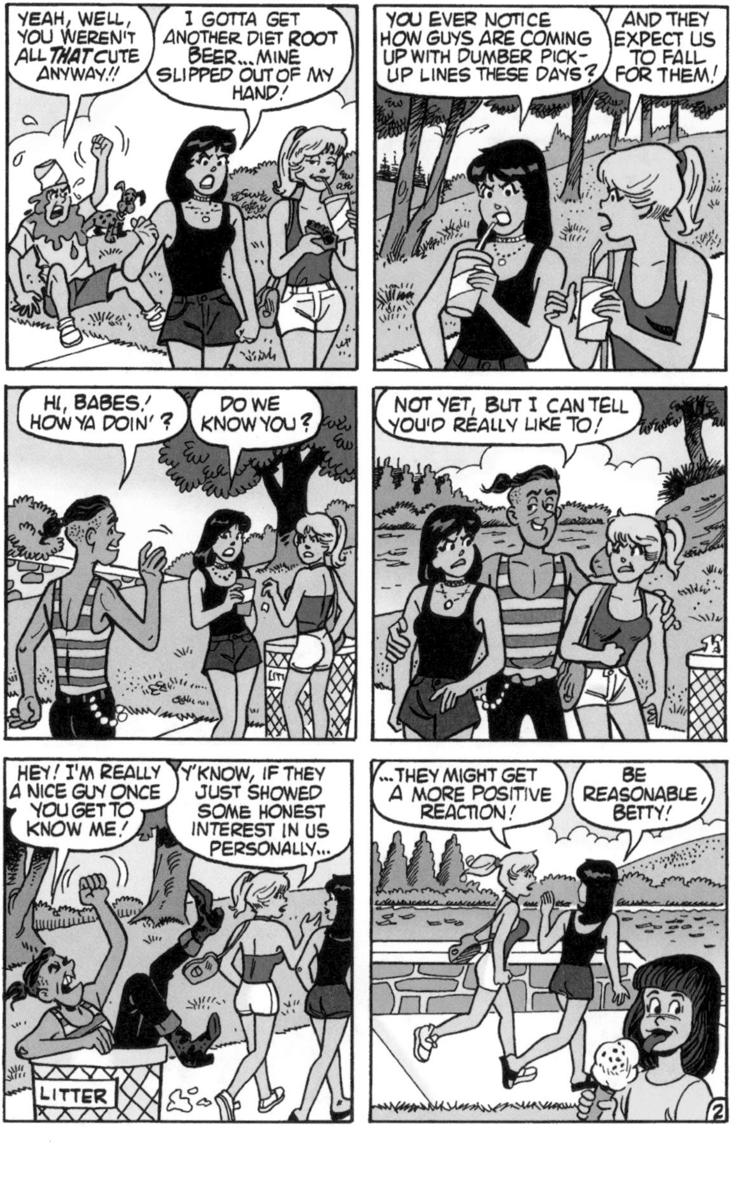

YEAH, WELL, YOU WEREN'T ALL THAT CUTE ANYWAY!!
I GOTTA GET ANOTHER DIET ROOT BEER...MINE SLIPPED OUT OF MY HAND!
YOU EVER NOTICE HOW GUYS ARE COMING UP WITH DUMBER PICK-UP LINES THESE DAYS?
AND THEY EXPECT US TO FALL FOR THEM!
HI, BABES! HOW YA DOIN'?
DO WE KNOW YOU?
NOT YET, BUT I CAN TELL YOU'D REALLY LIKE TO!
HEY! I'M REALLY A NICE GUY ONCE YOU GET TO KNOW ME!
Y'KNOW, IF THEY JUST SHOWED SOME HONEST INTEREST IN US PERSONALLY...
LITTER
...THEY MIGHT GET A MORE POSITIVE REACTION!
BE REASONABLE, BETTY!
2

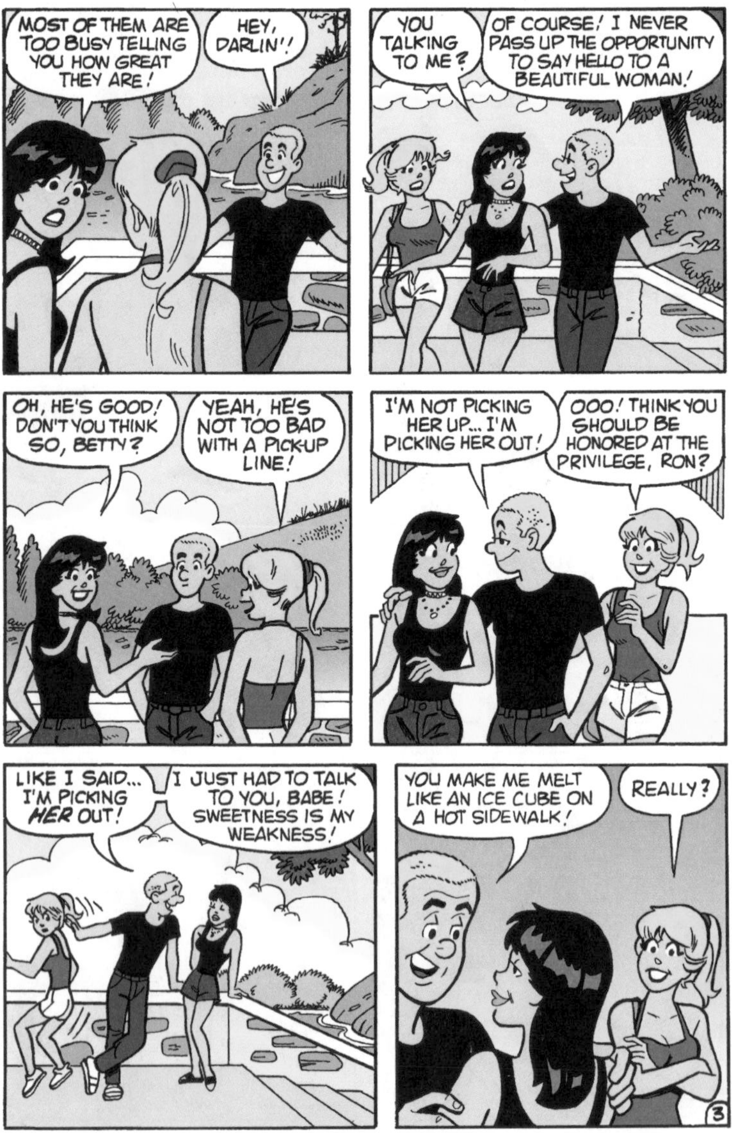
MOST OF THEM ARE TOO BUSY TELLING YOU HOW GREAT THEY ARE!
HEY, DARLIN'!
YOU TALKING TO ME?
OF COURSE! I NEVER PASS UP THE OPPORTUNITY TO SAY HELLO TO A BEAUTIFUL WOMAN!
OH, HE'S GOOD! DON'T YOU THINK SO, BETTY?
YEAH, HE'S NOT TOO BAD WITH A PICK-UP LINE!
I'M NOT PICKING HER UP... I'M PICKING HER OUT!
OOO! THINK YOU SHOULD BE HONORED AT THE PRIVILEGE, RON?
LIKE I SAID... I'M PICKING **HER** OUT!
I JUST HAD TO TALK TO YOU, BABE! SWEETNESS IS MY WEAKNESS!
YOU MAKE ME MELT LIKE AN ICE CUBE ON A HOT SIDEWALK!
REALLY?
3

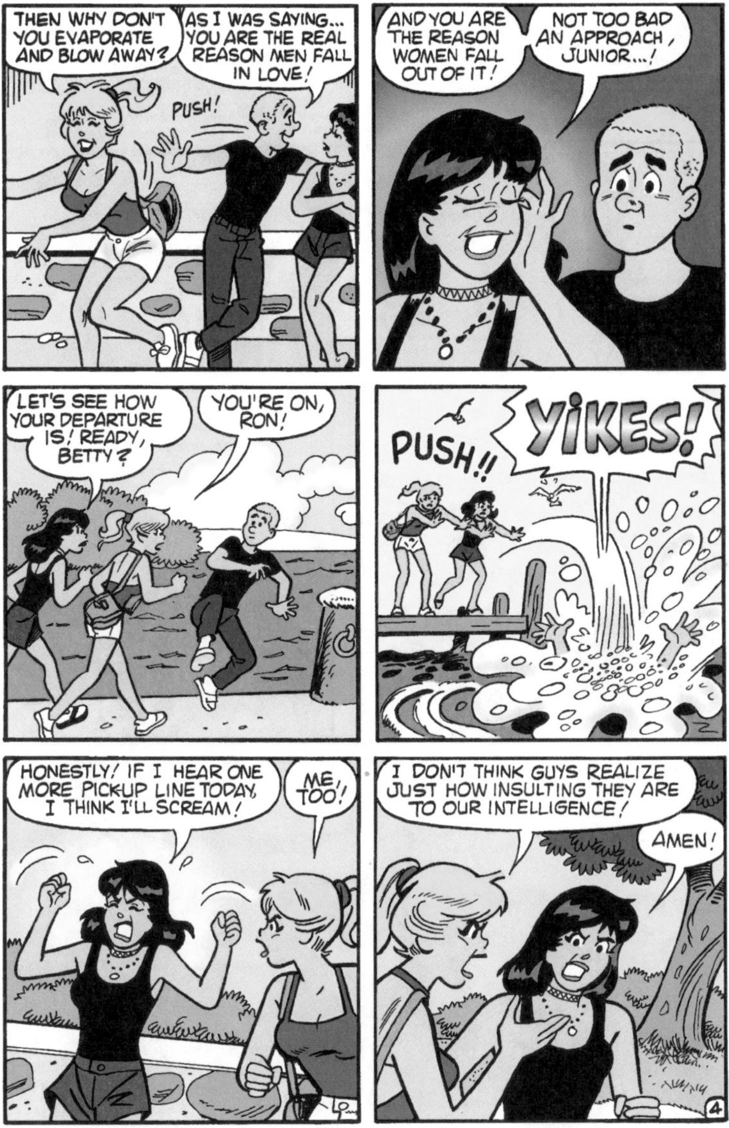

THEN WHY DON'T YOU EVAPORATE AND BLOW AWAY?
AS I WAS SAYING... YOU ARE THE REAL REASON MEN FALL IN LOVE!
PUSH!
AND YOU ARE THE REASON WOMEN FALL OUT OF IT!
NOT TOO BAD AN APPROACH, JUNIOR...!
LET'S SEE HOW YOUR DEPARTURE IS! READY, BETTY?
YOU'RE ON, RON!
PUSH!!
YIKES!
HONESTLY! IF I HEAR ONE MORE PICKUP LINE TODAY, I THINK I'LL SCREAM!
ME, TOO!
I DON'T THINK GUYS REALIZE JUST HOW INSULTING THEY ARE TO OUR INTELLIGENCE!
AMEN!
4

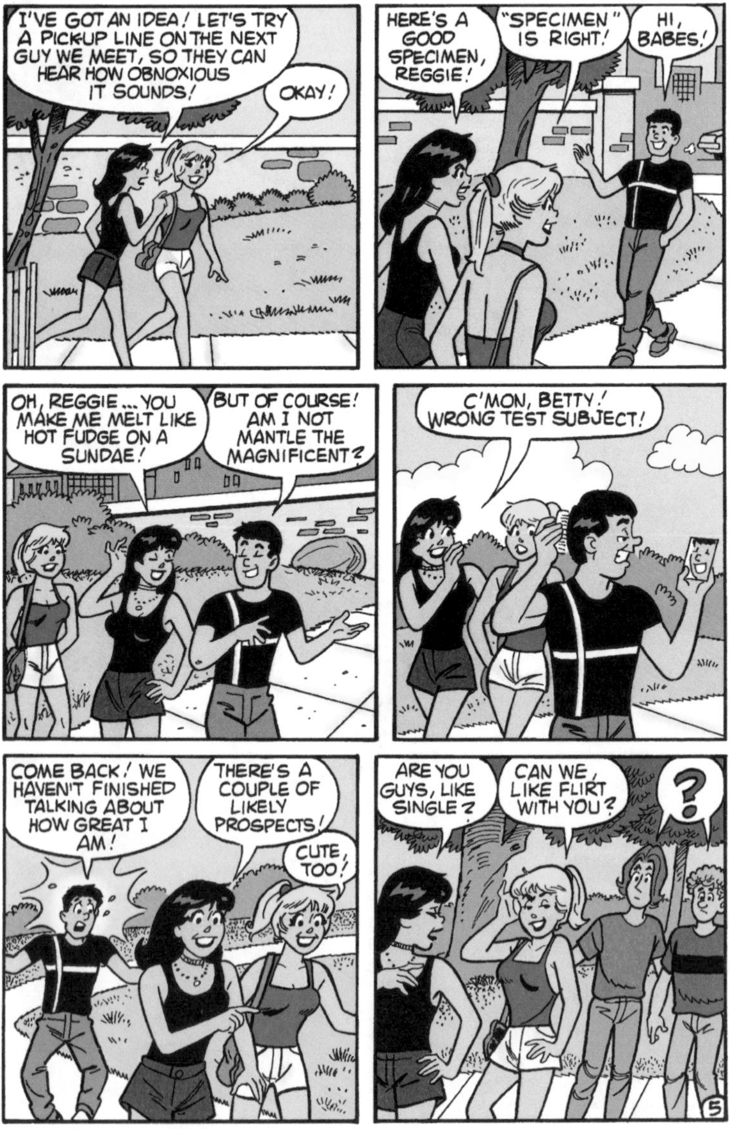
I'VE GOT AN IDEA! LET'S TRY A PICK-UP LINE ON THE NEXT GUY WE MEET, SO THEY CAN HEAR HOW OBNOXIOUS IT SOUNDS!
OKAY!
HERE'S A GOOD SPECIMEN, REGGIE!
"SPECIMEN" IS RIGHT!
HI, BABES!
OH, REGGIE... YOU MAKE ME MELT LIKE HOT FUDGE ON A SUNDAE!
BUT OF COURSE! AM I NOT MANTLE THE MAGNIFICENT?
C'MON, BETTY! WRONG TEST SUBJECT!
COME BACK! WE HAVEN'T FINISHED TALKING ABOUT HOW GREAT I AM!
THERE'S A COUPLE OF LIKELY PROSPECTS!
CUTE, TOO!
ARE YOU GUYS, LIKE SINGLE?
CAN WE, LIKE FLIRT WITH YOU?
?
5

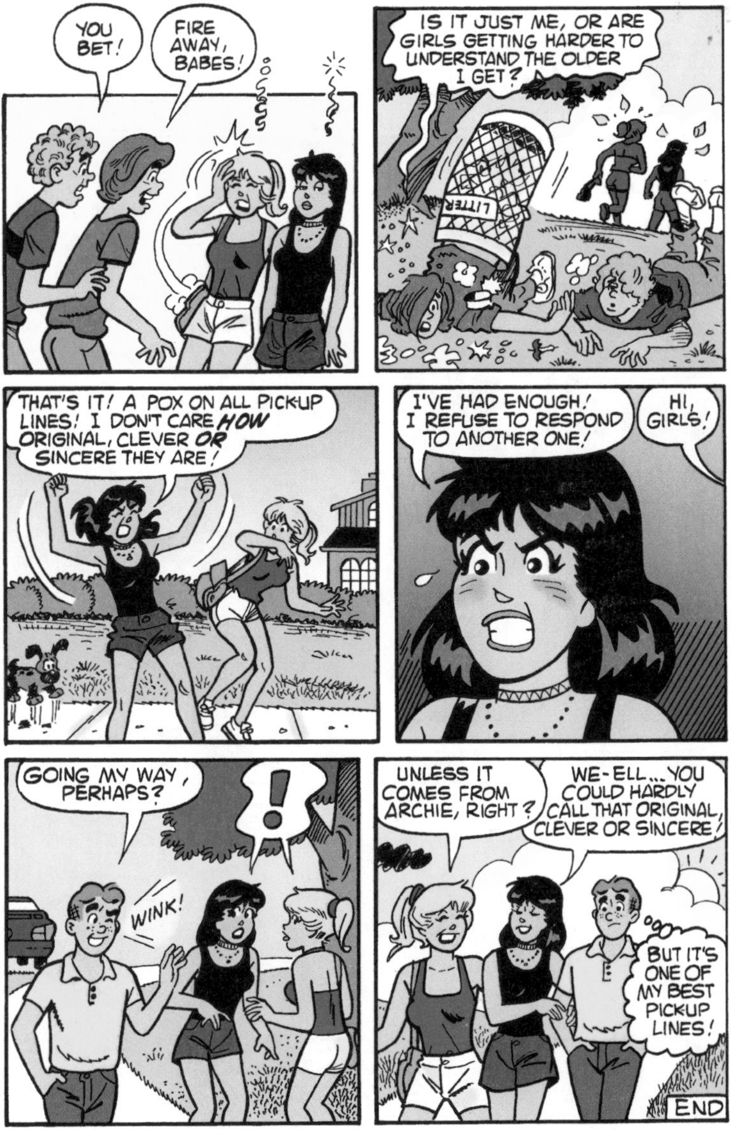
YOU BET!
FIRE AWAY, BABES!
IS IT JUST ME, OR ARE GIRLS GETTING HARDER TO UNDERSTAND THE OLDER I GET?
LITTER
THAT'S IT! A POX ON ALL PICK-UP LINES! I DON'T CARE HOW ORIGINAL, CLEVER OR SINCERE THEY ARE!
I'VE HAD ENOUGH! I REFUSE TO RESPOND TO ANOTHER ONE!
HI, GIRLS!
GOING MY WAY, PERHAPS?
!
WINK!
UNLESS IT COMES FROM ARCHIE, RIGHT?
WE-ELL... YOU COULD HARDLY CALL THAT ORIGINAL, CLEVER OR SINCERE!
BUT IT'S ONE OF MY BEST PICKUP LINES!
END

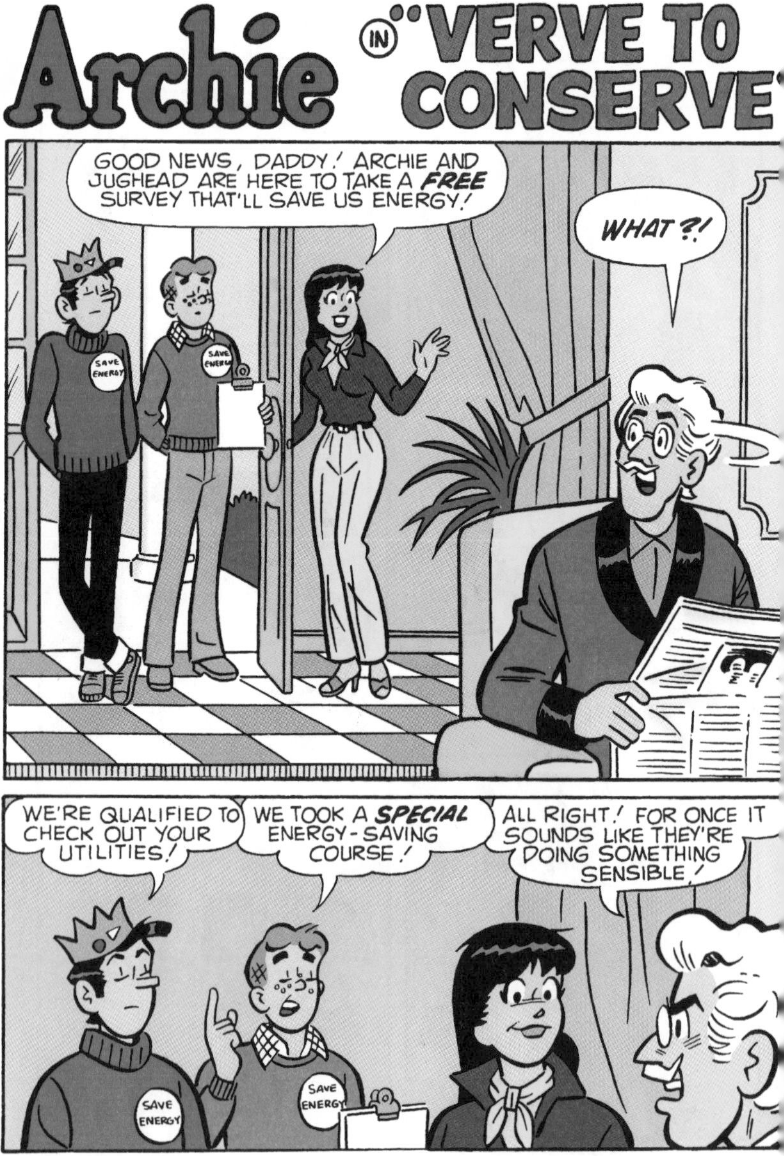
Archie IN "VERVE TO CONSERVE"
GOOD NEWS, DADDY! ARCHIE AND JUGHEAD ARE HERE TO TAKE A FREE SURVEY THAT'LL SAVE US ENERGY!
WHAT?!
SAVE ENERGY
SAVE ENERGY
WE'RE QUALIFIED TO CHECK OUT YOUR UTILITIES!
WE TOOK A SPECIAL ENERGY-SAVING COURSE!
ALL RIGHT! FOR ONCE IT SOUNDS LIKE THEY'RE DOING SOMETHING SENSIBLE!
SAVE ENERGY
SAVE ENERGY

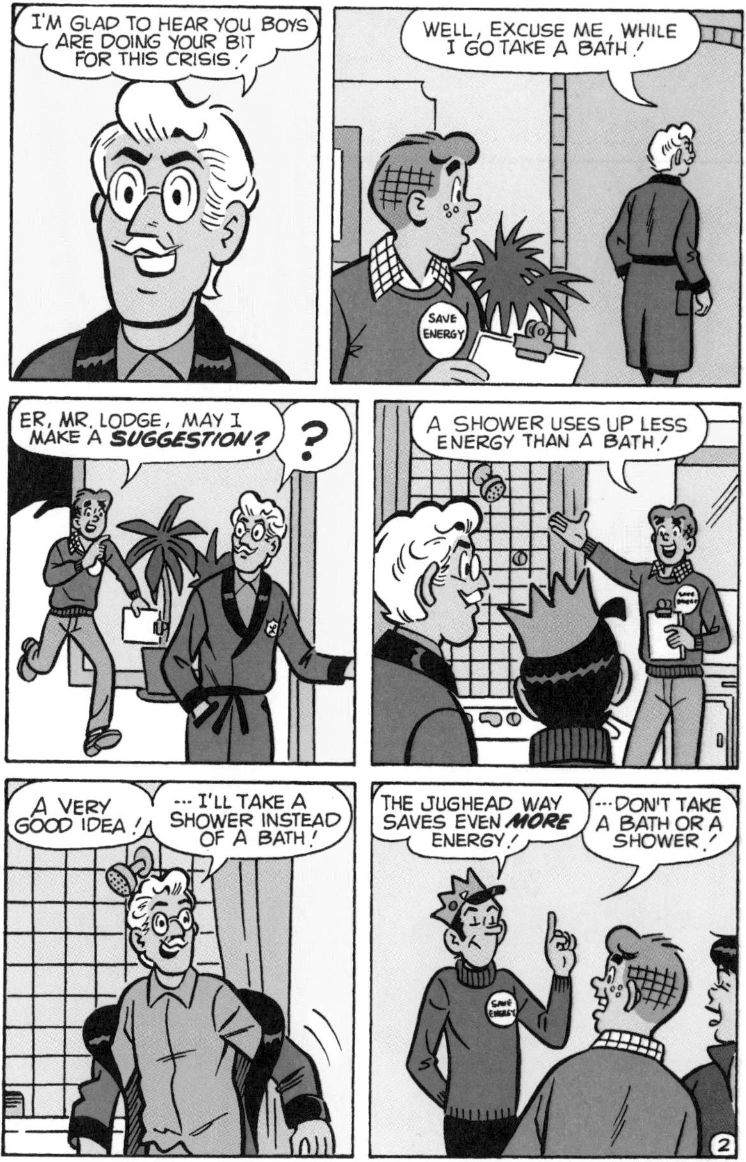

I'M GLAD TO HEAR YOU BOYS ARE DOING YOUR BIT FOR THIS CRISIS!
WELL, EXCUSE ME, WHILE I GO TAKE A BATH!
SAVE ENERGY
ER, MR. LODGE, MAY I MAKE A SUGGESTION?
?
A SHOWER USES UP LESS ENERGY THAN A BATH!
A VERY GOOD IDEA!
--- I'LL TAKE A SHOWER INSTEAD OF A BATH!
THE JUGHEAD WAY SAVES EVEN MORE ENERGY!
---DON'T TAKE A BATH OR A SHOWER!
SAVE ENERGY
2

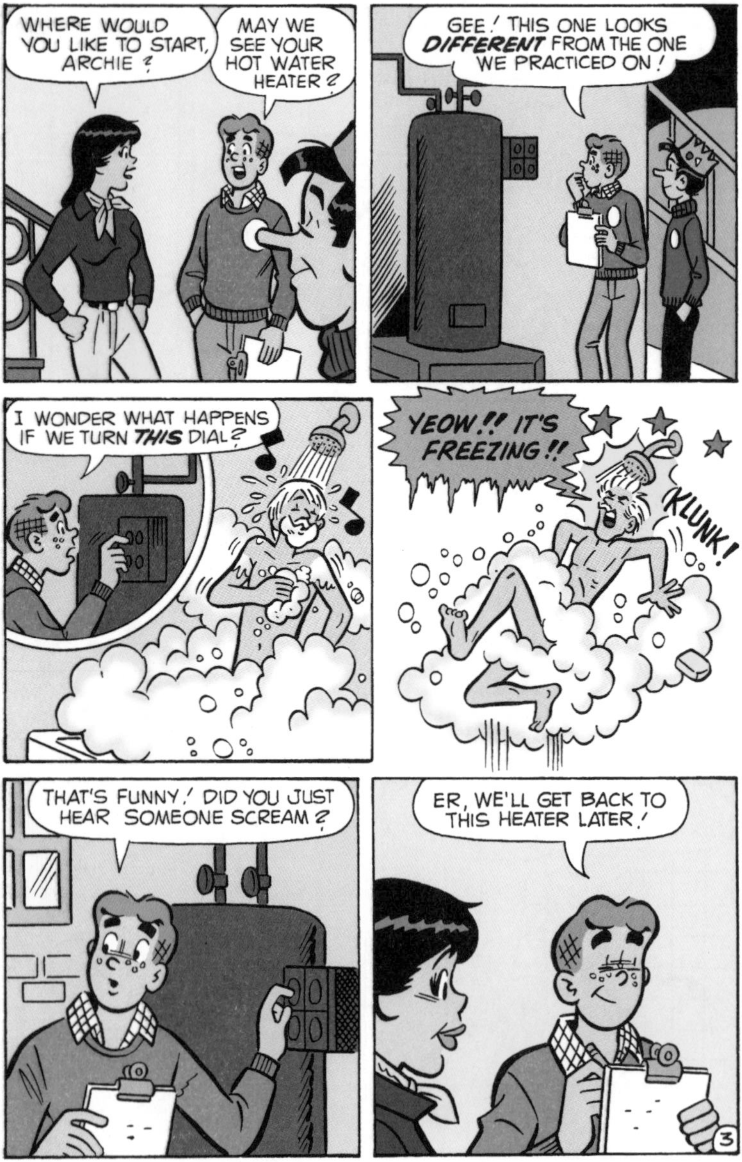
WHERE WOULD YOU LIKE TO START, ARCHIE?
MAY WE SEE YOUR HOT WATER HEATER?
GEE! THIS ONE LOOKS DIFFERENT FROM THE ONE WE PRACTICED ON!
I WONDER WHAT HAPPENS IF WE TURN THIS DIAL?
YEOW!!! IT'S FREEZING!!
KLUNK!
THAT'S FUNNY! DID YOU JUST HEAR SOMEONE SCREAM?
ER, WE'LL GET BACK TO THIS HEATER LATER!
3

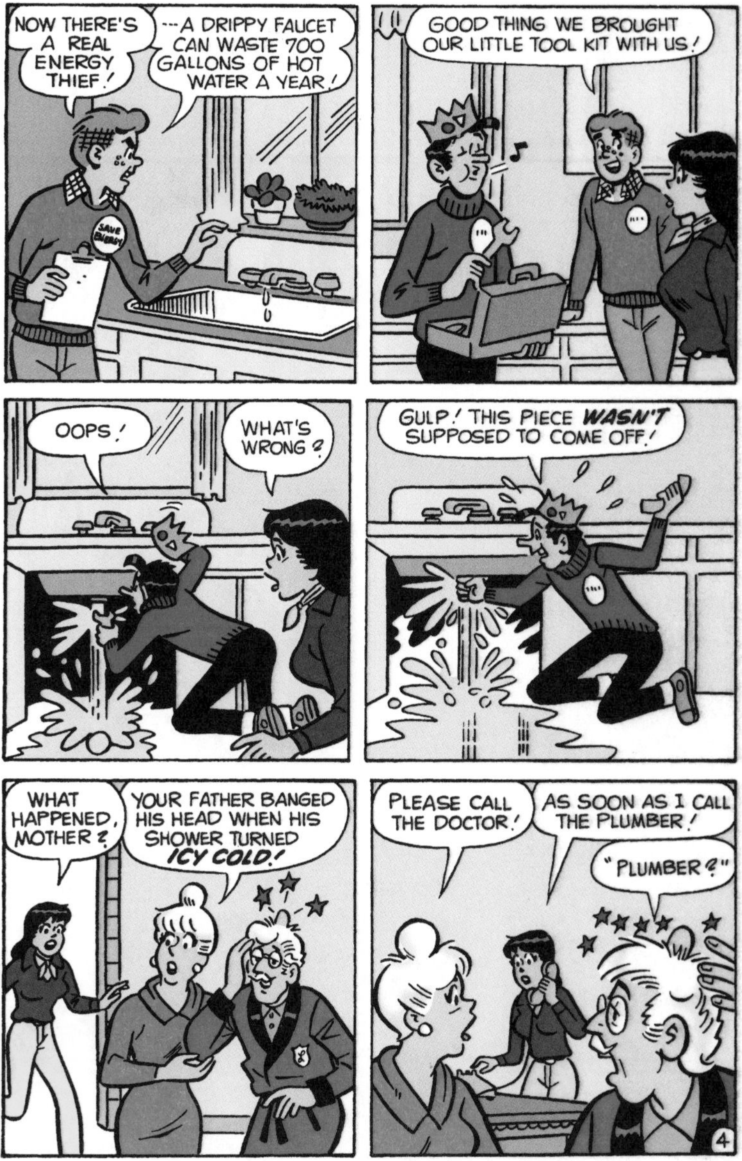
NOW THERE'S A REAL ENERGY THIEF!
---A DRIPPY FAUCET CAN WASTE 700 GALLONS OF HOT WATER A YEAR!
GOOD THING WE BROUGHT OUR LITTLE TOOL KIT WITH US!
OOPS!
WHAT'S WRONG?
GULP! THIS PIECE WASN'T SUPPOSED TO COME OFF!
WHAT HAPPENED, MOTHER?
YOUR FATHER BANGED HIS HEAD WHEN HIS SHOWER TURNED ICY COLD!
PLEASE CALL THE DOCTOR!
AS SOON AS I CALL THE PLUMBER!
"PLUMBER?"
4

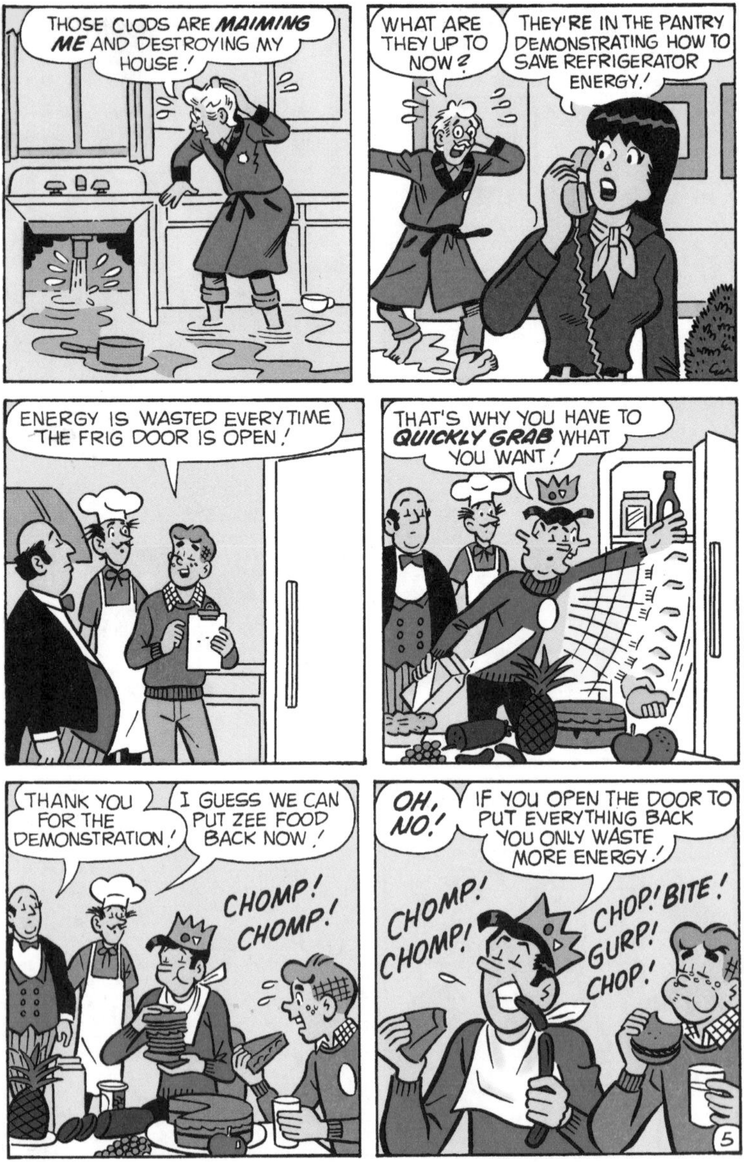

THOSE CLODS ARE MAIMING ME AND DESTROYING MY HOUSE!
WHAT ARE THEY UP TO NOW?
THEY'RE IN THE PANTRY DEMONSTRATING HOW TO SAVE REFRIGERATOR ENERGY!
ENERGY IS WASTED EVERY TIME THE FRIG DOOR IS OPEN!
THAT'S WHY YOU HAVE TO QUICKLY GRAB WHAT YOU WANT!
THANK YOU FOR THE DEMONSTRATION!
I GUESS WE CAN PUT ZEE FOOD BACK NOW!
CHOMP! CHOMP!
OH, NO!
IF YOU OPEN THE DOOR TO PUT EVERYTHING BACK YOU ONLY WASTE MORE ENERGY!
CHOMP! CHOMP!
CHOP! BITE! GURP! CHOP!
5

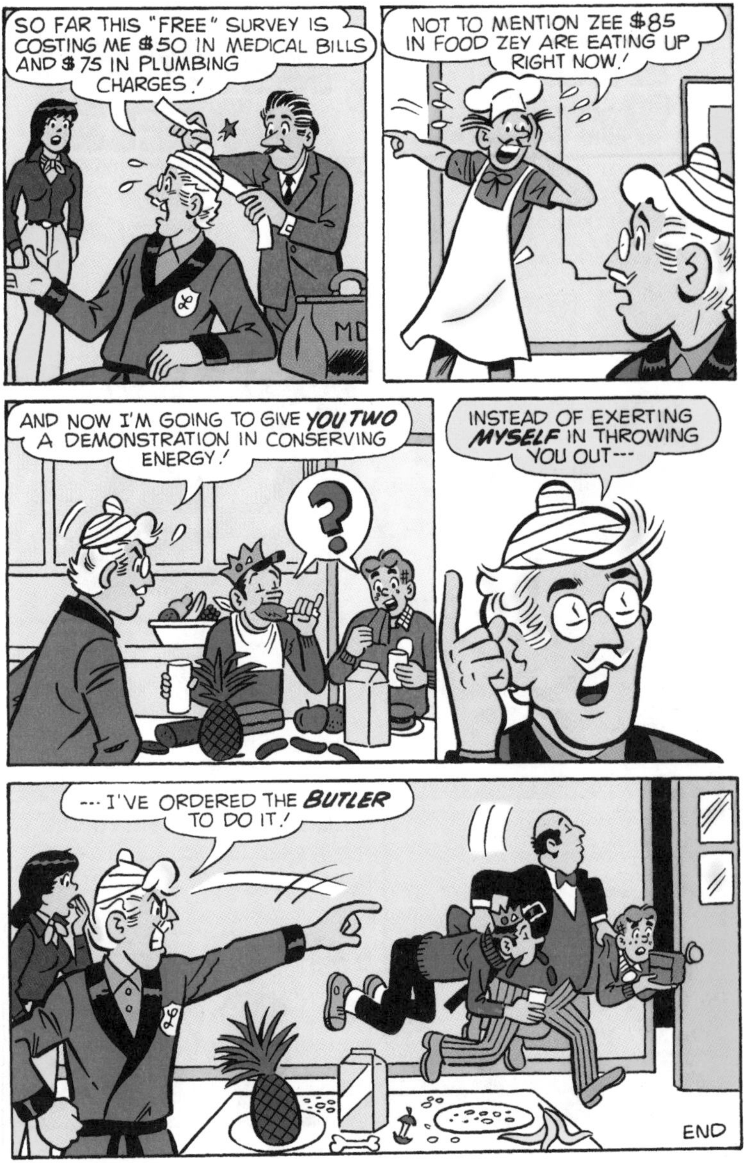
SO FAR THIS "FREE" SURVEY IS COSTING ME $50 IN MEDICAL BILLS AND $75 IN PLUMBING CHARGES!
NOT TO MENTION ZEE $85 IN FOOD ZEY ARE EATING UP RIGHT NOW!
MD
AND NOW I'M GOING TO GIVE YOU TWO A DEMONSTRATION IN CONSERVING ENERGY!
?
INSTEAD OF EXERTING MYSELF IN THROWING YOU OUT---
--- I'VE ORDERED THE BUTLER TO DO IT!
END

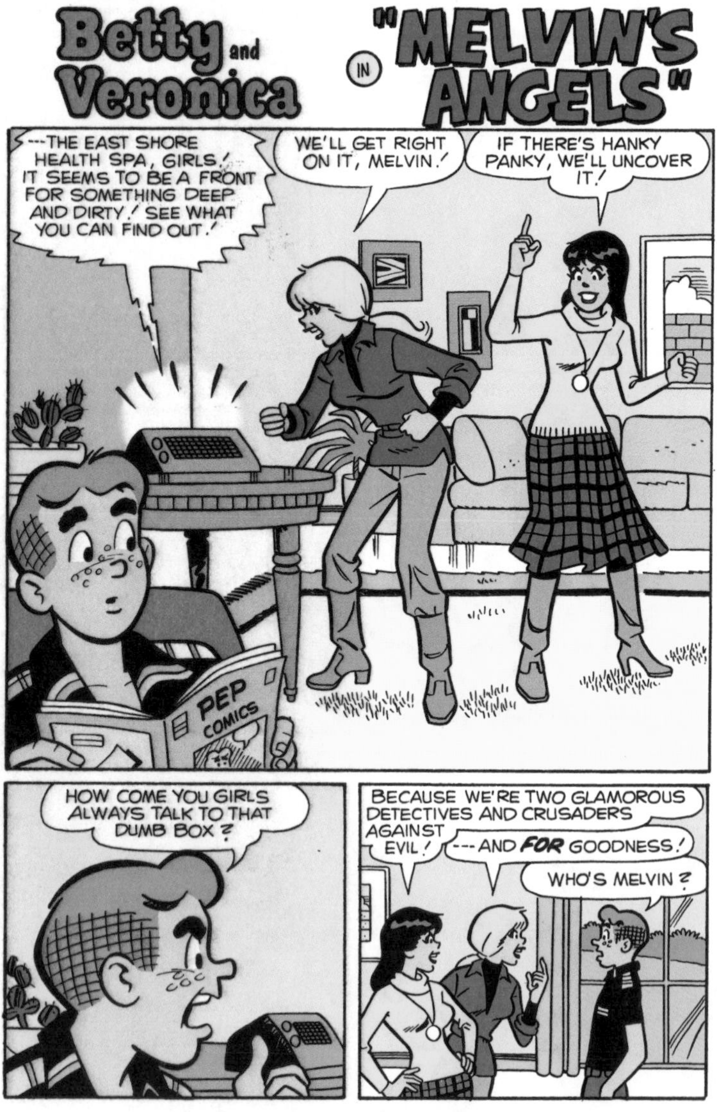
Betty and Veronica IN "MELVIN'S ANGELS"
---THE EAST SHORE HEALTH SPA, GIRLS! IT SEEMS TO BE A FRONT FOR SOMETHING DEEP AND DIRTY! SEE WHAT YOU CAN FIND OUT!
WE'LL GET RIGHT ON IT, MELVIN!
IF THERE'S HANKY PANKY, WE'LL UNCOVER IT!
PEP COMICS
HOW COME YOU GIRLS ALWAYS TALK TO THAT DUMB BOX?
BECAUSE WE'RE TWO GLAMOROUS DETECTIVES AND CRUSADERS AGAINST EVIL!
---AND FOR GOODNESS!
WHO'S MELVIN?

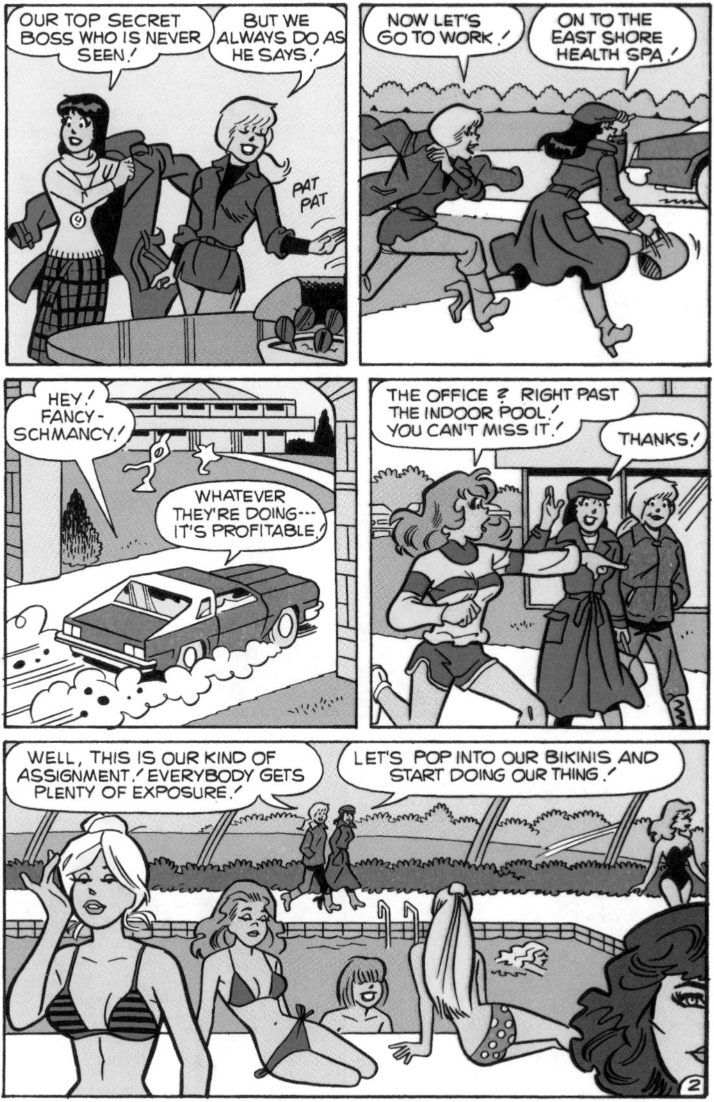
OUR TOP SECRET BOSS WHO IS NEVER SEEN!
BUT WE ALWAYS DO AS HE SAYS!
PAT PAT
NOW LET'S GO TO WORK!
ON TO THE EAST SHORE HEALTH SPA!
HEY! FANCY-SCHMANCY!
WHATEVER THEY'RE DOING--- IT'S PROFITABLE!
THE OFFICE? RIGHT PAST THE INDOOR POOL! YOU CAN'T MISS IT!
THANKS!
WELL, THIS IS OUR KIND OF ASSIGNMENT! EVERYBODY GETS PLENTY OF EXPOSURE!
LET'S POP INTO OUR BIKINIS AND START DOING OUR THING!
2

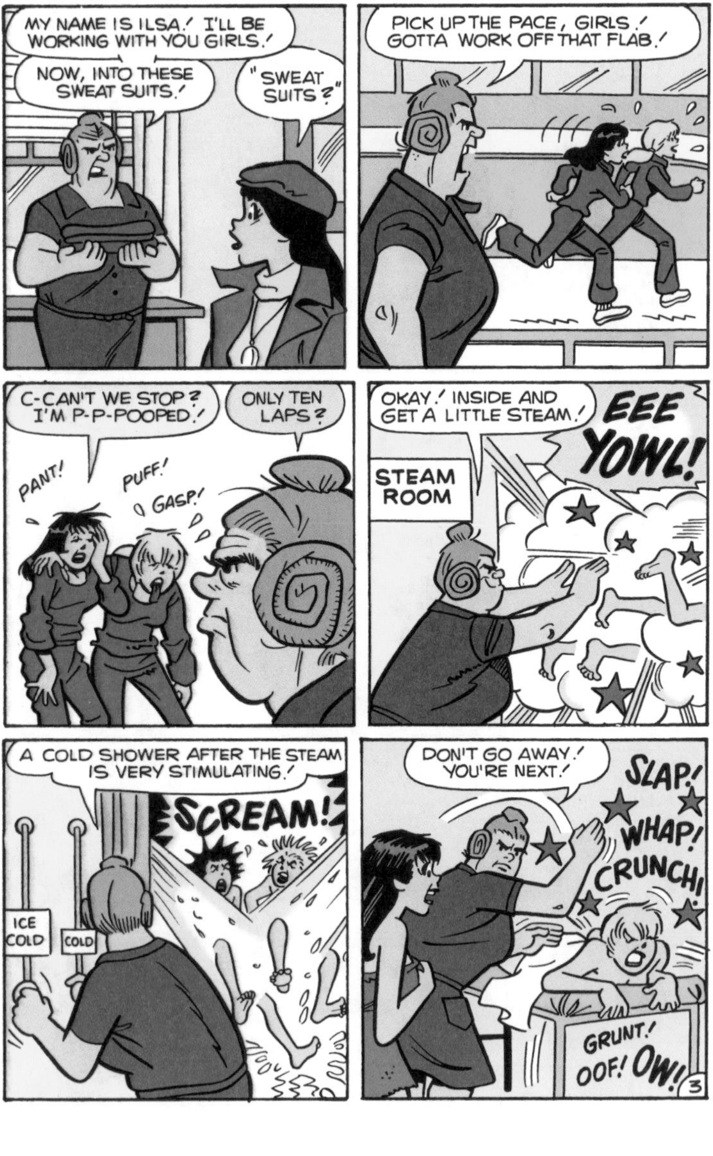

MY NAME IS ILSA! I'LL BE WORKING WITH YOU GIRLS!
NOW, INTO THESE SWEAT SUITS!
"SWEAT SUITS?"
PICK UP THE PACE, GIRLS! GOTTA WORK OFF THAT FLAB!
C-CAN'T WE STOP? I'M P-P-POOPED!
ONLY TEN LAPS?
PANT!
PUFF!
GASP!
OKAY! INSIDE AND GET A LITTLE STEAM!
STEAM ROOM
EEE YOWL!
A COLD SHOWER AFTER THE STEAM IS VERY STIMULATING!
SCREAM!
ICE COLD
COLD
DON'T GO AWAY! YOU'RE NEXT!
SLAP!
WHAP!
CRUNCH!
GRUNT!
OOF! OW!
3

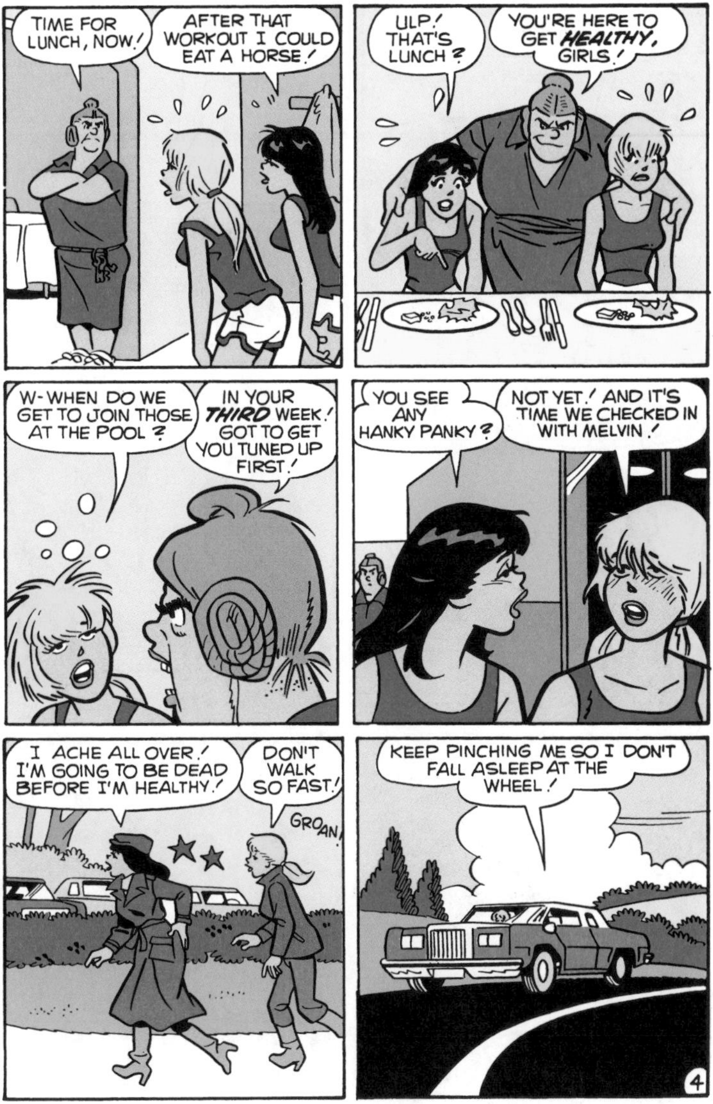
TIME FOR LUNCH, NOW!
AFTER THAT WORKOUT I COULD EAT A HORSE!
ULP! THAT'S LUNCH?
YOU'RE HERE TO GET HEALTHY, GIRLS!
W-WHEN DO WE GET TO JOIN THOSE AT THE POOL?
IN YOUR THIRD WEEK! GOT TO GET YOU TUNED UP FIRST!
YOU SEE ANY HANKY PANKY?
NOT YET! AND IT'S TIME WE CHECKED IN WITH MELVIN!
I ACHE ALL OVER! I'M GOING TO BE DEAD BEFORE I'M HEALTHY!
DON'T WALK SO FAST!
GROAN!
KEEP PINCHING ME SO I DON'T FALL ASLEEP AT THE WHEEL!
4

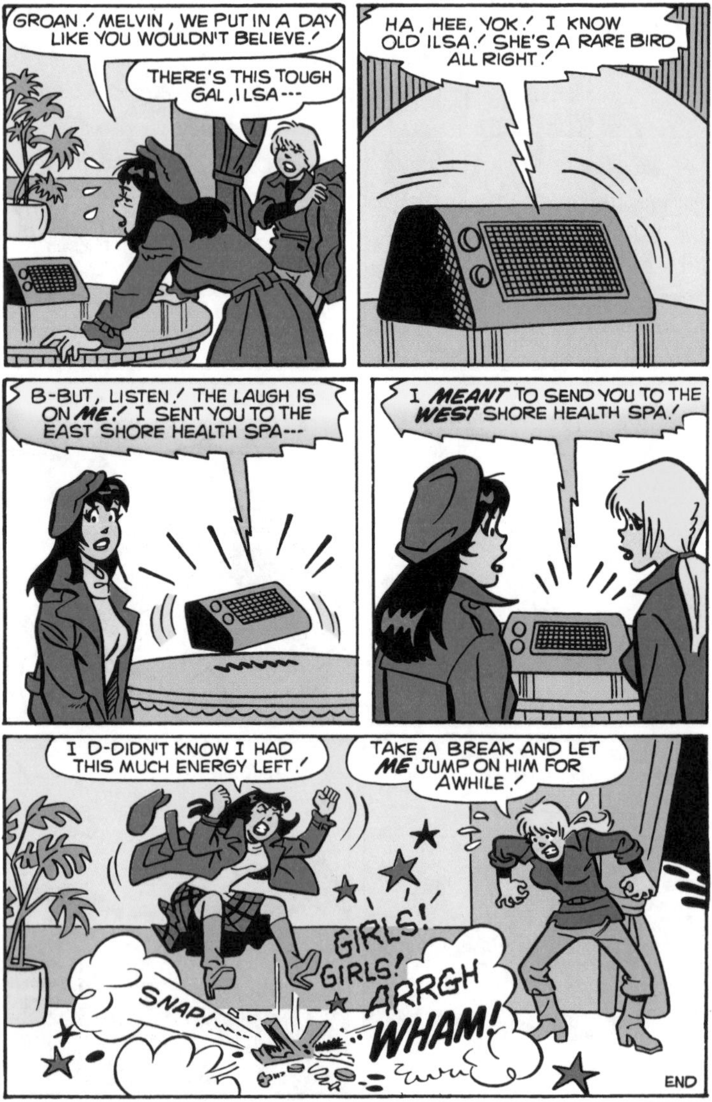
GROAN! MELVIN, WE PUT IN A DAY LIKE YOU WOULDN'T BELIEVE!
THERE'S THIS TOUGH GAL, ILSA---
HA, HEE, YOK! I KNOW OLD ILSA! SHE'S A RARE BIRD ALL RIGHT!
B-BUT, LISTEN! THE LAUGH IS ON ME! I SENT YOU TO THE EAST SHORE HEALTH SPA---
I MEANT TO SEND YOU TO THE WEST SHORE HEALTH SPA!
I D-DIDN'T KNOW I HAD THIS MUCH ENERGY LEFT!
TAKE A BREAK AND LET ME JUMP ON HIM FOR AWHILE!
GIRLS!
GIRLS!
ARRGH
SNAP!
WHAM!
END

### Double Play
*Betty & Veronica* #140, 1999
by Angelo DeCesare, Dan DeCarlo,
Henry Scarpelli, Barry Grossman and Bill Yoshida

My parents were big on reading and not-so-big on candy, so I always had access to Archie Comics. I suspect it was less of a threat to family peace to sit me somewhere with a Double Digest than to risk the tantrums of a daughter in the throes of a Dubble Bubble sugar high. And Archie Comics were so nice; what other collection of stories of high school students would you happily hand to a child without fear?

**Brenna Clarke Gray**
*Writer and Educator*

### The Art Lesson
*Betty's Diary* #1, 1987
by Kathleen Webb, Dan DeCarlo,
Jim DeCarlo and Bill Yoshida

As a kid, I spent many lazy afternoons with an Archie Digest— and some recent afternoons as well! When I was asked to recommend a story for this book, I knew I wanted to recommend a story from *Betty's Diary*. While Betty and Veronica are famous for fghting over Archie, Betty's Diary is where we learned more about Betty's life outside of romance. "The Art Lesson" is a great example—it shows the reader how important it is to be true to yourself—especially facing peer pressure.

**Grace Randolph**
*Host and Writer, **Think About the Ink / Supurbia***

~BONUS COVER~
*Betty & Veronica* #257, February 2012

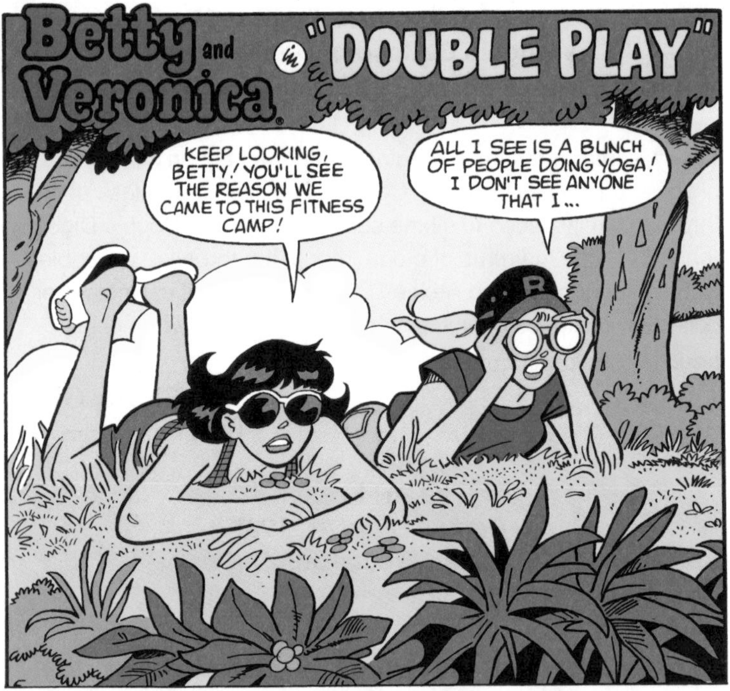
Betty and Veronica in "DOUBLE PLAY"
KEEP LOOKING, BETTY! YOU'LL SEE THE REASON WE CAME TO THIS FITNESS CAMP!
ALL I SEE IS A BUNCH OF PEOPLE DOING YOGA! I DON'T SEE ANYONE THAT I...

SCRIPT: ANGELO DECESARE PENCILS: DAN DECARLO INKING: HENRY SCARPELLI LETTERING: BILL YOSHIDA COLORING: BARRY GROSSMAN

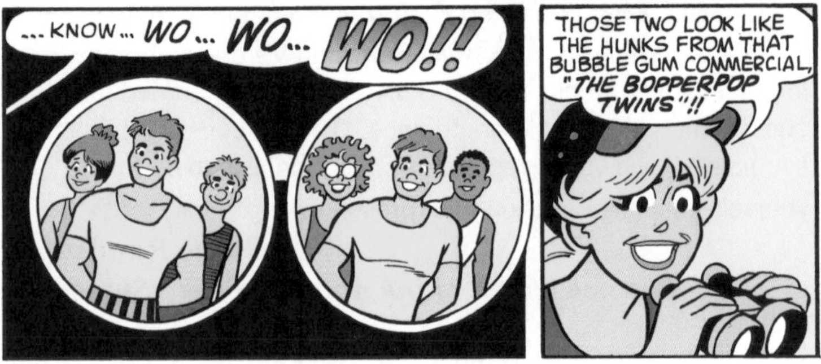
... KNOW... WO... WO... WO!!
THOSE TWO LOOK LIKE THE HUNKS FROM THAT BUBBLE GUM COMMERCIAL, "THE BOPPERPOP TWINS"!!

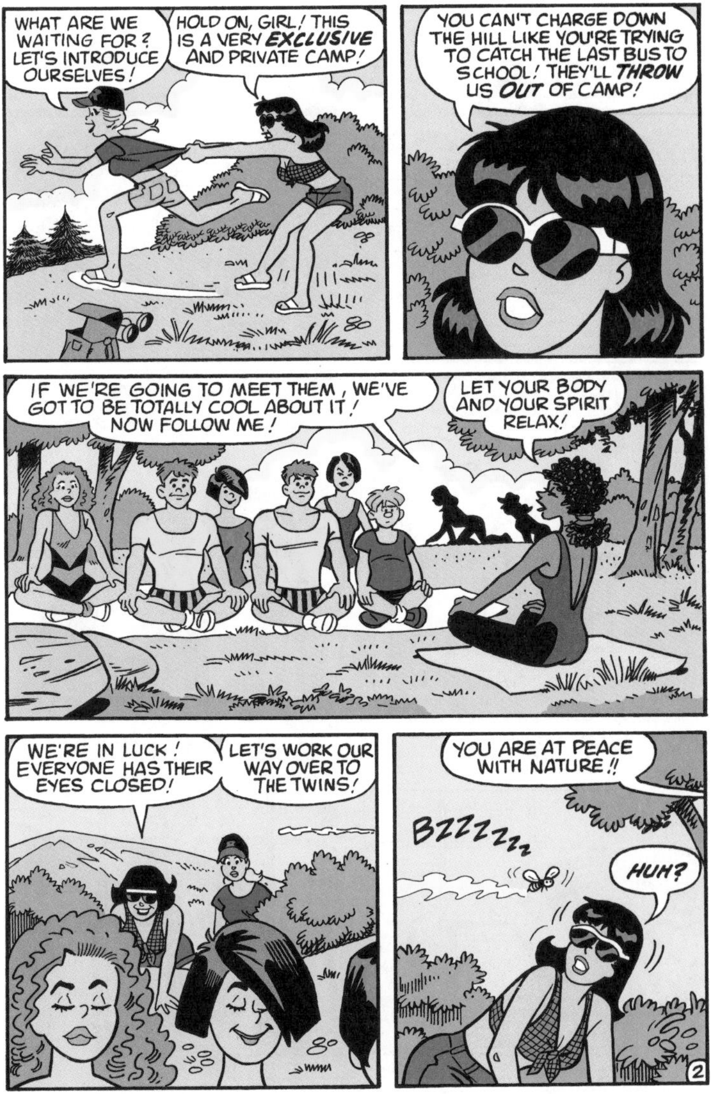
WHAT ARE WE WAITING FOR? LET'S INTRODUCE OURSELVES!
HOLD ON, GIRL! THIS IS A VERY EXCLUSIVE AND PRIVATE CAMP!
YOU CAN'T CHARGE DOWN THE HILL LIKE YOU'RE TRYING TO CATCH THE LAST BUS TO SCHOOL! THEY'LL THROW US OUT OF CAMP!
IF WE'RE GOING TO MEET THEM, WE'VE GOT TO BE TOTALLY COOL ABOUT IT! NOW FOLLOW ME!
LET YOUR BODY AND YOUR SPIRIT RELAX!
WE'RE IN LUCK! EVERYONE HAS THEIR EYES CLOSED!
LET'S WORK OUR WAY OVER TO THE TWINS!
YOU ARE AT PEACE WITH NATURE!!
BZZZZzz
HUH?
2

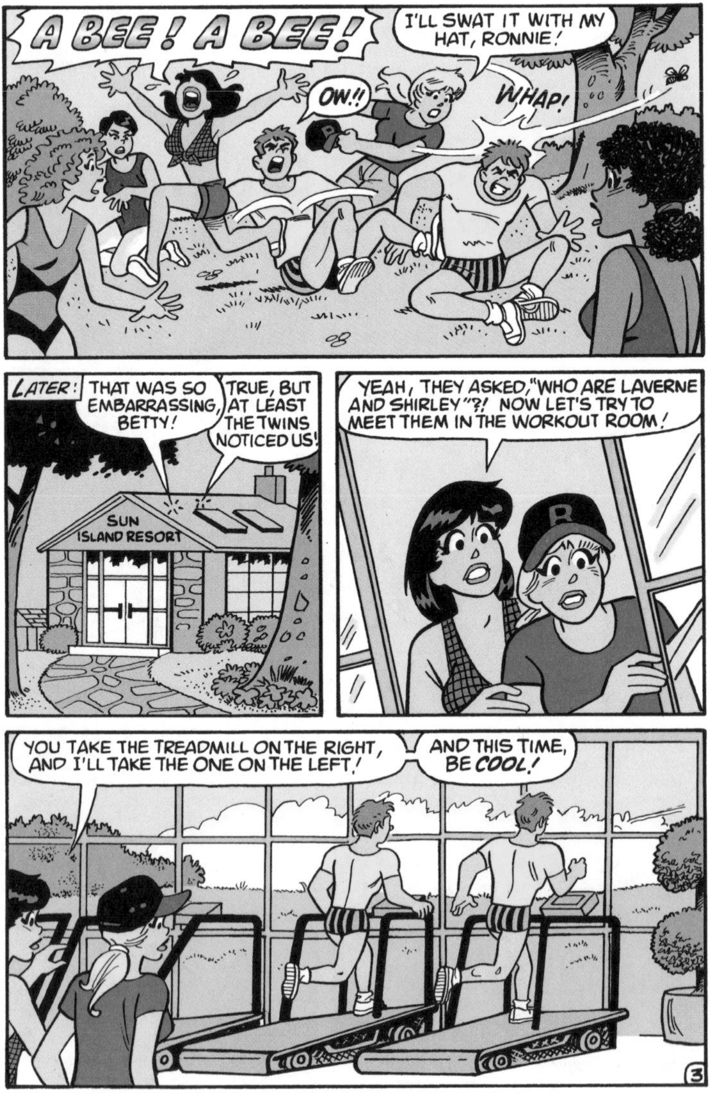
A BEE! A BEE!
I'LL SWAT IT WITH MY HAT, RONNIE!
OW!!
WHAP!
LATER:
THAT WAS SO EMBARRASSING, BETTY!
TRUE, BUT AT LEAST THE TWINS NOTICED US!
SUN ISLAND RESORT
YEAH, THEY ASKED, "WHO ARE LAVERNE AND SHIRLEY"?! NOW LET'S TRY TO MEET THEM IN THE WORKOUT ROOM!
YOU TAKE THE TREADMILL ON THE RIGHT, AND I'LL TAKE THE ONE ON THE LEFT!
AND THIS TIME, BE COOL!
3

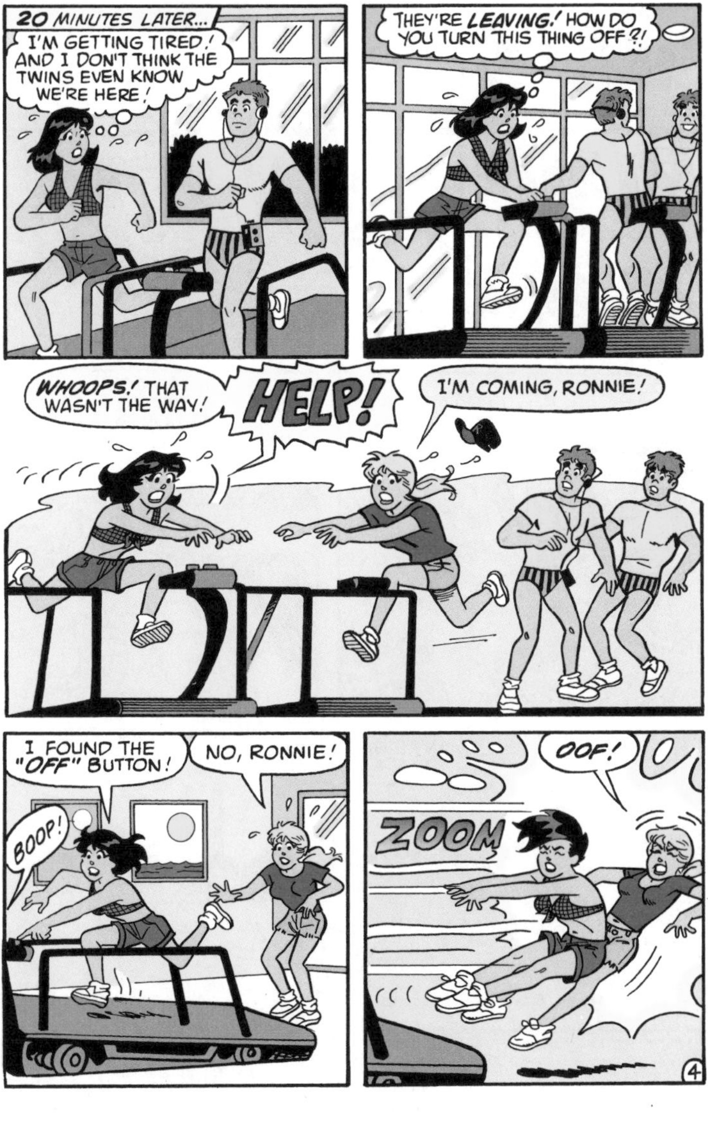

20 MINUTES LATER...
I'M GETTING TIRED! AND I DON'T THINK THE TWINS EVEN KNOW WE'RE HERE!
THEY'RE LEAVING! HOW DO YOU TURN THIS THING OFF?!
WHOOPS! THAT WASN'T THE WAY!
HELP!
I'M COMING, RONNIE!
I FOUND THE "OFF" BUTTON!
NO, RONNIE!
BOOP!
OOF!
ZOOM
4

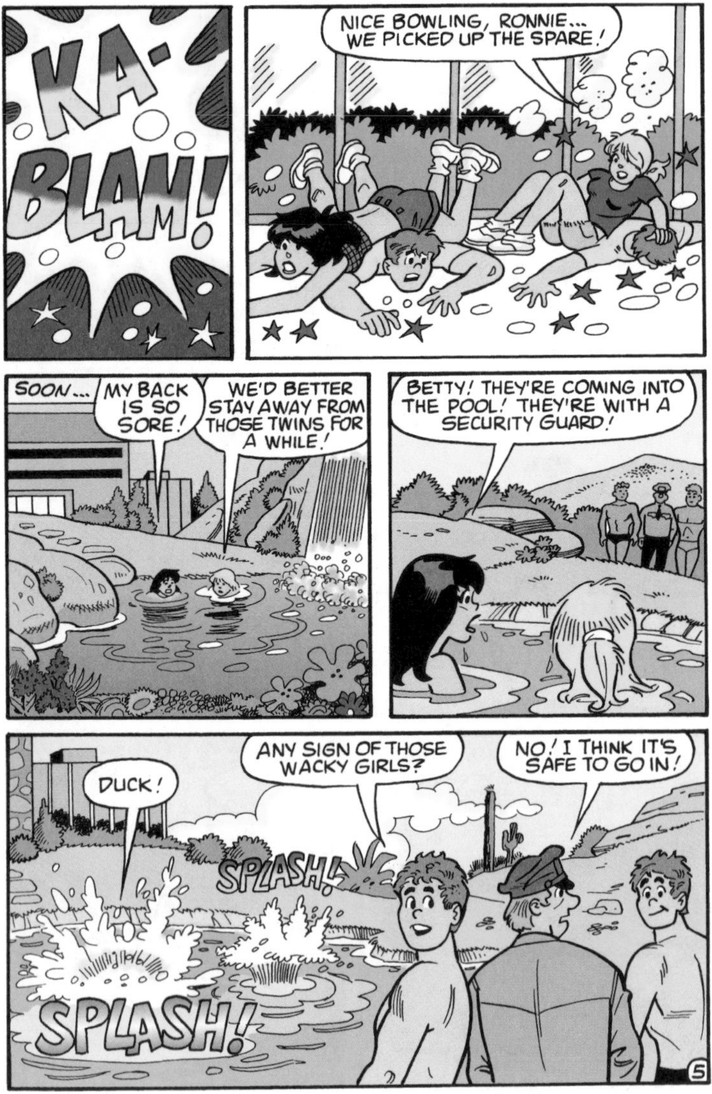
KA-
BLAM!
NICE BOWLING, RONNIE... WE PICKED UP THE SPARE!
SOON...
MY BACK IS SO SORE!
WE'D BETTER STAY AWAY FROM THOSE TWINS FOR A WHILE!
BETTY! THEY'RE COMING INTO THE POOL! THEY'RE WITH A SECURITY GUARD!
DUCK!
ANY SIGN OF THOSE WACKY GIRLS?
NO! I THINK IT'S SAFE TO GO IN!
SPLASH!
SPLASH!
5

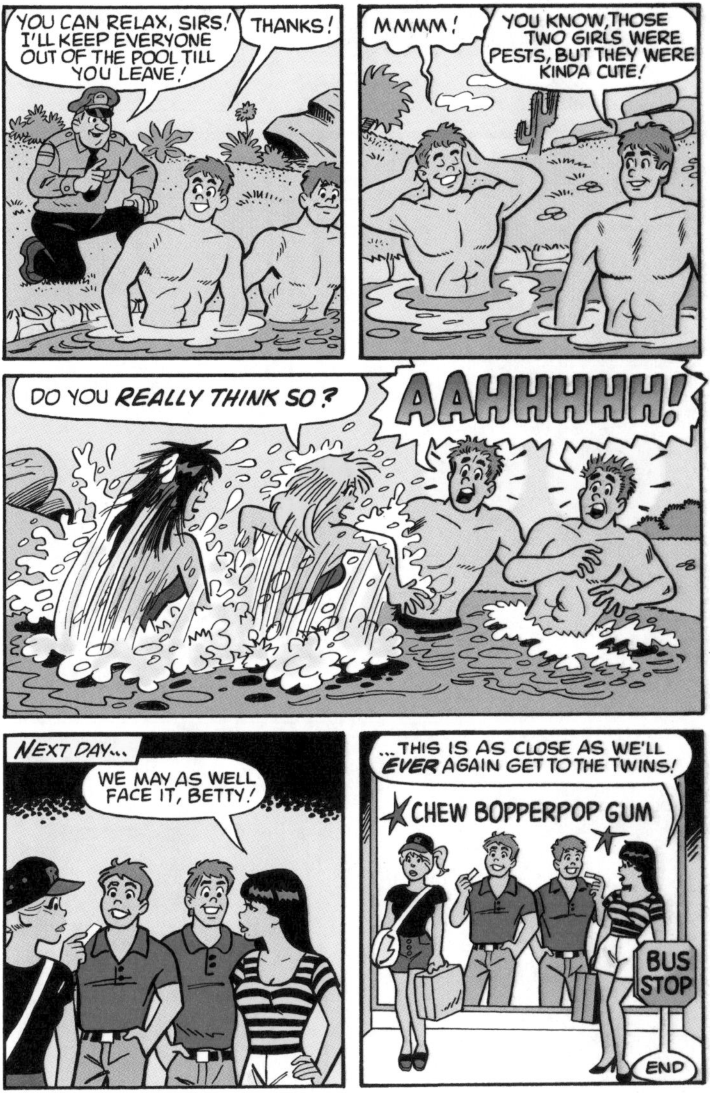
YOU CAN RELAX, SIRS! I'LL KEEP EVERYONE OUT OF THE POOL TILL YOU LEAVE!
THANKS!
MMMM!
YOU KNOW, THOSE TWO GIRLS WERE PESTS, BUT THEY WERE KINDA CUTE!
DO YOU REALLY THINK SO?
AAHHHHH!
NEXT DAY...
WE MAY AS WELL FACE IT, BETTY!
...THIS IS AS CLOSE AS WE'LL EVER AGAIN GET TO THE TWINS!
CHEW BOPPERPOP GUM
BUS STOP
END

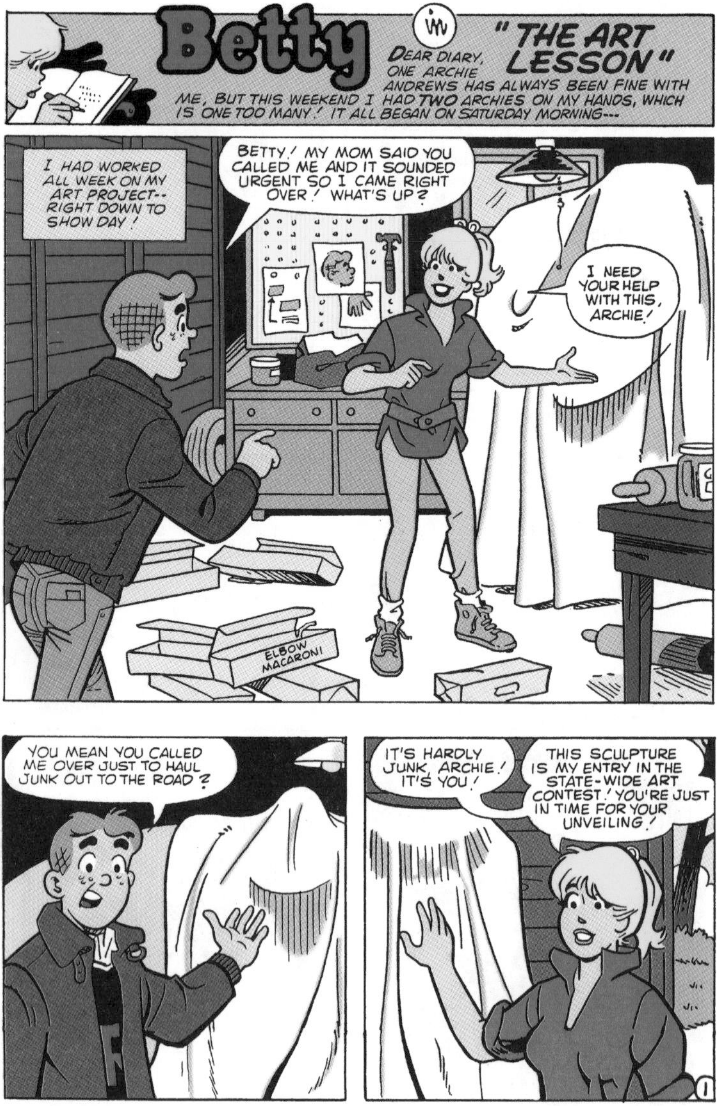
Betty
"THE ART LESSON"
DEAR DIARY, ONE ARCHIE ANDREWS HAS ALWAYS BEEN FINE WITH ME, BUT THIS WEEKEND I HAD TWO ARCHIES ON MY HANDS, WHICH IS ONE TOO MANY! IT ALL BEGAN ON SATURDAY MORNING---
I HAD WORKED ALL WEEK ON MY ART PROJECT-- RIGHT DOWN TO SHOW DAY!
BETTY! MY MOM SAID YOU CALLED ME AND IT SOUNDED URGENT SO I CAME RIGHT OVER! WHAT'S UP?
I NEED YOUR HELP WITH THIS, ARCHIE!
ELBOW MACARONI
YOU MEAN YOU CALLED ME OVER JUST TO HAUL JUNK OUT TO THE ROAD?
IT'S HARDLY JUNK, ARCHIE! IT'S YOU!
THIS SCULPTURE IS MY ENTRY IN THE STATE-WIDE ART CONTEST! YOU'RE JUST IN TIME FOR YOUR UNVEILING!
1

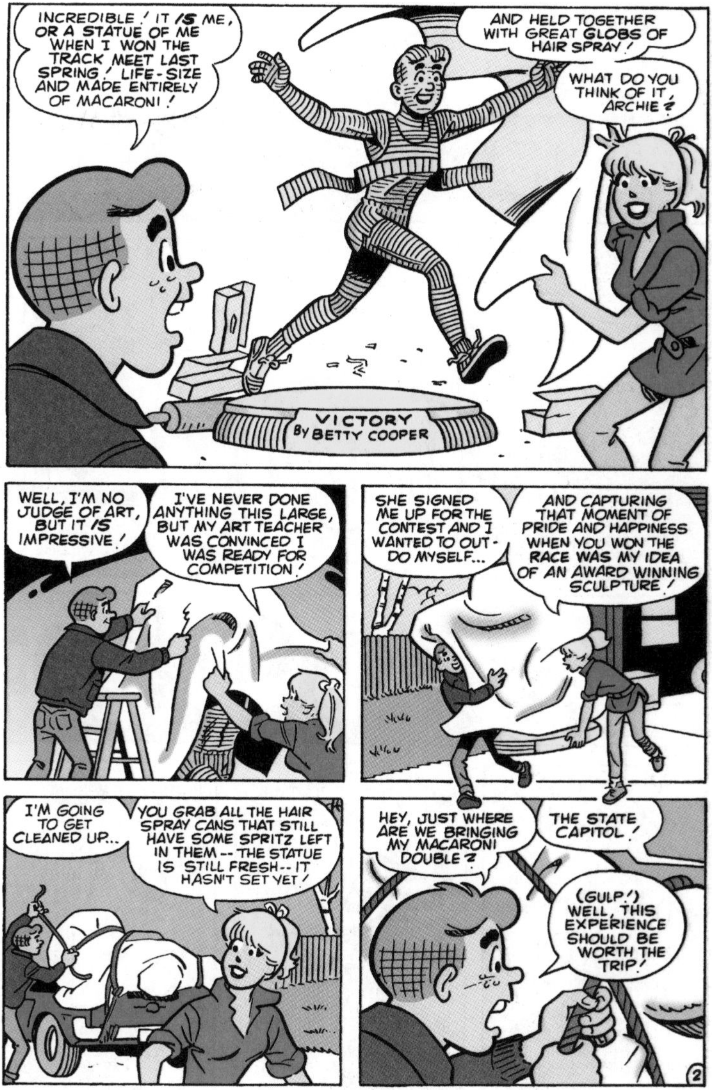
INCREDIBLE! IT IS ME, OR A STATUE OF ME WHEN I WON THE TRACK MEET LAST SPRING! LIFE-SIZE AND MADE ENTIRELY OF MACARONI!
AND HELD TOGETHER WITH GREAT GLOBS OF HAIR SPRAY!
WHAT DO YOU THINK OF IT, ARCHIE?
VICTORY BY BETTY COOPER
WELL, I'M NO JUDGE OF ART, BUT IT IS IMPRESSIVE!
I'VE NEVER DONE ANYTHING THIS LARGE, BUT MY ART TEACHER WAS CONVINCED I WAS READY FOR COMPETITION!
SHE SIGNED ME UP FOR THE CONTEST AND I WANTED TO OUT-DO MYSELF...
AND CAPTURING THAT MOMENT OF PRIDE AND HAPPINESS WHEN YOU WON THE RACE WAS MY IDEA OF AN AWARD WINNING SCULPTURE!
I'M GOING TO GET CLEANED UP...
YOU GRAB ALL THE HAIR SPRAY CANS THAT STILL HAVE SOME SPRITZ LEFT IN THEM -- THE STATUE IS STILL FRESH -- IT HASN'T SET YET!
HEY, JUST WHERE ARE WE BRINGING MY MACARONI DOUBLE?
THE STATE CAPITOL!
(GULP!) WELL, THIS EXPERIENCE SHOULD BE WORTH THE TRIP!
2

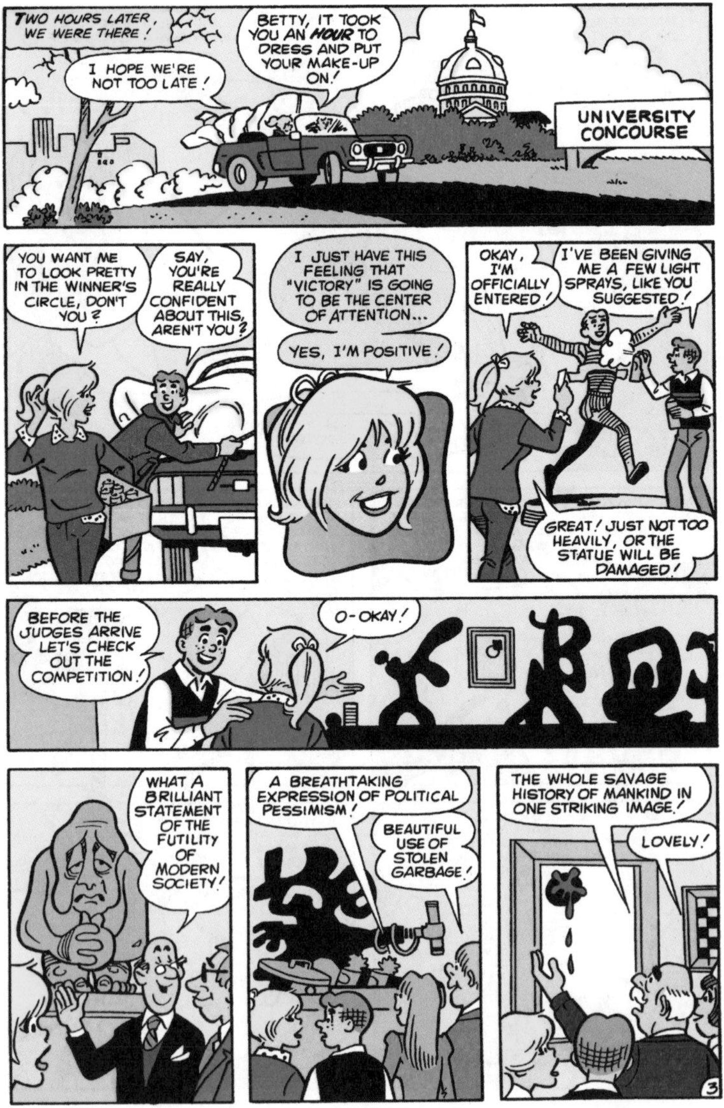
TWO HOURS LATER, WE WERE THERE!
I HOPE WE'RE NOT TOO LATE!
BETTY, IT TOOK YOU AN HOUR TO DRESS AND PUT YOUR MAKE-UP ON!
UNIVERSITY CONCOURSE
YOU WANT ME TO LOOK PRETTY IN THE WINNER'S CIRCLE, DON'T YOU?
SAY, YOU'RE REALLY CONFIDENT ABOUT THIS, AREN'T YOU?
I JUST HAVE THIS FEELING THAT "VICTORY" IS GOING TO BE THE CENTER OF ATTENTION...
YES, I'M POSITIVE!
OKAY, I'M OFFICIALLY ENTERED!
I'VE BEEN GIVING ME A FEW LIGHT SPRAYS, LIKE YOU SUGGESTED!
GREAT! JUST NOT TOO HEAVILY, OR THE STATUE WILL BE DAMAGED!
BEFORE THE JUDGES ARRIVE LET'S CHECK OUT THE COMPETITION!
O-OKAY!
WHAT A BRILLIANT STATEMENT OF THE FUTILITY OF MODERN SOCIETY!
A BREATHTAKING EXPRESSION OF POLITICAL PESSIMISM!
BEAUTIFUL USE OF STOLEN GARBAGE!
THE WHOLE SAVAGE HISTORY OF MANKIND IN ONE STRIKING IMAGE!
LOVELY!
3

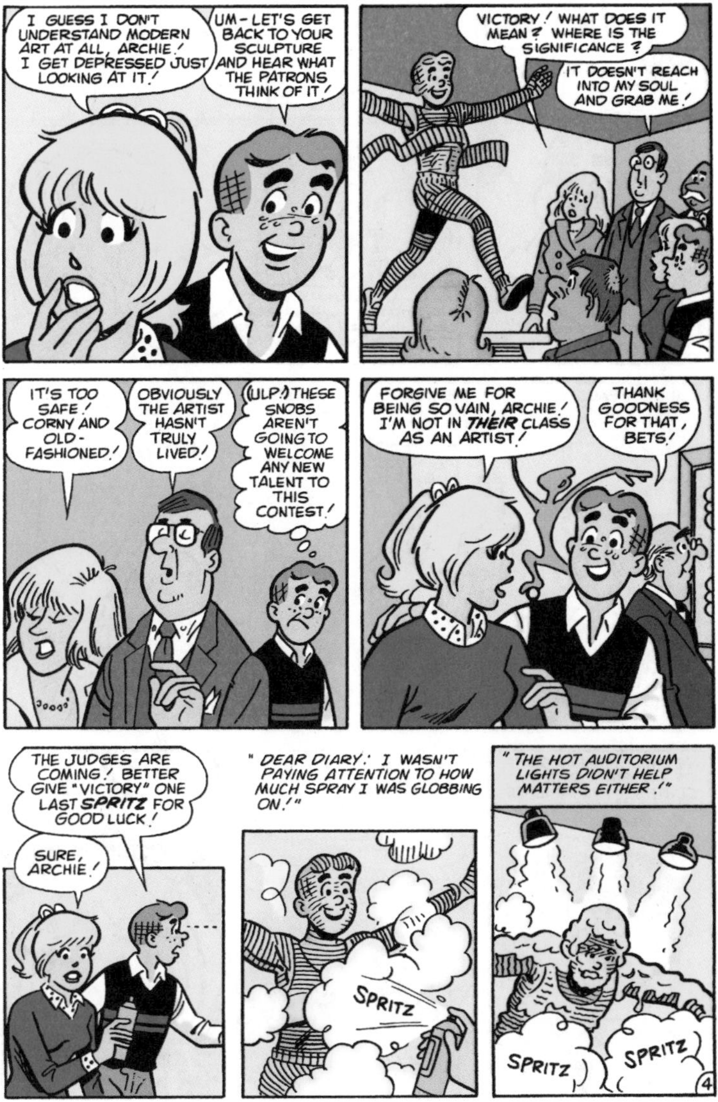
I GUESS I DON'T UNDERSTAND MODERN ART AT ALL, ARCHIE! I GET DEPRESSED JUST LOOKING AT IT!
UM-LET'S GET BACK TO YOUR SCULPTURE AND HEAR WHAT THE PATRONS THINK OF IT!
VICTORY! WHAT DOES IT MEAN? WHERE IS THE SIGNIFICANCE?
IT DOESN'T REACH INTO MY SOUL AND GRAB ME!
IT'S TOO SAFE! CORNY AND OLD-FASHIONED!
OBVIOUSLY THE ARTIST HASN'T TRULY LIVED!
(ULP!) THESE SNOBS AREN'T GOING TO WELCOME ANY NEW TALENT TO THIS CONTEST!
FORGIVE ME FOR BEING SO VAIN, ARCHIE! I'M NOT IN *THEIR* CLASS AS AN ARTIST!
THANK GOODNESS FOR THAT, BETS!
THE JUDGES ARE COMING! BETTER GIVE "VICTORY" ONE LAST *SPRITZ* FOR GOOD LUCK!
SURE, ARCHIE!
"*DEAR DIARY: I WASN'T PAYING ATTENTION TO HOW MUCH SPRAY I WAS GLOBBING ON!*"
SPRITZ
"*THE HOT AUDITORIUM LIGHTS DIDN'T HELP MATTERS EITHER!*"
SPRITZ
SPRITZ
4

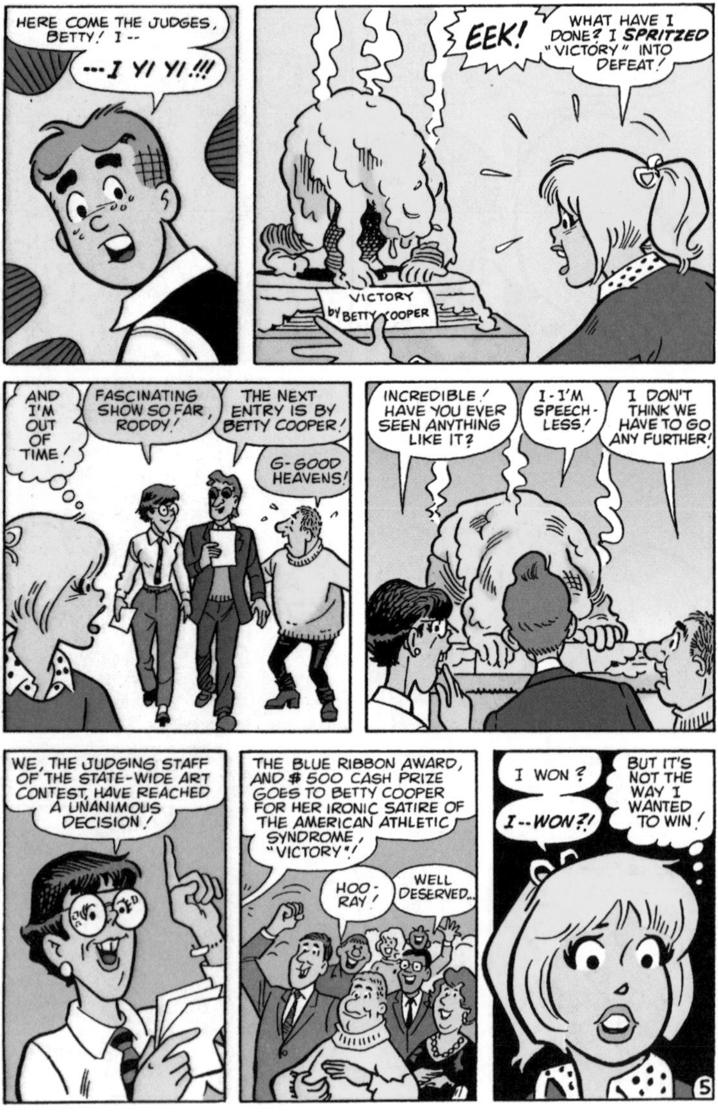

HERE COME THE JUDGES, BETTY! I --
--- I YI YI !!!
EEK!
WHAT HAVE I DONE? I SPRITZED "VICTORY" INTO DEFEAT!
VICTORY by BETTY COOPER
AND I'M OUT OF TIME!
FASCINATING SHOW SO FAR, RODDY!
THE NEXT ENTRY IS BY BETTY COOPER!
G-GOOD HEAVENS!
INCREDIBLE! HAVE YOU EVER SEEN ANYTHING LIKE IT?
I-I'M SPEECH-LESS!
I DON'T THINK WE HAVE TO GO ANY FURTHER!
WE, THE JUDGING STAFF OF THE STATE-WIDE ART CONTEST, HAVE REACHED A UNANIMOUS DECISION!
THE BLUE RIBBON AWARD, AND $ 500 CASH PRIZE GOES TO BETTY COOPER FOR HER IRONIC SATIRE OF THE AMERICAN ATHLETIC SYNDROME, "VICTORY"!
HOO-RAY!
WELL DESERVED...
I WON?
I--WON?!
BUT IT'S NOT THE WAY I WANTED TO WIN!
5

OH, ARCHIE... WHATEVER YOU DECIDE, HON, YOU KNOW I'LL BE RIGHT WITH YOU!

OKAY!

THAT'S IT!

JUST A *COTTON PICKIN'* MINUTE!

JUST A SECOND, YOUNG LADY!

WAIT, RODDY, IT'S OUR BRILLIANT NEW ART FIND!

MY STATUE WAS DAMAGED-- IT ISN'T WHAT I SET OUT TO DO! I DISQUALIFY MYSELF!

NONSENSE, THE END RESULT IS WONDERFUL! YOU'VE CAPTURED THE GLOOMY GRIM REALITY OF MODERN LIFE FOR ALL TO SEE!

THAT'S THE BIG PROBLEM! THAT'S NOT THE WAY I SEE IT!"

I THINK LIFE IS BRIGHT AND BEAUTIFUL AND THAT'S THE KIND OF ART I BELIEVE IN AND TRY TO DO!

THE MODERN ART YOU LIKE SO MUCH IS JUST PLAIN UGLY... AND A LITTLE SAD!

I GUESS ART REALLY IS IN THE EYES OF THE BEHOLDER... AND WE JUST DON'T SEE EYE TO EYE!

DEAR DIARY: YOU GUESSED IT! NO BLUE RIBBON, NO CASH PRIZE! ARCHIE AND I CAME BACK TO RIVERDALE EMPTY-HANDED...

KLUNK

AFTER DEPOSITING "VICTORY" IN THE SCRAP HEAP!

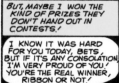

BUT, MAYBE I WON THE KIND OF PRIZES THEY DON'T HAND OUT IN CONTESTS!

I KNOW IT WAS HARD FOR YOU TODAY, BETS, BUT IF IT'S ANY CONSOLATION, I'M VERY PROUD OF YOU! YOU'RE THE REAL WINNER, RIBBON OR NOT!

"AND I WAS TOTALLY HONEST...ABOUT MYSELF AND MY ART"

BUT NEXT TIME, I'M GONNA GET A BETTER BRAND OF HAIR SPRAY!

DIARY

END

Archie COMICS

# Betty and Veronica®

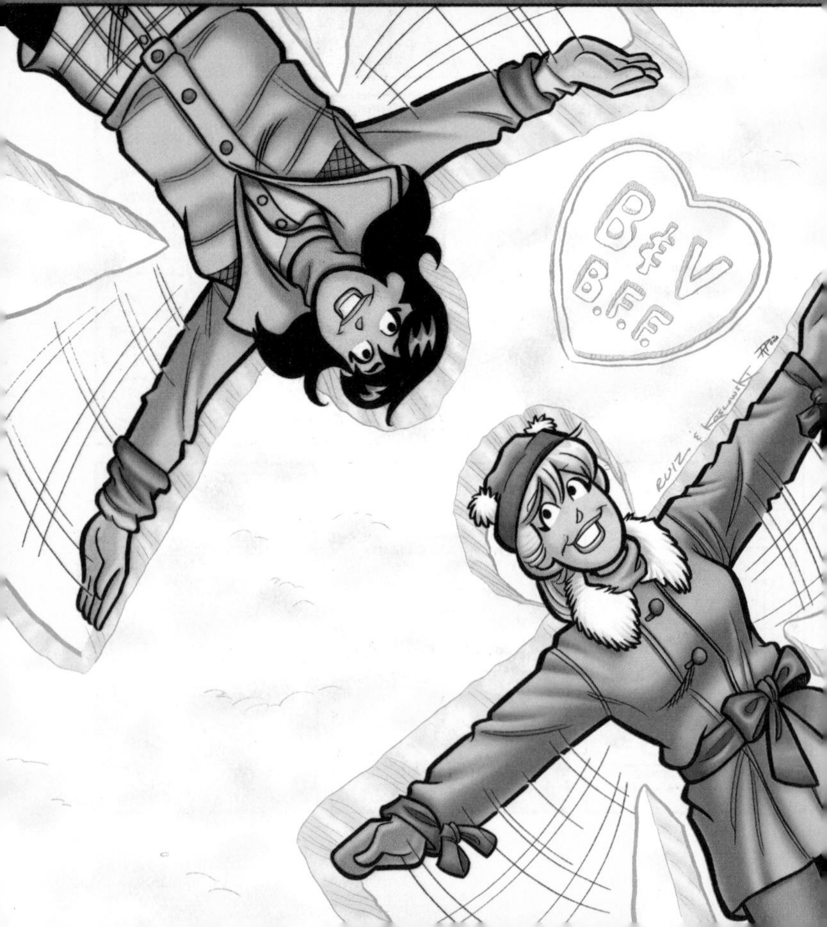
B & V
B.F.F.

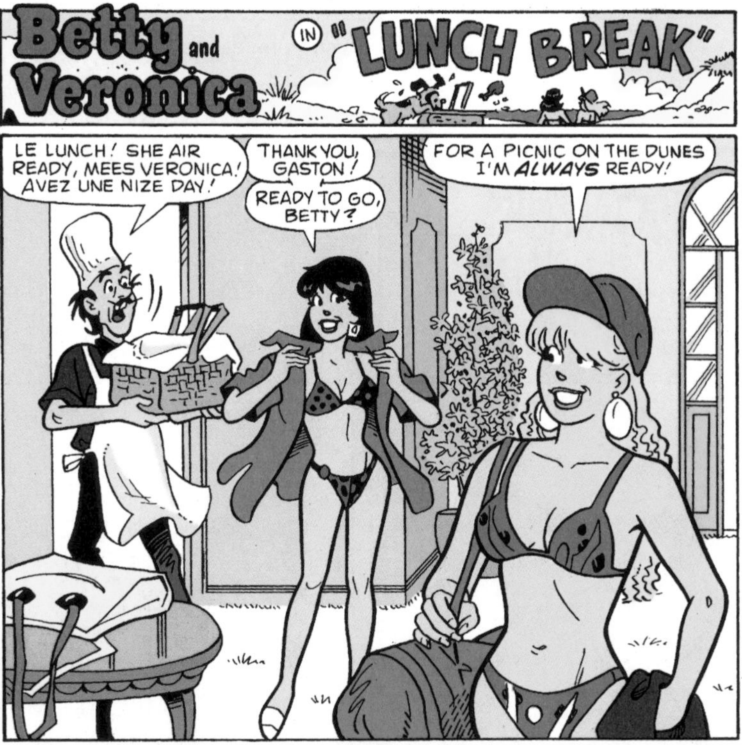
Betty and Veronica
IN "LUNCH BREAK"
LE LUNCH! SHE AIR READY, MEES VERONICA! AVEZ UNE NIZE DAY!
THANK YOU, GASTON!
READY TO GO, BETTY?
FOR A PICNIC ON THE DUNES I'M ALWAYS READY!

Script: Frank Doyle / Pencils: Dan DeCarlo / Inks: Alison Flood / Letters: Bill Yoshida / Colors: Barry Grossman

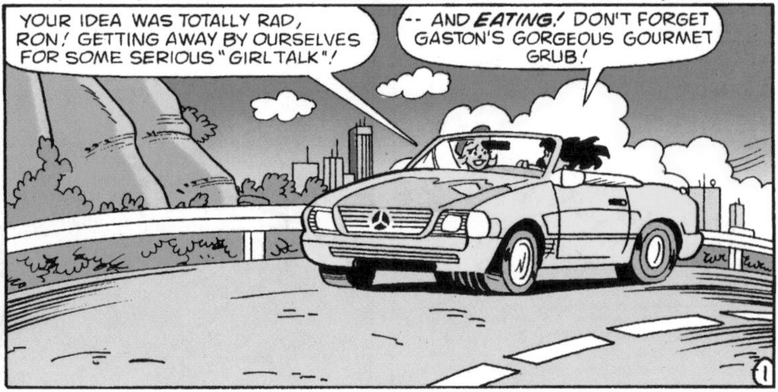
YOUR IDEA WAS TOTALLY RAD, RON! GETTING AWAY BY OURSELVES FOR SOME SERIOUS "GIRLTALK"!
-- AND EATING! DON'T FORGET GASTON'S GORGEOUS GOURMET GRUB!
1

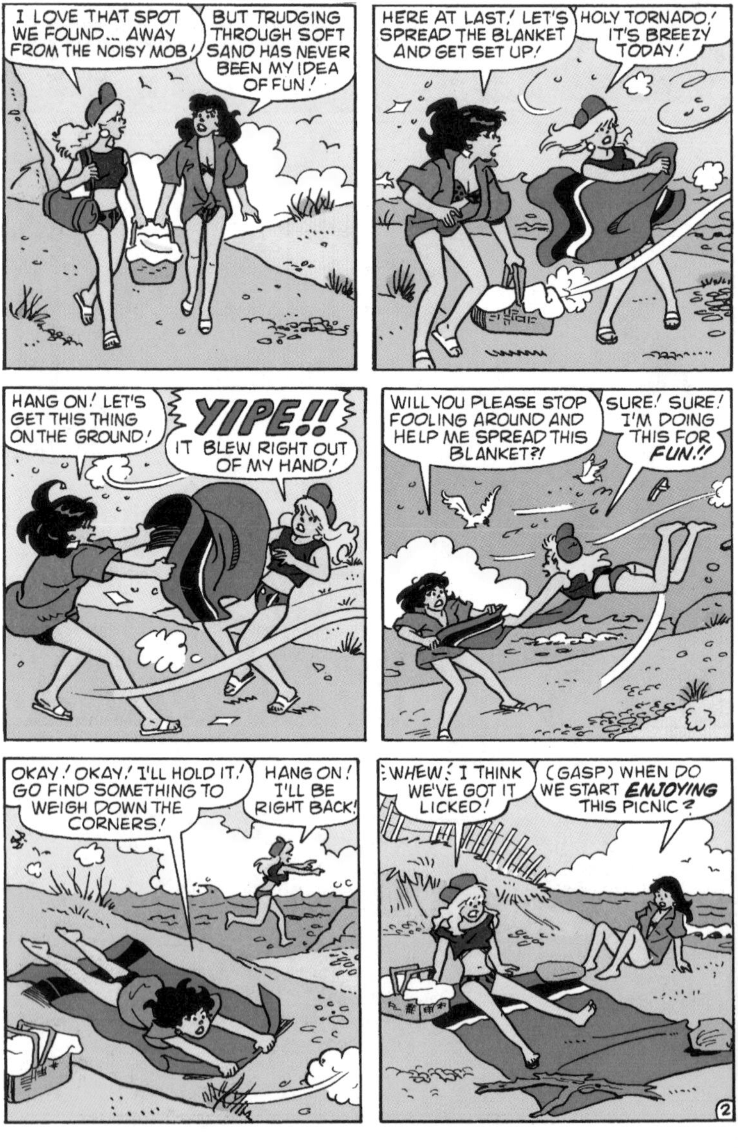

I LOVE THAT SPOT WE FOUND... AWAY FROM THE NOISY MOB!
BUT TRUDGING THROUGH SOFT SAND HAS NEVER BEEN MY IDEA OF FUN!
HERE AT LAST! LET'S SPREAD THE BLANKET AND GET SET UP!
HOLY TORNADO! IT'S BREEZY TODAY!
HANG ON! LET'S GET THIS THING ON THE GROUND!
YIPE!! IT BLEW RIGHT OUT OF MY HAND!
WILL YOU PLEASE STOP FOOLING AROUND AND HELP ME SPREAD THIS BLANKET?!
SURE! SURE! I'M DOING THIS FOR FUN!!
OKAY! OKAY! I'LL HOLD IT! GO FIND SOMETHING TO WEIGH DOWN THE CORNERS!
HANG ON! I'LL BE RIGHT BACK!
WHEW! I THINK WE'VE GOT IT LICKED!
(GASP) WHEN DO WE START ENJOYING THIS PICNIC?
2

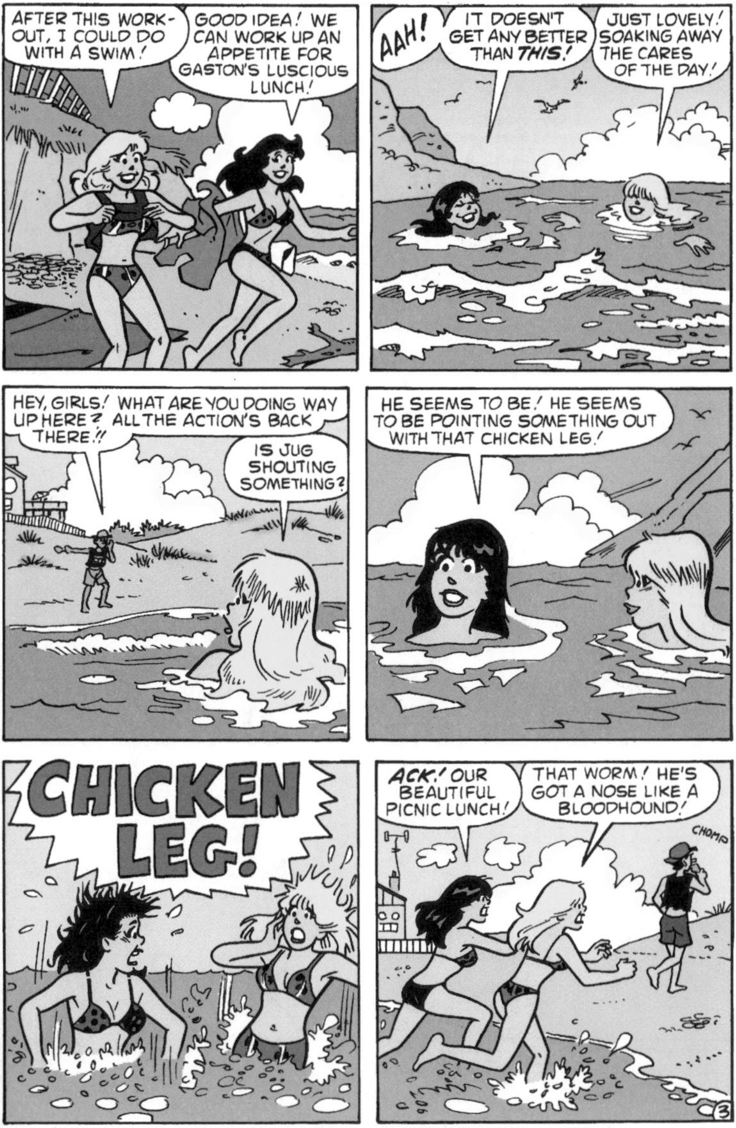
AFTER THIS WORK-OUT, I COULD DO WITH A SWIM!
GOOD IDEA! WE CAN WORK UP AN APPETITE FOR GASTON'S LUSCIOUS LUNCH!
AAH!
IT DOESN'T GET ANY BETTER THAN THIS!
JUST LOVELY! SOAKING AWAY THE CARES OF THE DAY!
HEY, GIRLS! WHAT ARE YOU DOING WAY UP HERE? ALL THE ACTION'S BACK THERE!!
IS JUG SHOUTING SOMETHING?
HE SEEMS TO BE! HE SEEMS TO BE POINTING SOMETHING OUT WITH THAT CHICKEN LEG!
CHICKEN LEG!
ACK! OUR BEAUTIFUL PICNIC LUNCH!
THAT WORM! HE'S GOT A NOSE LIKE A BLOODHOUND!
CHOMP
3

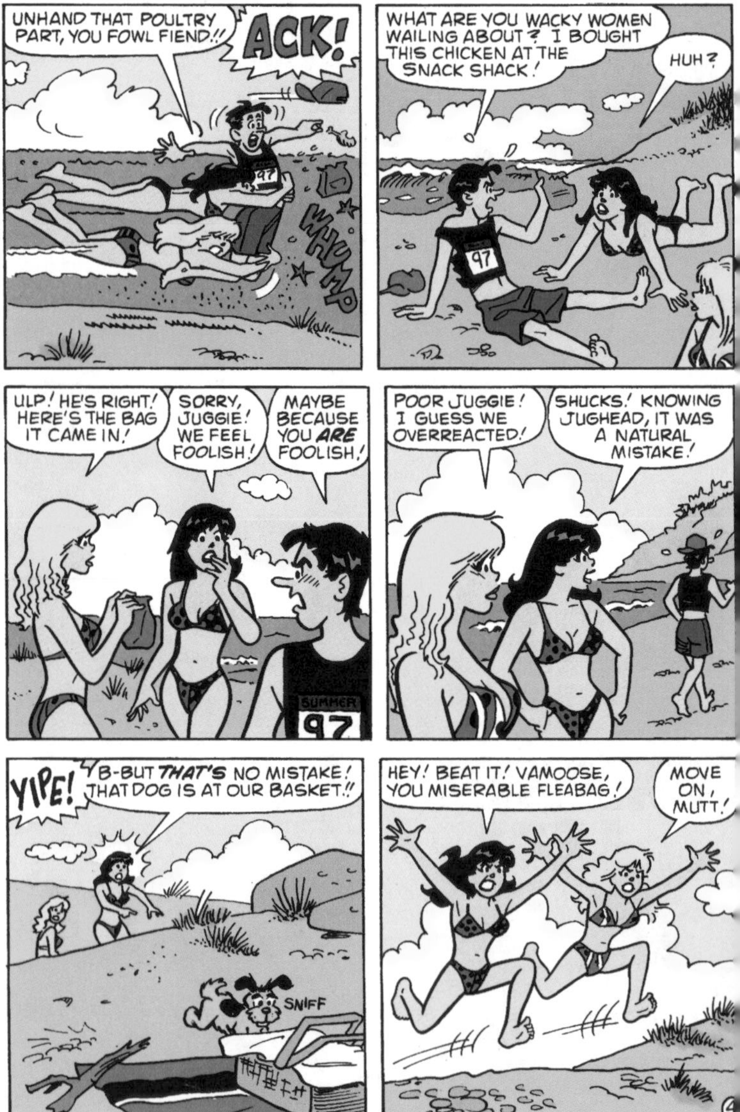
UNHAND THAT POULTRY PART, YOU FOWL FIEND!!
ACK!
WHUMP
WHAT ARE YOU WACKY WOMEN WAILING ABOUT? I BOUGHT THIS CHICKEN AT THE SNACK SHACK!
HUH?
97
ULP! HE'S RIGHT! HERE'S THE BAG IT CAME IN!
SORRY, JUGGIE! WE FEEL FOOLISH!
MAYBE BECAUSE YOU ***ARE*** FOOLISH!
SUMMER
97
POOR JUGGIE! I GUESS WE OVERREACTED!
SHUCKS! KNOWING JUGHEAD, IT WAS A NATURAL MISTAKE!
YIPE!
B-BUT ***THAT'S*** NO MISTAKE! THAT DOG IS AT OUR BASKET!!
SNIFF
HEY! BEAT IT! VAMOOSE, YOU MISERABLE FLEABAG!
MOVE ON, MUTT!

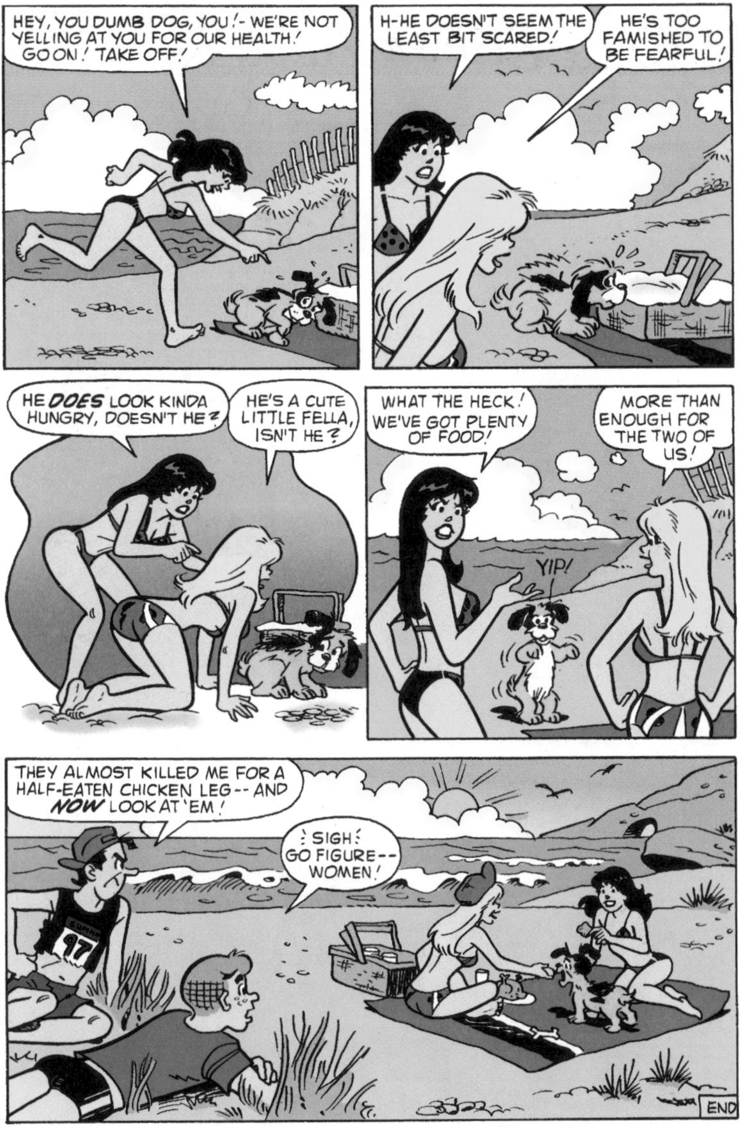
HEY, YOU DUMB DOG, YOU!- WE'RE NOT YELLING AT YOU FOR OUR HEALTH! GO ON! TAKE OFF!
H-HE DOESN'T SEEM THE LEAST BIT SCARED!
HE'S TOO FAMISHED TO BE FEARFUL!
HE DOES LOOK KINDA HUNGRY, DOESN'T HE?
HE'S A CUTE LITTLE FELLA, ISN'T HE?
WHAT THE HECK! WE'VE GOT PLENTY OF FOOD!
MORE THAN ENOUGH FOR THE TWO OF US!
YIP!
THEY ALMOST KILLED ME FOR A HALF-EATEN CHICKEN LEG -- AND NOW LOOK AT 'EM!
SIGH GO FIGURE-- WOMEN!
END

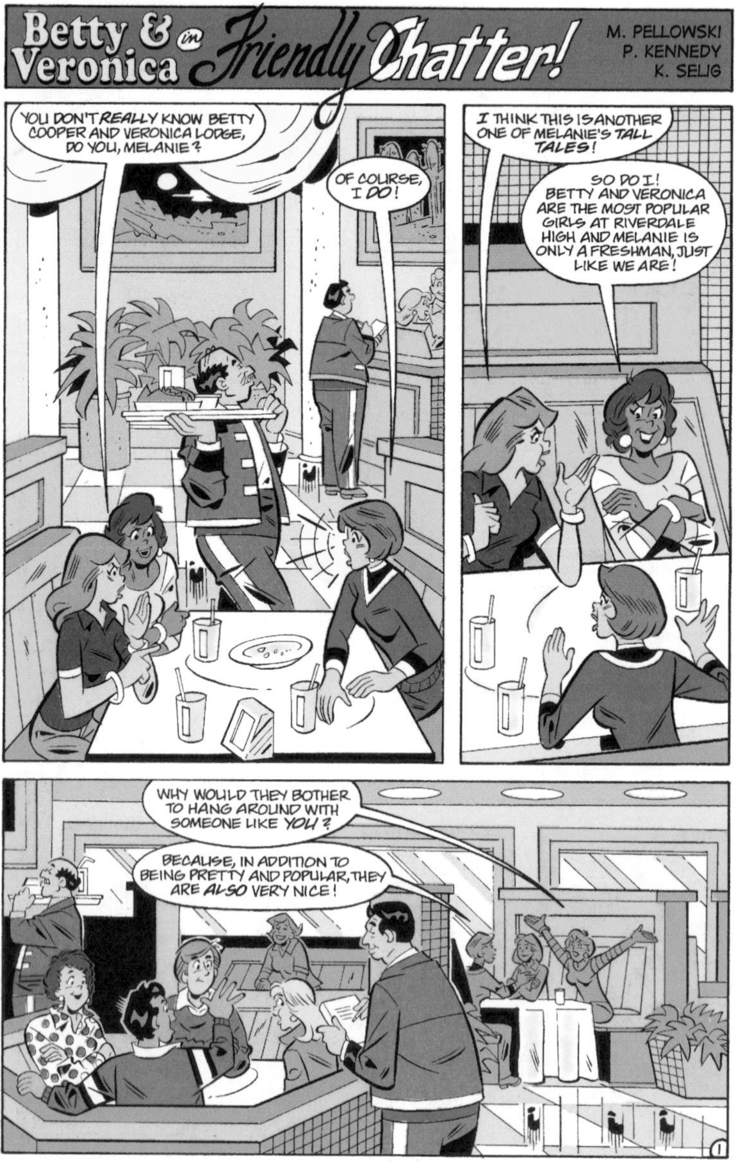
Betty & Veronica in Friendly Chatter!
M. PELLOWSKI
P. KENNEDY
K. SELIG
YOU DON'T REALLY KNOW BETTY COOPER AND VERONICA LODGE, DO YOU, MELANIE?
OF COURSE, I DO!
I THINK THIS IS ANOTHER ONE OF MELANIE'S TALL TALES!
SO DO I! BETTY AND VERONICA ARE THE MOST POPULAR GIRLS AT RIVERDALE HIGH AND MELANIE IS ONLY A FRESHMAN, JUST LIKE WE ARE!
WHY WOULD THEY BOTHER TO HANG AROUND WITH SOMEONE LIKE YOU?
BECAUSE, IN ADDITION TO BEING PRETTY AND POPULAR, THEY ARE ALSO VERY NICE!
1

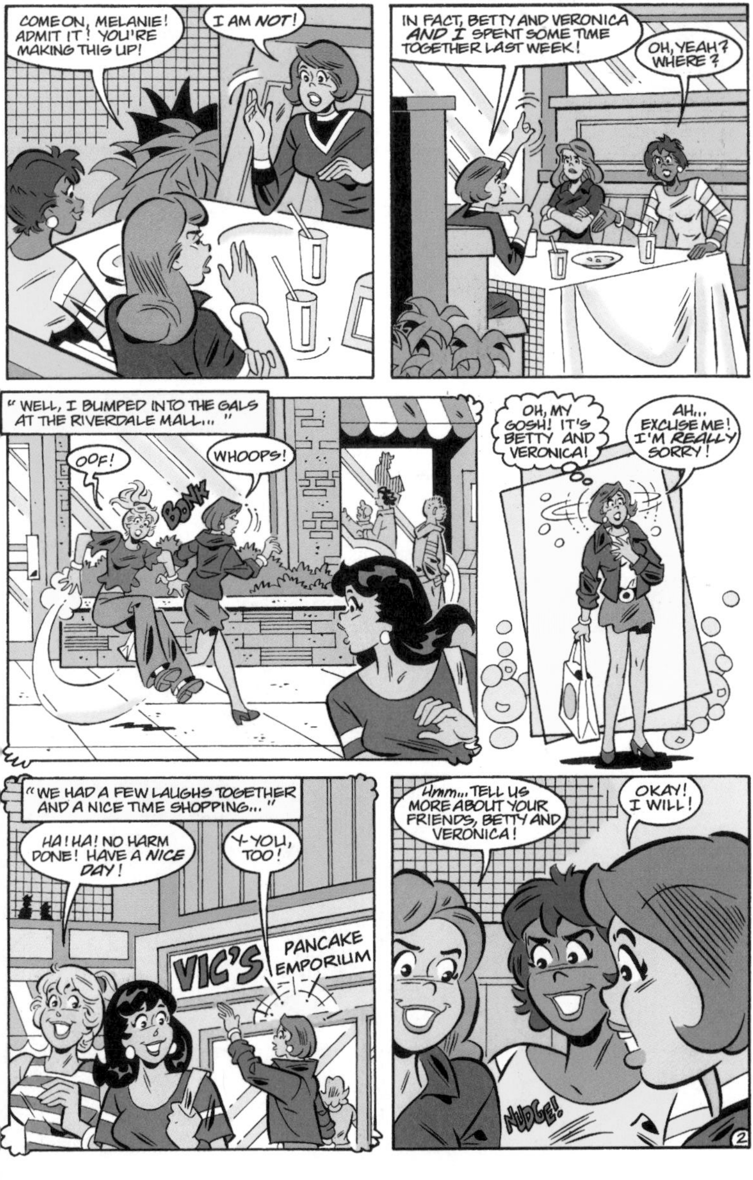
COME ON, MELANIE! ADMIT IT! YOU'RE MAKING THIS UP!
I AM NOT!
IN FACT, BETTY AND VERONICA AND I SPENT SOME TIME TOGETHER LAST WEEK!
OH, YEAH? WHERE?
" WELL, I BUMPED INTO THE GALS AT THE RIVERDALE MALL... "
OOF!
BONK
WHOOPS!
OH, MY GOSH! IT'S BETTY AND VERONICA!
AH... EXCUSE ME! I'M REALLY SORRY!
" WE HAD A FEW LAUGHS TOGETHER AND A NICE TIME SHOPPING... "
HA! HA! NO HARM DONE! HAVE A NICE DAY!
Y-YOU, TOO!
VIC'S
PANCAKE EMPORIUM
Hmm... TELL US MORE ABOUT YOUR FRIENDS, BETTY AND VERONICA!
OKAY! I WILL!
NUDGE!
2

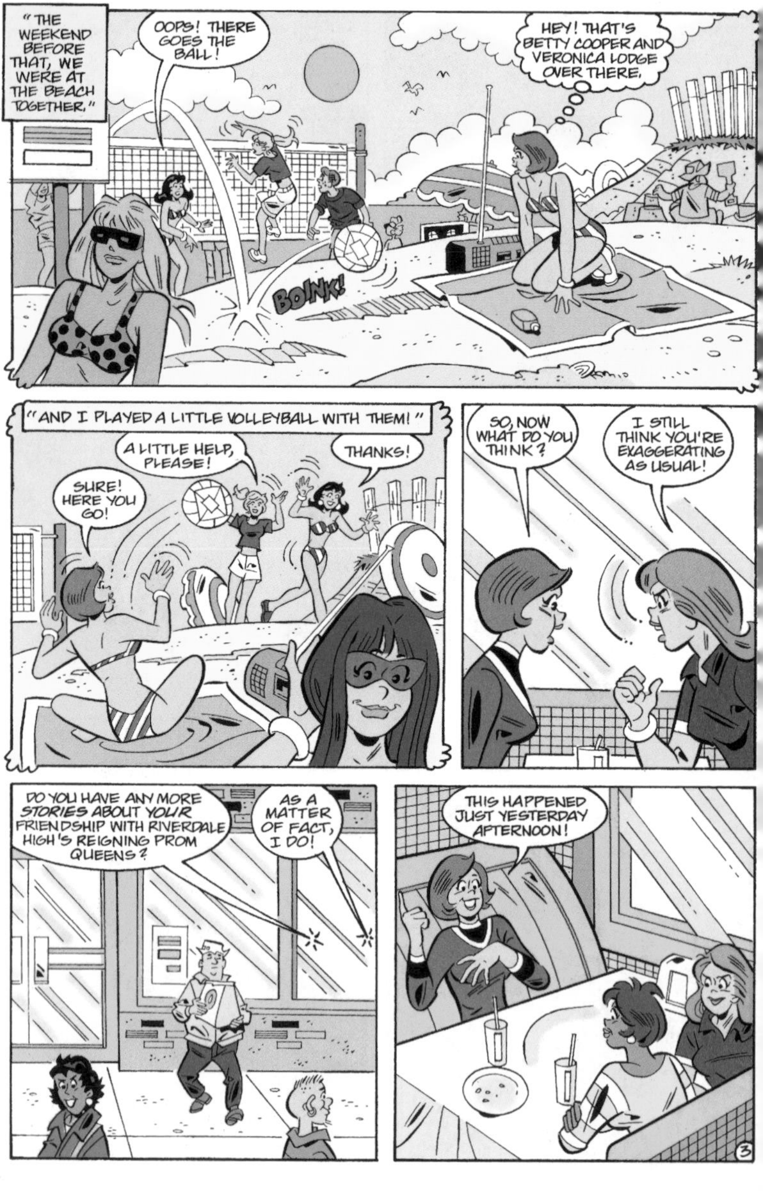
"THE WEEKEND BEFORE THAT, WE WERE AT THE BEACH TOGETHER."
OOPS! THERE GOES THE BALL!
HEY! THAT'S BETTY COOPER AND VERONICA LODGE OVER THERE.
BOINK!
"AND I PLAYED A LITTLE VOLLEYBALL WITH THEM!"
A LITTLE HELP, PLEASE!
THANKS!
SURE! HERE YOU GO!
SO, NOW WHAT DO YOU THINK?
I STILL THINK YOU'RE EXAGGERATING AS USUAL!
DO YOU HAVE ANY MORE STORIES ABOUT YOUR FRIENDSHIP WITH RIVERDALE HIGH'S REIGNING PROM QUEENS?
AS A MATTER OF FACT, I DO!
THIS HAPPENED JUST YESTERDAY AFTERNOON!
3

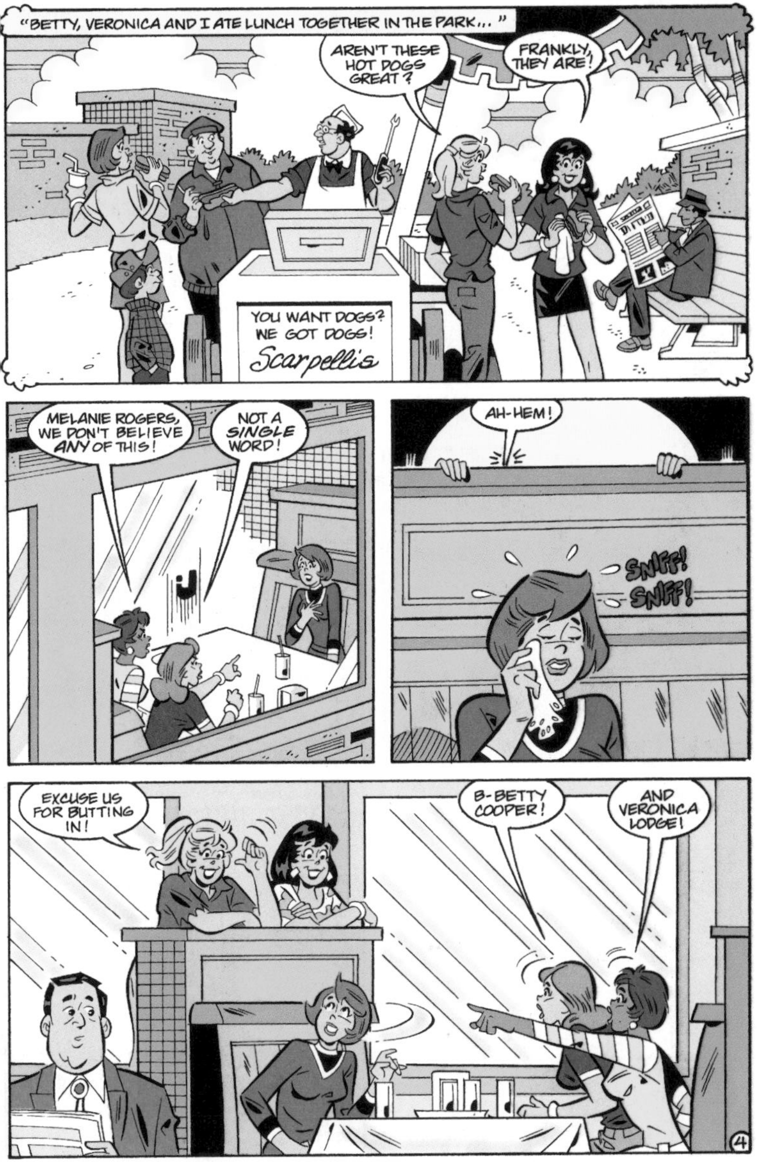
"BETTY, VERONICA AND I ATE LUNCH TOGETHER IN THE PARK..."
AREN'T THESE HOT DOGS GREAT?
FRANKLY, THEY ARE!
YOU WANT DOGS? WE GOT DOGS!
Scarpelli's
MELANIE ROGERS, WE DON'T BELIEVE ANY OF THIS!
NOT A SINGLE WORD!
AH-HEM!
SNIFF! SNIFF!
EXCUSE US FOR BUTTING IN!
B-BETTY COOPER!
AND VERONICA LODGE!
4

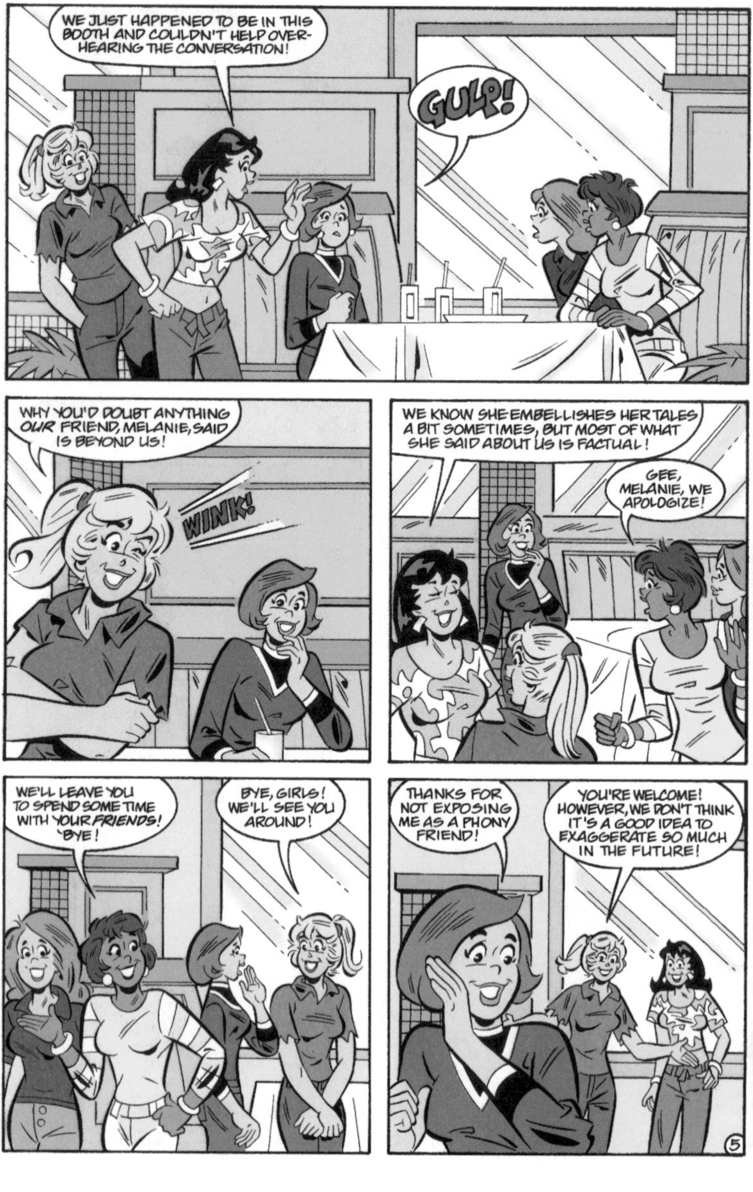
WE JUST HAPPENED TO BE IN THIS BOOTH AND COULDN'T HELP OVER-HEARING THE CONVERSATION!
GULP!
WHY YOU'D DOUBT ANYTHING OUR FRIEND, MELANIE, SAID IS BEYOND US!
WINK!
WE KNOW SHE EMBELLISHES HER TALES A BIT SOMETIMES, BUT MOST OF WHAT SHE SAID ABOUT US IS FACTUAL!
GEE, MELANIE, WE APOLOGIZE!
WE'LL LEAVE YOU TO SPEND SOME TIME WITH YOUR FRIENDS! 'BYE!
BYE, GIRLS! WE'LL SEE YOU AROUND!
THANKS FOR NOT EXPOSING ME AS A PHONY FRIEND!
YOU'RE WELCOME! HOWEVER, WE DON'T THINK IT'S A GOOD IDEA TO EXAGGERATE SO MUCH IN THE FUTURE!

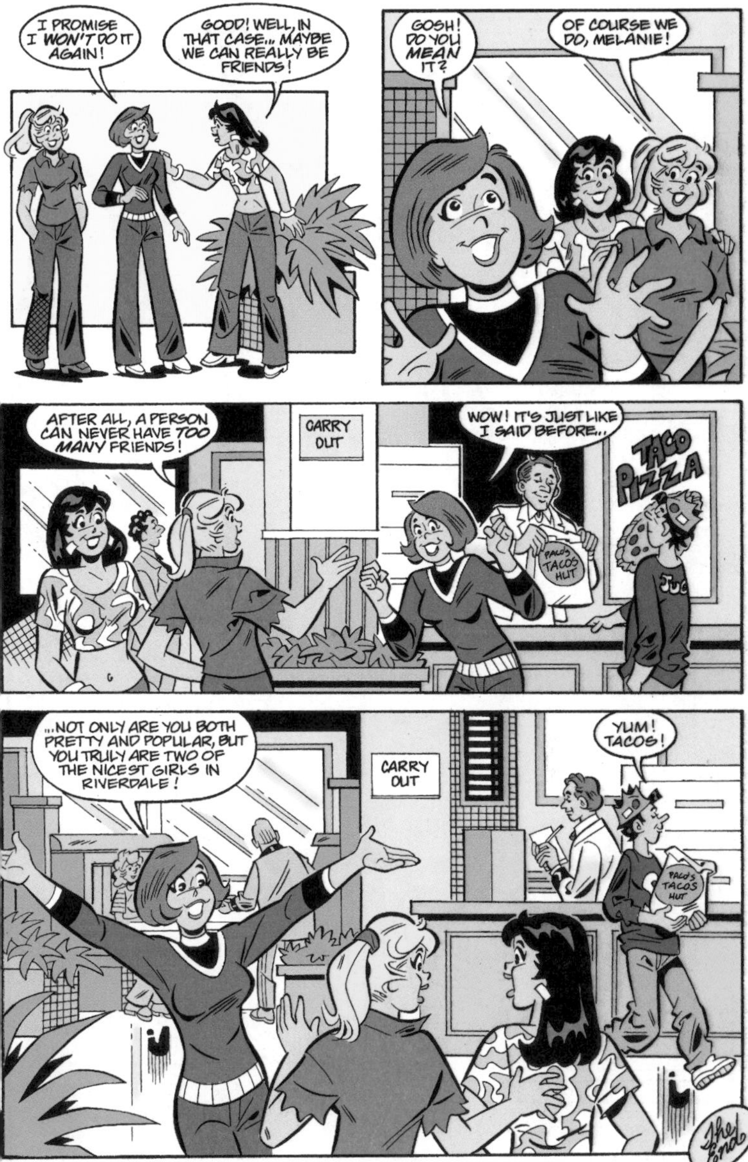
I PROMISE I WON'T DO IT AGAIN!
GOOD! WELL, IN THAT CASE... MAYBE WE CAN REALLY BE FRIENDS!
GOSH! DO YOU MEAN IT?
OF COURSE WE DO, MELANIE!
AFTER ALL, A PERSON CAN NEVER HAVE TOO MANY FRIENDS!
CARRY OUT
WOW! IT'S JUST LIKE I SAID BEFORE...
TACO PIZZA
PACO'S TACOS HUT
...NOT ONLY ARE YOU BOTH PRETTY AND POPULAR, BUT YOU TRULY ARE TWO OF THE NICEST GIRLS IN RIVERDALE!
CARRY OUT
YUM! TACOS!
PACO'S TACOS HUT
The End

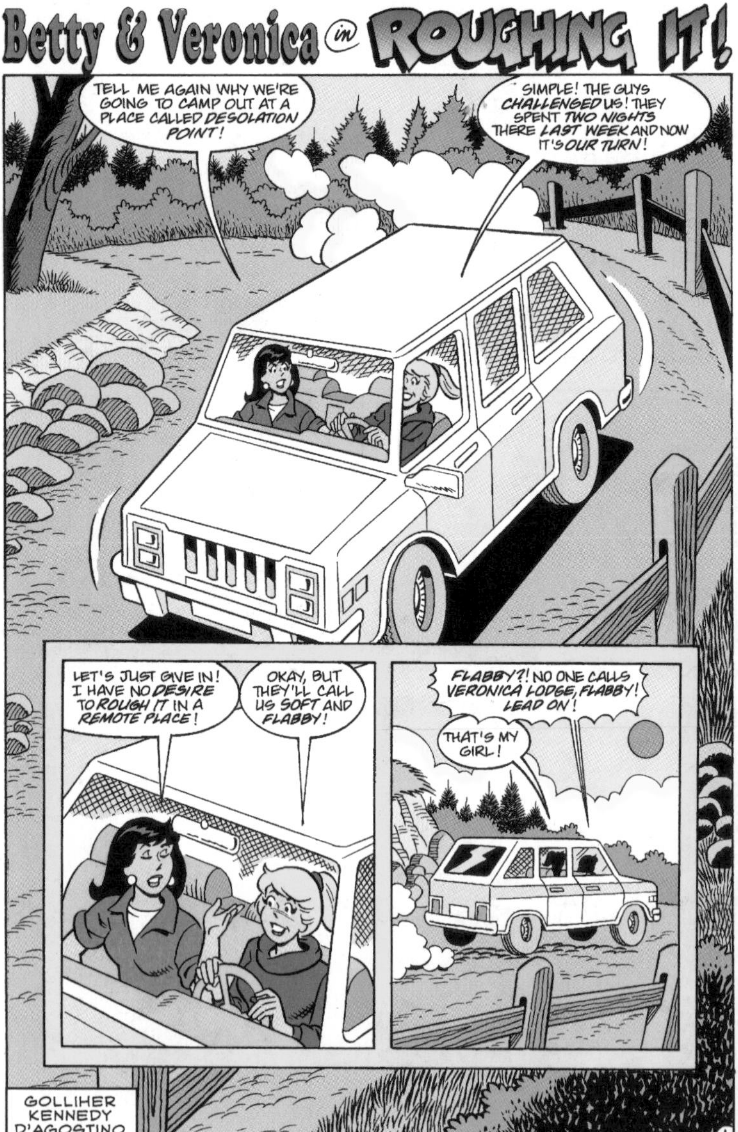
Betty & Veronica in ROUGHING IT!
TELL ME AGAIN WHY WE'RE GOING TO CAMP OUT AT A PLACE CALLED DESOLATION POINT!
SIMPLE! THE GUYS CHALLENGED US! THEY SPENT TWO NIGHTS THERE LAST WEEK AND NOW IT'S OUR TURN!
LET'S JUST GIVE IN! I HAVE NO DESIRE TO ROUGH IT IN A REMOTE PLACE!
OKAY, BUT THEY'LL CALL US SOFT AND FLABBY!
FLABBY?! NO ONE CALLS VERONICA LODGE, FLABBY! LEAD ON!
THAT'S MY GIRL!
GOLLIHER
KENNEDY
D'AGOSTINO
1

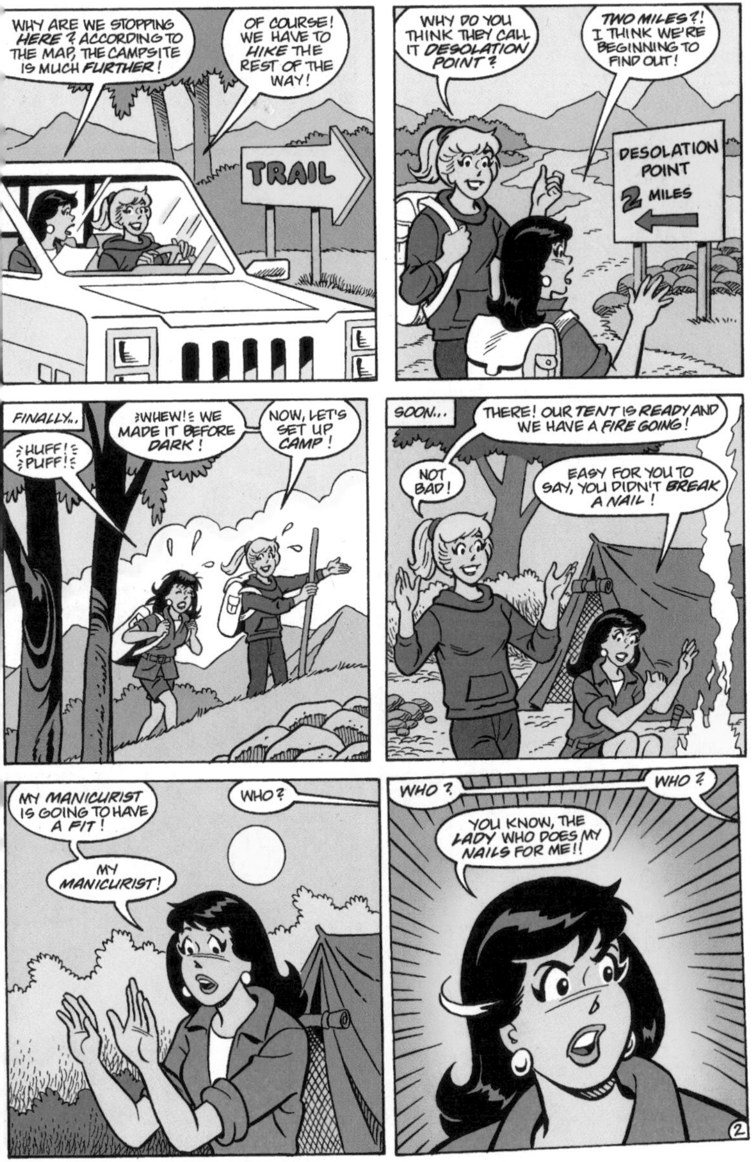
WHY ARE WE STOPPING HERE? ACCORDING TO THE MAP, THE CAMPSITE IS MUCH FURTHER!
OF COURSE! WE HAVE TO HIKE THE REST OF THE WAY!
TRAIL
WHY DO YOU THINK THEY CALL IT DESOLATION POINT?
TWO MILES?! I THINK WE'RE BEGINNING TO FIND OUT!
DESOLATION POINT 2 MILES
FINALLY...
HUFF! PUFF!
WHEW! WE MADE IT BEFORE DARK!
NOW, LET'S SET UP CAMP!
SOON...
THERE! OUR TENT IS READY AND WE HAVE A FIRE GOING!
NOT BAD!
EASY FOR YOU TO SAY, YOU DIDN'T BREAK A NAIL!
MY MANICURIST IS GOING TO HAVE A FIT!
WHO?
MY MANICURIST!
WHO?
WHO?
YOU KNOW, THE LADY WHO DOES MY NAILS FOR ME!!
2

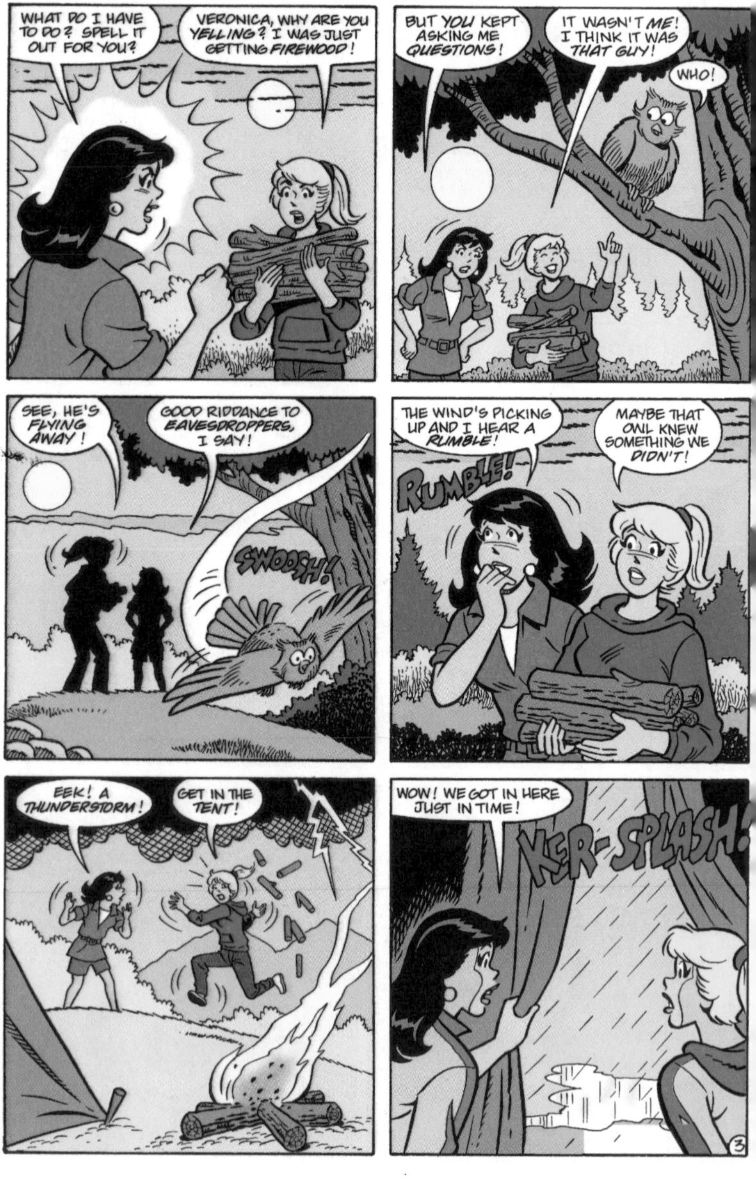
WHAT DO I HAVE TO DO? SPELL IT OUT FOR YOU?
VERONICA, WHY ARE YOU YELLING? I WAS JUST GETTING FIREWOOD!
BUT YOU KEPT ASKING ME QUESTIONS!
IT WASN'T ME! I THINK IT WAS THAT GUY!
WHO!
SEE, HE'S FLYING AWAY!
GOOD RIDDANCE TO EAVESDROPPERS, I SAY!
SWOOSH!
THE WIND'S PICKING UP AND I HEAR A RUMBLE!
MAYBE THAT OWL KNEW SOMETHING WE DIDN'T!
RUMBLE!
EEK! A THUNDERSTORM!
GET IN THE TENT!
WOW! WE GOT IN HERE JUST IN TIME!
KER-SPLASH!
3

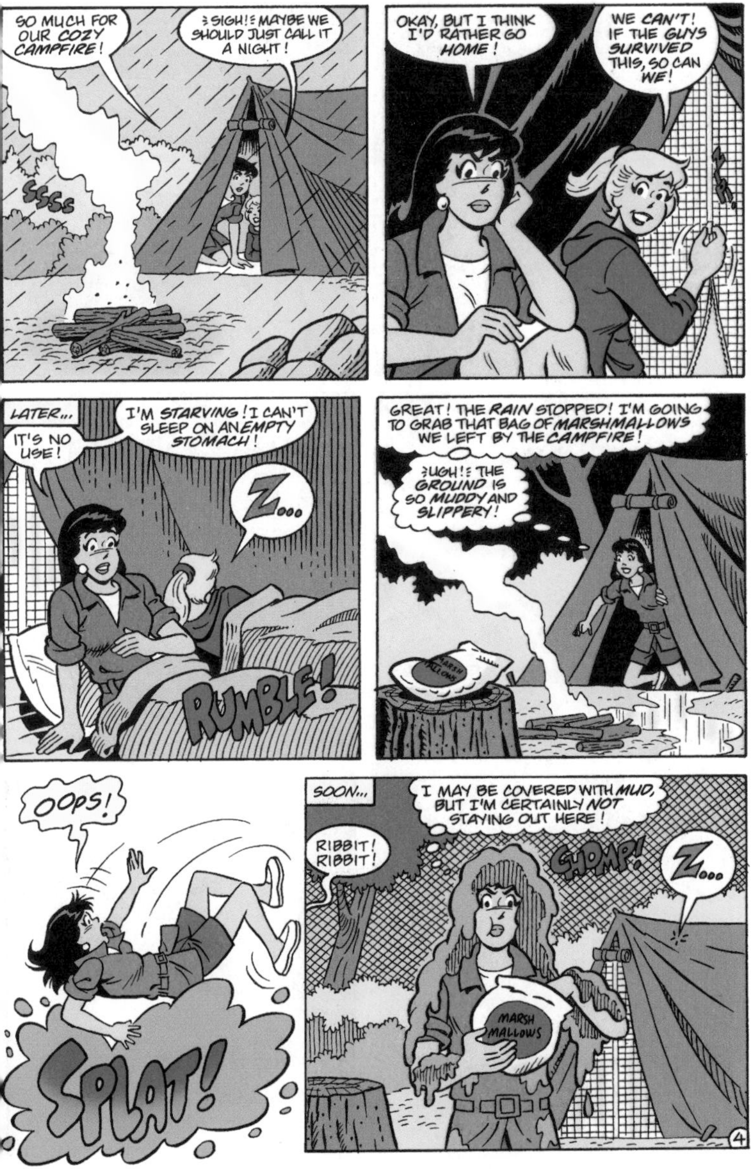
SO MUCH FOR OUR COZY CAMPFIRE!
SIGH! MAYBE WE SHOULD JUST CALL IT A NIGHT!
SSSSS
OKAY, BUT I THINK I'D RATHER GO HOME!
WE CAN'T! IF THE GUYS SURVIVED THIS, SO CAN WE!
LATER...
IT'S NO USE!
I'M STARVING! I CAN'T SLEEP ON AN EMPTY STOMACH!
Zooo
RUMBLE!
GREAT! THE RAIN STOPPED! I'M GOING TO GRAB THAT BAG OF MARSHMALLOWS WE LEFT BY THE CAMPFIRE!
UGH! THE GROUND IS SO MUDDY AND SLIPPERY!
MARSH MALLOWS
OOPS!
SPLAT!
SOON...
I MAY BE COVERED WITH MUD, BUT I'M CERTAINLY NOT STAYING OUT HERE!
RIBBIT! RIBBIT!
CHOMP!
Zooo
MARSH MALLOWS
4

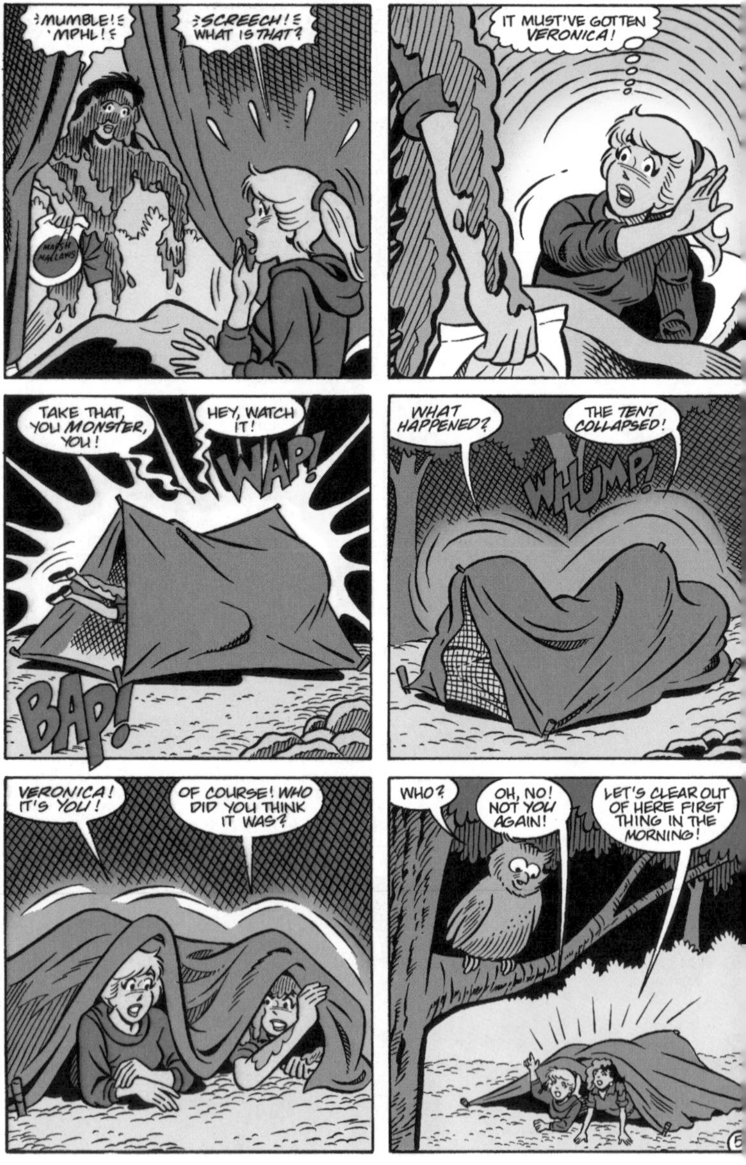
MUMBLE! 'MPHL!
SCREECH! WHAT IS THAT?
MARSH MALLOWS
IT MUST'VE GOTTEN VERONICA!
TAKE THAT, YOU MONSTER, YOU!
HEY, WATCH IT!
WAP!
BAP!
WHAT HAPPENED?
THE TENT COLLAPSED!
WHUMP!
VERONICA! IT'S YOU!
OF COURSE! WHO DID YOU THINK IT WAS?
WHO?
OH, NO! NOT YOU AGAIN!
LET'S CLEAR OUT OF HERE FIRST THING IN THE MORNING!

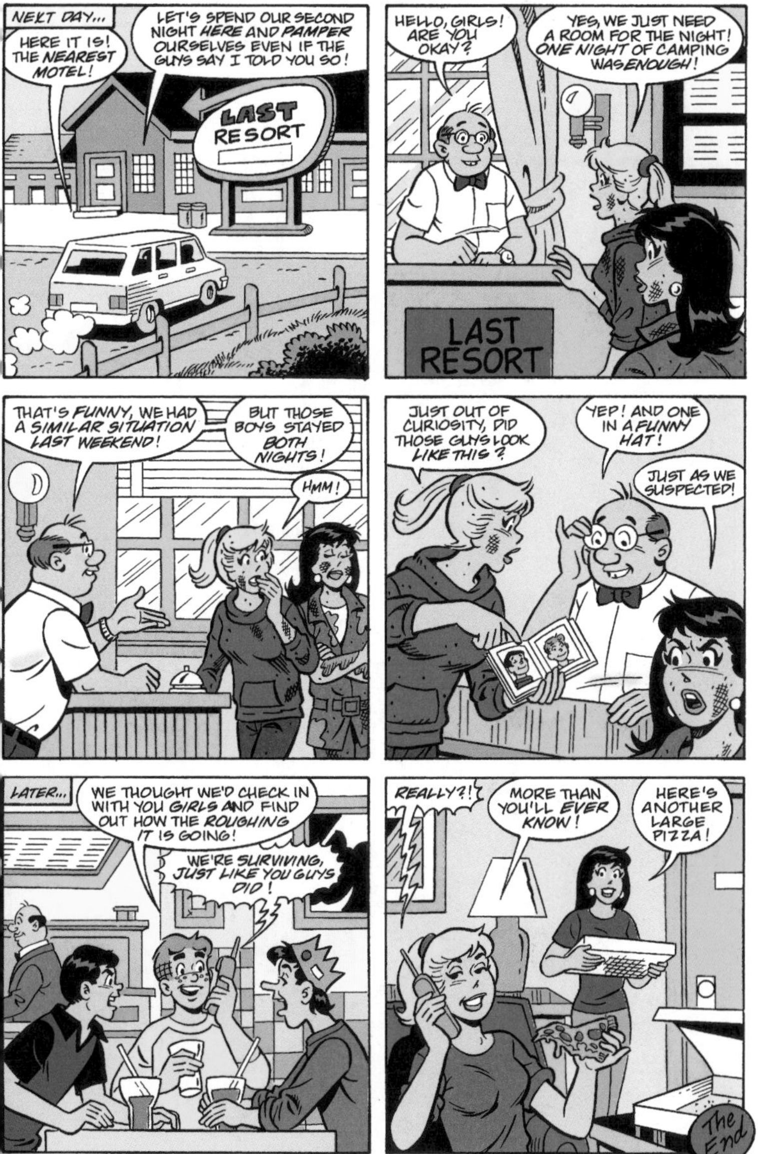
NEXT DAY...
HERE IT IS! THE NEAREST MOTEL!
LET'S SPEND OUR SECOND NIGHT HERE AND PAMPER OURSELVES EVEN IF THE GUYS SAY I TOLD YOU SO!
LAST RESORT
HELLO, GIRLS! ARE YOU OKAY?
YES, WE JUST NEED A ROOM FOR THE NIGHT! ONE NIGHT OF CAMPING WAS ENOUGH!
LAST RESORT
THAT'S FUNNY, WE HAD A SIMILAR SITUATION LAST WEEKEND!
BUT THOSE BOYS STAYED BOTH NIGHTS!
HMM!
JUST OUT OF CURIOSITY, DID THOSE GUYS LOOK LIKE THIS?
YEP! AND ONE IN A FUNNY HAT!
JUST AS WE SUSPECTED!
LATER...
WE THOUGHT WE'D CHECK IN WITH YOU GIRLS AND FIND OUT HOW THE ROUGHING IT IS GOING!
WE'RE SURVIVING, JUST LIKE YOU GUYS DID!
REALLY?!
MORE THAN YOU'LL EVER KNOW!
HERE'S ANOTHER LARGE PIZZA!
The End

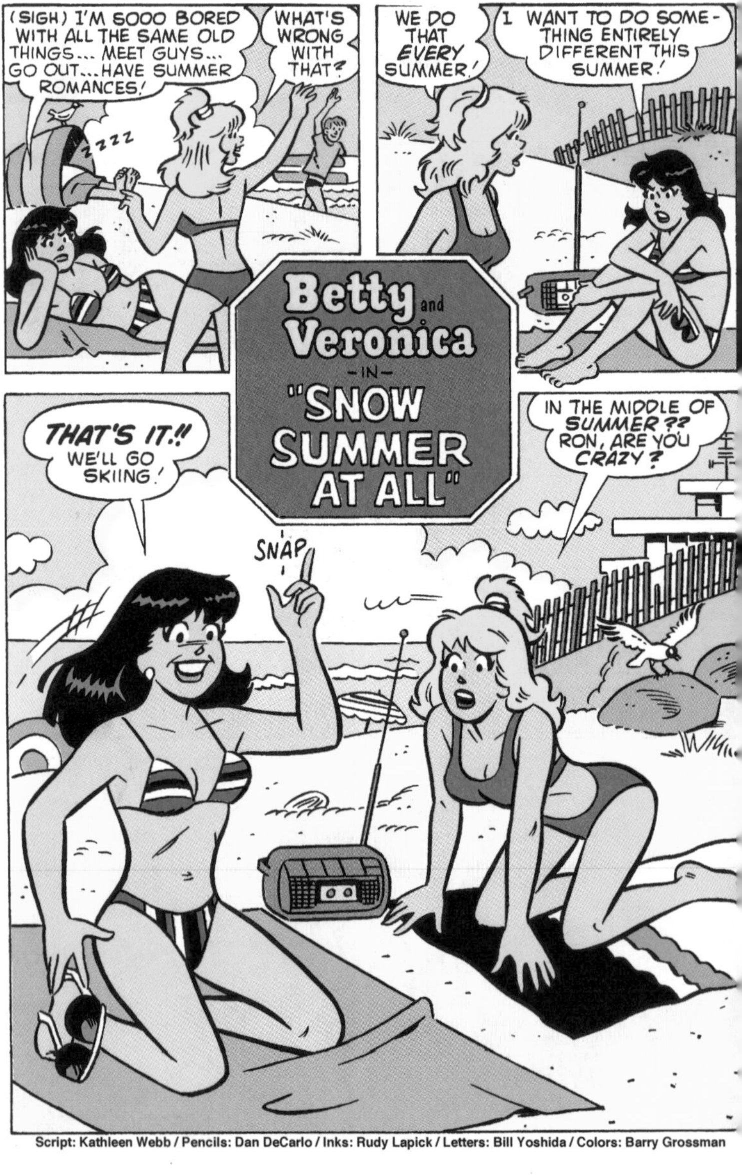
(SIGH) I'M SOOO BORED WITH ALL THE SAME OLD THINGS... MEET GUYS... GO OUT...HAVE SUMMER ROMANCES!
WHAT'S WRONG WITH THAT?
ZZZZ
WE DO THAT *EVERY* SUMMER!
I WANT TO DO SOMETHING ENTIRELY DIFFERENT THIS SUMMER!
Betty and Veronica
-IN-
"SNOW SUMMER AT ALL"
*THAT'S IT!!* WE'LL GO SKIING!
SNAP
IN THE MIDDLE OF *SUMMER??* RON, ARE YOU *CRAZY?*

Script: Kathleen Webb / Pencils: Dan DeCarlo / Inks: Rudy Lapick / Letters: Bill Yoshida / Colors: Barry Grossman

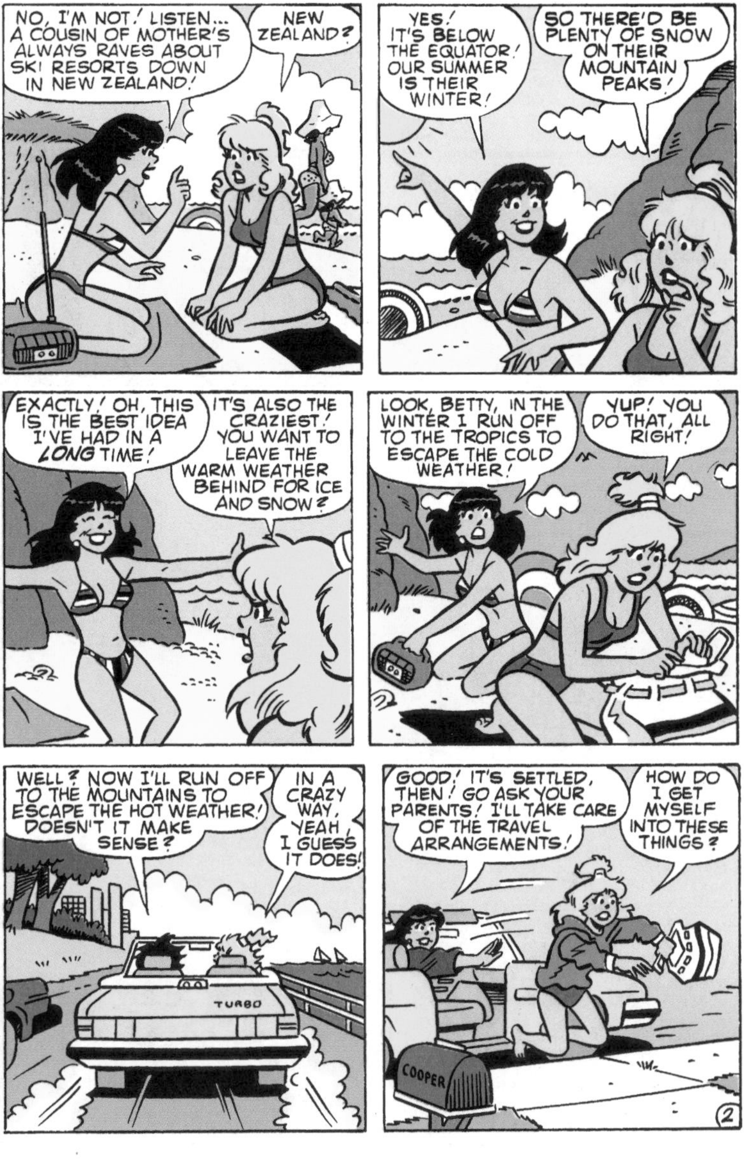
NO, I'M NOT! LISTEN... A COUSIN OF MOTHER'S ALWAYS RAVES ABOUT SKI RESORTS DOWN IN NEW ZEALAND!
NEW ZEALAND?
YES! IT'S BELOW THE EQUATOR! OUR SUMMER IS THEIR WINTER!
SO THERE'D BE PLENTY OF SNOW ON THEIR MOUNTAIN PEAKS!
EXACTLY! OH, THIS IS THE BEST IDEA I'VE HAD IN A LONG TIME!
IT'S ALSO THE CRAZIEST! YOU WANT TO LEAVE THE WARM WEATHER BEHIND FOR ICE AND SNOW?
LOOK, BETTY, IN THE WINTER I RUN OFF TO THE TROPICS TO ESCAPE THE COLD WEATHER!
YUP! YOU DO THAT, ALL RIGHT!
WELL? NOW I'LL RUN OFF TO THE MOUNTAINS TO ESCAPE THE HOT WEATHER! DOESN'T IT MAKE SENSE?
IN A CRAZY WAY, YEAH, I GUESS IT DOES!
TURBO
GOOD! IT'S SETTLED, THEN! GO ASK YOUR PARENTS! I'LL TAKE CARE OF THE TRAVEL ARRANGEMENTS!
HOW DO I GET MYSELF INTO THESE THINGS?
COOPER
2

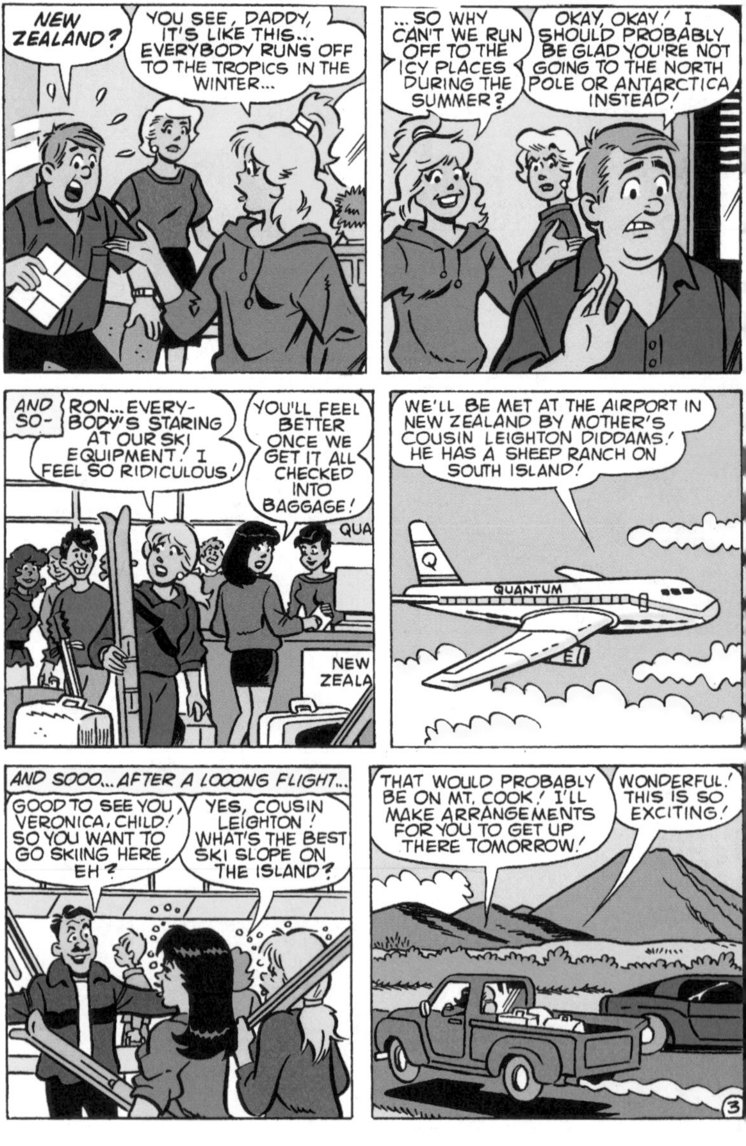
NEW ZEALAND?
YOU SEE, DADDY, IT'S LIKE THIS... EVERYBODY RUNS OFF TO THE TROPICS IN THE WINTER...
...SO WHY CAN'T WE RUN OFF TO THE ICY PLACES DURING THE SUMMER?
OKAY, OKAY! I SHOULD PROBABLY BE GLAD YOU'RE NOT GOING TO THE NORTH POLE OR ANTARCTICA INSTEAD!
AND SO-
RON...EVERYBODY'S STARING AT OUR SKI EQUIPMENT! I FEEL SO RIDICULOUS!
YOU'LL FEEL BETTER ONCE WE GET IT ALL CHECKED INTO BAGGAGE!
QUA
NEW ZEALA
WE'LL BE MET AT THE AIRPORT IN NEW ZEALAND BY MOTHER'S COUSIN LEIGHTON DIDDAMS! HE HAS A SHEEP RANCH ON SOUTH ISLAND!
QUANTUM
AND SOOO...AFTER A LOOONG FLIGHT...
GOOD TO SEE YOU, VERONICA, CHILD! SO YOU WANT TO GO SKIING HERE, EH?
YES, COUSIN LEIGHTON! WHAT'S THE BEST SKI SLOPE ON THE ISLAND?
THAT WOULD PROBABLY BE ON MT. COOK! I'LL MAKE ARRANGEMENTS FOR YOU TO GET UP THERE TOMORROW!
WONDERFUL! THIS IS SO EXCITING!
3

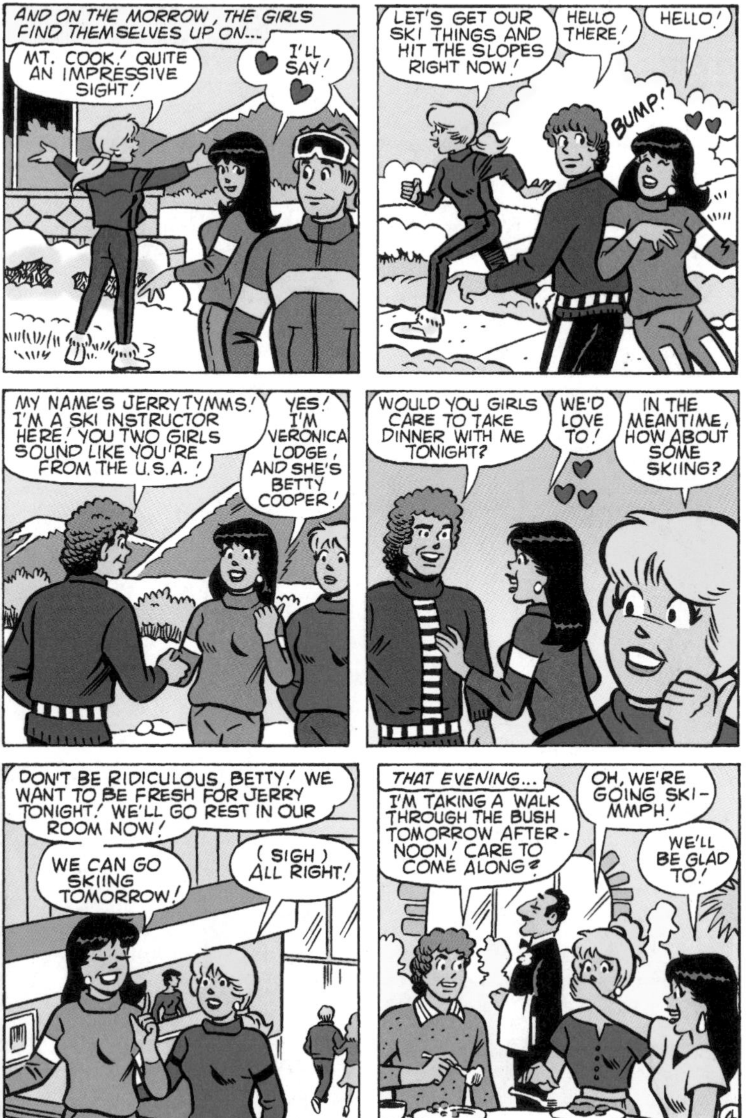
AND ON THE MORROW, THE GIRLS FIND THEMSELVES UP ON...
MT. COOK! QUITE AN IMPRESSIVE SIGHT!
I'LL SAY!
LET'S GET OUR SKI THINGS AND HIT THE SLOPES RIGHT NOW!
HELLO THERE!
HELLO!
BUMP!
MY NAME'S JERRY TYMMS! I'M A SKI INSTRUCTOR HERE! YOU TWO GIRLS SOUND LIKE YOU'RE FROM THE U.S.A.!
YES! I'M VERONICA LODGE, AND SHE'S BETTY COOPER!
WOULD YOU GIRLS CARE TO TAKE DINNER WITH ME TONIGHT?
WE'D LOVE TO!
IN THE MEANTIME, HOW ABOUT SOME SKIING?
DON'T BE RIDICULOUS, BETTY! WE WANT TO BE FRESH FOR JERRY TONIGHT! WE'LL GO REST IN OUR ROOM NOW!
WE CAN GO SKIING TOMORROW!
( SIGH ) ALL RIGHT!
THAT EVENING...
I'M TAKING A WALK THROUGH THE BUSH TOMORROW AFTER-NOON! CARE TO COME ALONG?
OH, WE'RE GOING SKI-MMPH!
WE'LL BE GLAD TO!
4

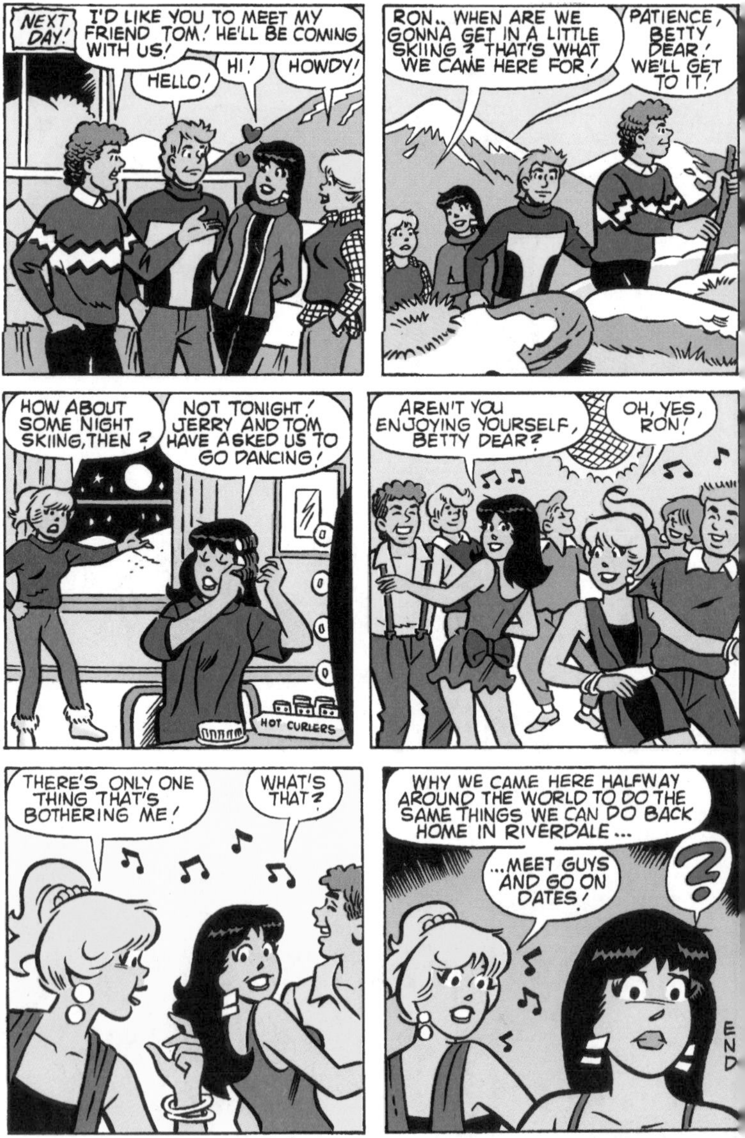
NEXT DAY!
I'D LIKE YOU TO MEET MY FRIEND TOM! HE'LL BE COMING WITH US!
HELLO!
HI!
HOWDY!
RON.. WHEN ARE WE GONNA GET IN A LITTLE SKIING? THAT'S WHAT WE CAME HERE FOR!
PATIENCE, BETTY DEAR! WE'LL GET TO IT!
HOW ABOUT SOME NIGHT SKIING, THEN?
NOT TONIGHT! JERRY AND TOM HAVE ASKED US TO GO DANCING!
HOT CURLERS
AREN'T YOU ENJOYING YOURSELF, BETTY DEAR?
OH, YES, RON!
THERE'S ONLY ONE THING THAT'S BOTHERING ME!
WHAT'S THAT?
WHY WE CAME HERE HALFWAY AROUND THE WORLD TO DO THE SAME THINGS WE CAN DO BACK HOME IN RIVERDALE...
...MEET GUYS AND GO ON DATES!
END

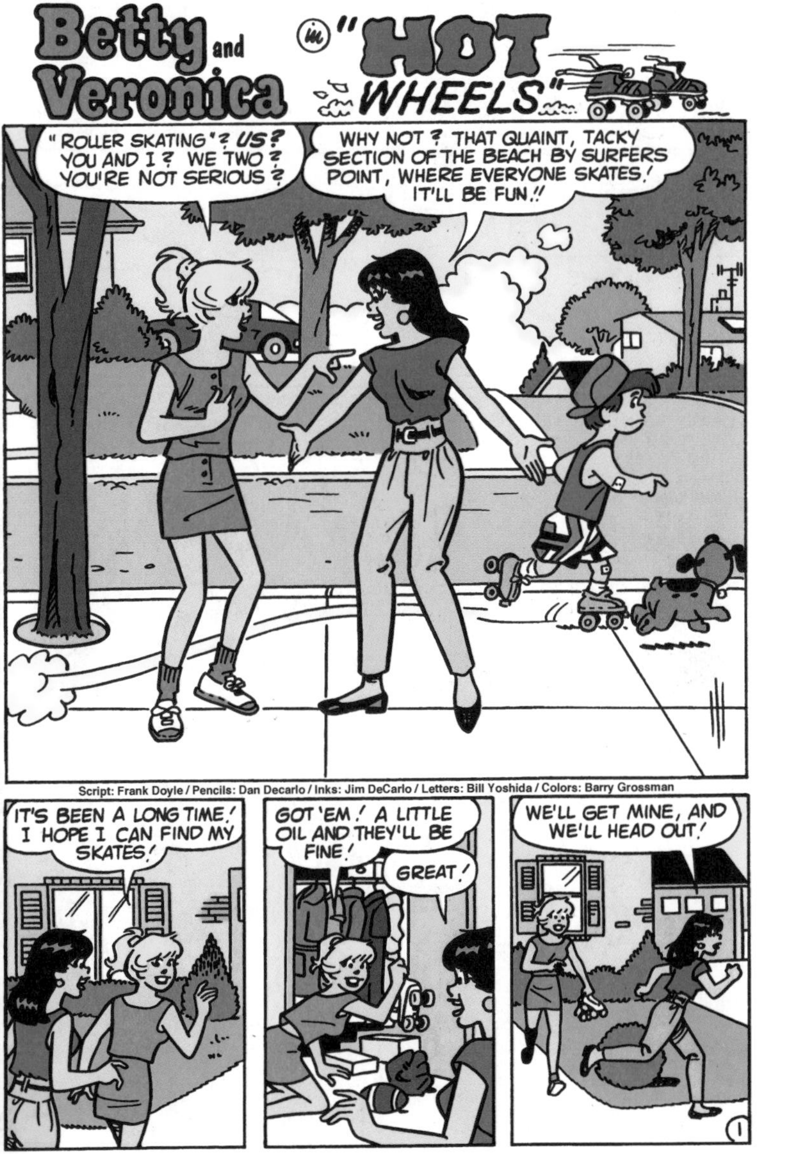

Betty and Veronica
in "HOT WHEELS"
"ROLLER SKATING"? US? YOU AND I? WE TWO? YOU'RE NOT SERIOUS?
WHY NOT? THAT QUAINT, TACKY SECTION OF THE BEACH BY SURFERS POINT, WHERE EVERYONE SKATES! IT'LL BE FUN!!
Script: Frank Doyle / Pencils: Dan Decarlo / Inks: Jim DeCarlo / Letters: Bill Yoshida / Colors: Barry Grossman
IT'S BEEN A LONG TIME! I HOPE I CAN FIND MY SKATES!
GOT 'EM! A LITTLE OIL AND THEY'LL BE FINE!
GREAT!
WE'LL GET MINE, AND WE'LL HEAD OUT!
1

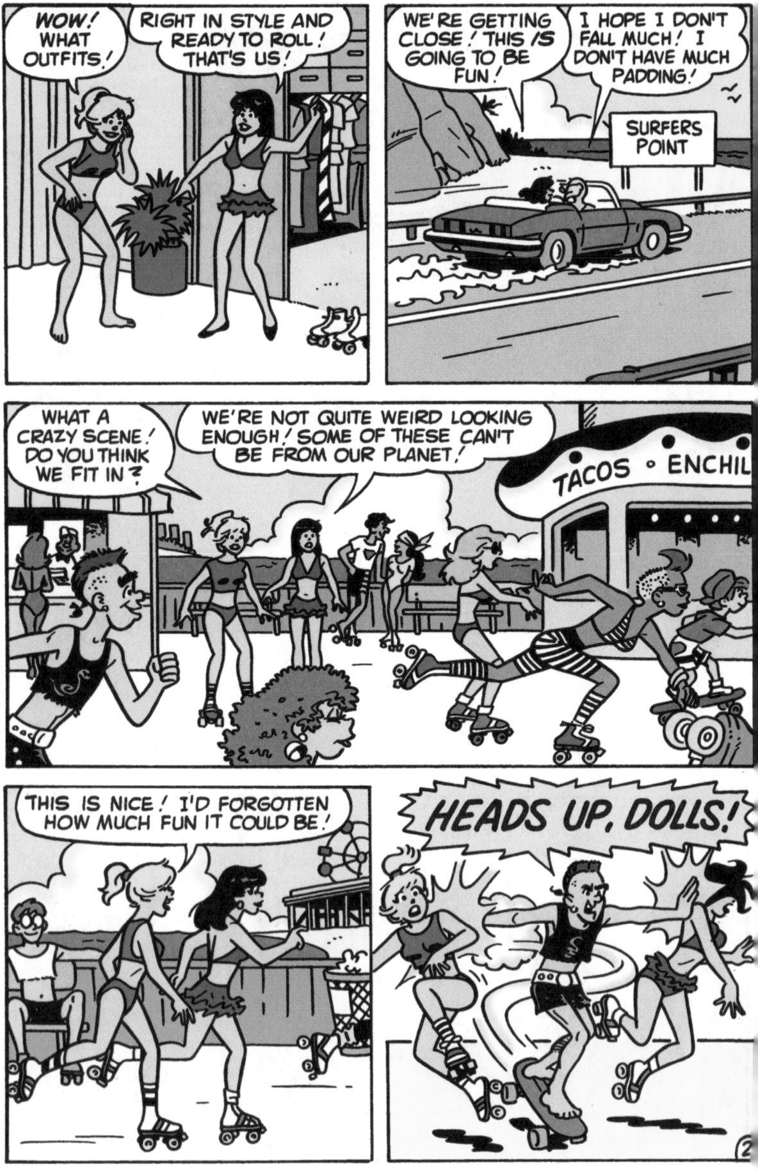
WOW! WHAT OUTFITS!
RIGHT IN STYLE AND READY TO ROLL! THAT'S US!
WE'RE GETTING CLOSE! THIS IS GOING TO BE FUN!
I HOPE I DON'T FALL MUCH! I DON'T HAVE MUCH PADDING!
SURFERS POINT
WHAT A CRAZY SCENE! DO YOU THINK WE FIT IN?
WE'RE NOT QUITE WEIRD LOOKING ENOUGH! SOME OF THESE CAN'T BE FROM OUR PLANET!
TACOS • ENCHIL
THIS IS NICE! I'D FORGOTTEN HOW MUCH FUN IT COULD BE!
HEADS UP, DOLLS!

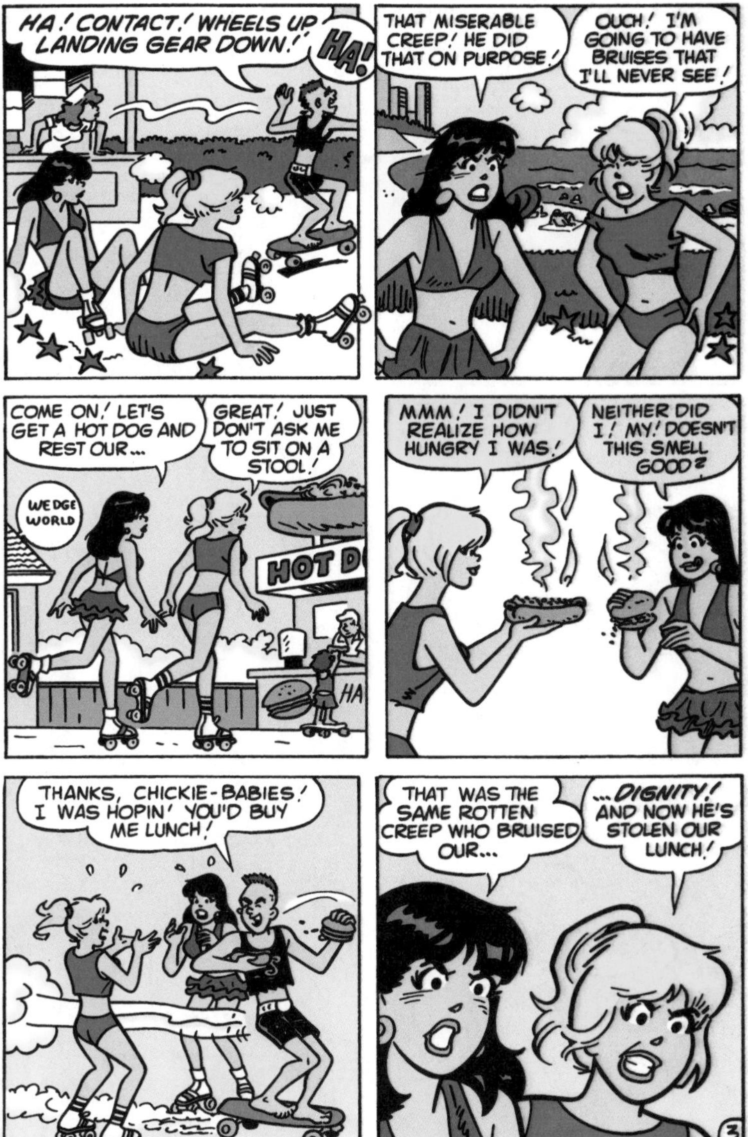
HA! CONTACT! WHEELS UP LANDING GEAR DOWN!
HA!
THAT MISERABLE CREEP! HE DID THAT ON PURPOSE!
OUCH! I'M GOING TO HAVE BRUISES THAT I'LL NEVER SEE!
COME ON! LET'S GET A HOT DOG AND REST OUR...
GREAT! JUST DON'T ASK ME TO SIT ON A STOOL!
WEDGE WORLD
HOT D
HA
MMM! I DIDN'T REALIZE HOW HUNGRY I WAS!
NEITHER DID I! MY! DOESN'T THIS SMELL GOOD?
THANKS, CHICKIE-BABIES! I WAS HOPIN' YOU'D BUY ME LUNCH!
THAT WAS THE SAME ROTTEN CREEP WHO BRUISED OUR...
...DIGNITY! AND NOW HE'S STOLEN OUR LUNCH!
3

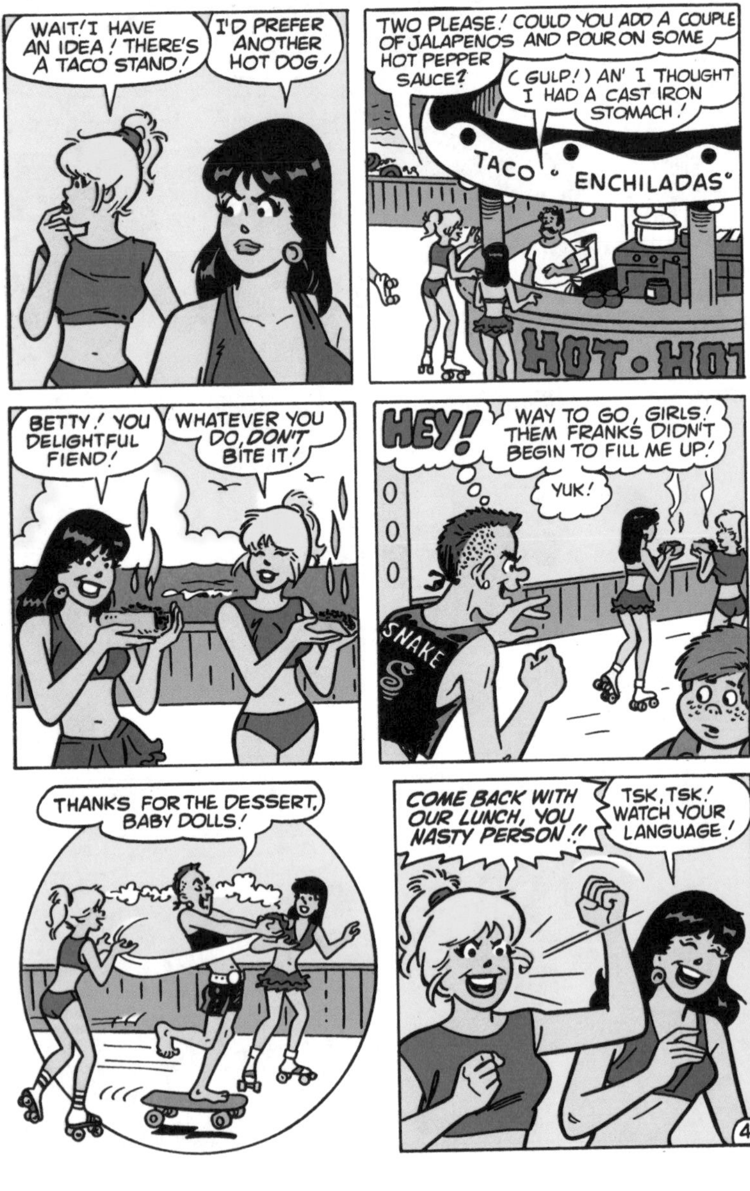
WAIT! I HAVE AN IDEA! THERE'S A TACO STAND!
I'D PREFER ANOTHER HOT DOG!
TWO PLEASE! COULD YOU ADD A COUPLE OF JALAPENOS AND POUR ON SOME HOT PEPPER SAUCE?
(GULP!) AN' I THOUGHT I HAD A CAST IRON STOMACH!
TACO • ENCHILADAS
HOT • HOT
BETTY! YOU DELIGHTFUL FIEND!
WHATEVER YOU DO, DON'T BITE IT!
HEY!
WAY TO GO, GIRLS! THEM FRANKS DIDN'T BEGIN TO FILL ME UP!
YUK!
SNAKE
THANKS FOR THE DESSERT, BABY DOLLS!
COME BACK WITH OUR LUNCH, YOU NASTY PERSON!!
TSK, TSK! WATCH YOUR LANGUAGE!

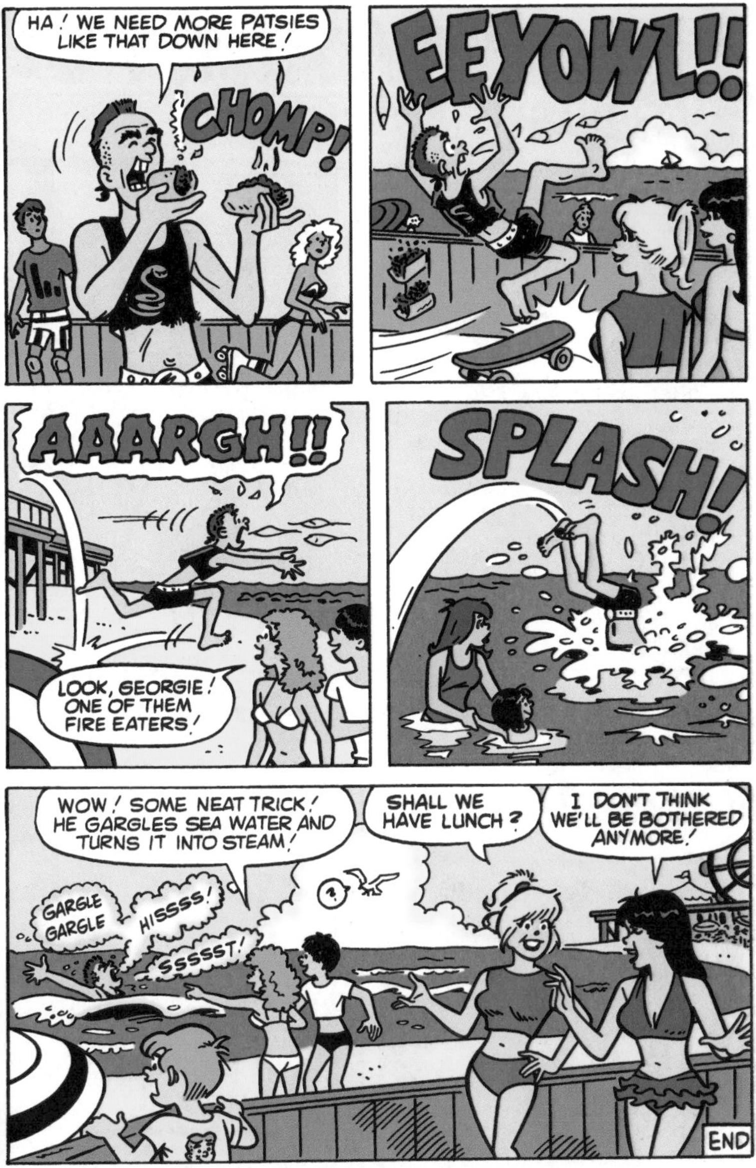
HA! WE NEED MORE PATSIES LIKE THAT DOWN HERE!
CHOMP!
EEYOWL!!
AAARGH!!
LOOK, GEORGIE! ONE OF THEM FIRE EATERS!
SPLASH!
WOW! SOME NEAT TRICK! HE GARGLES SEA WATER AND TURNS IT INTO STEAM!
SHALL WE HAVE LUNCH?
I DON'T THINK WE'LL BE BOTHERED ANYMORE!
GARGLE GARGLE
HISSSS!
SSSSST!
?
END

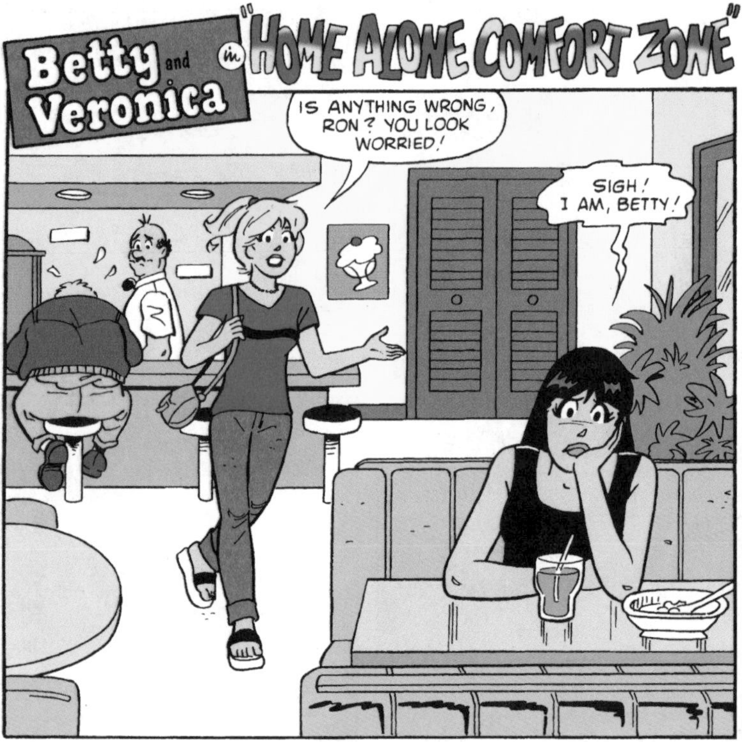
Betty and Veronica in "HOME ALONE COMFORT ZONE"
IS ANYTHING WRONG, RON? YOU LOOK WORRIED!
SIGH! I AM, BETTY!

Script: Mike Pellowski / Art: Dan DeCarlo / Letters: Bill Yoshida / Colors: Barry Grossman

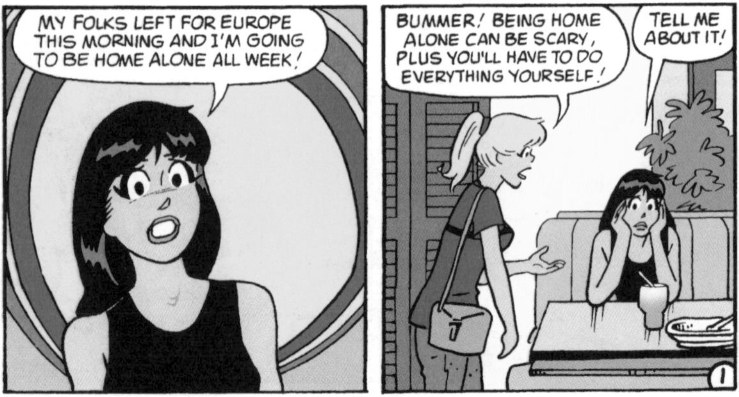
MY FOLKS LEFT FOR EUROPE THIS MORNING AND I'M GOING TO BE HOME ALONE ALL WEEK!
BUMMER! BEING HOME ALONE CAN BE SCARY, PLUS YOU'LL HAVE TO DO EVERYTHING YOURSELF!
TELL ME ABOUT IT!
1

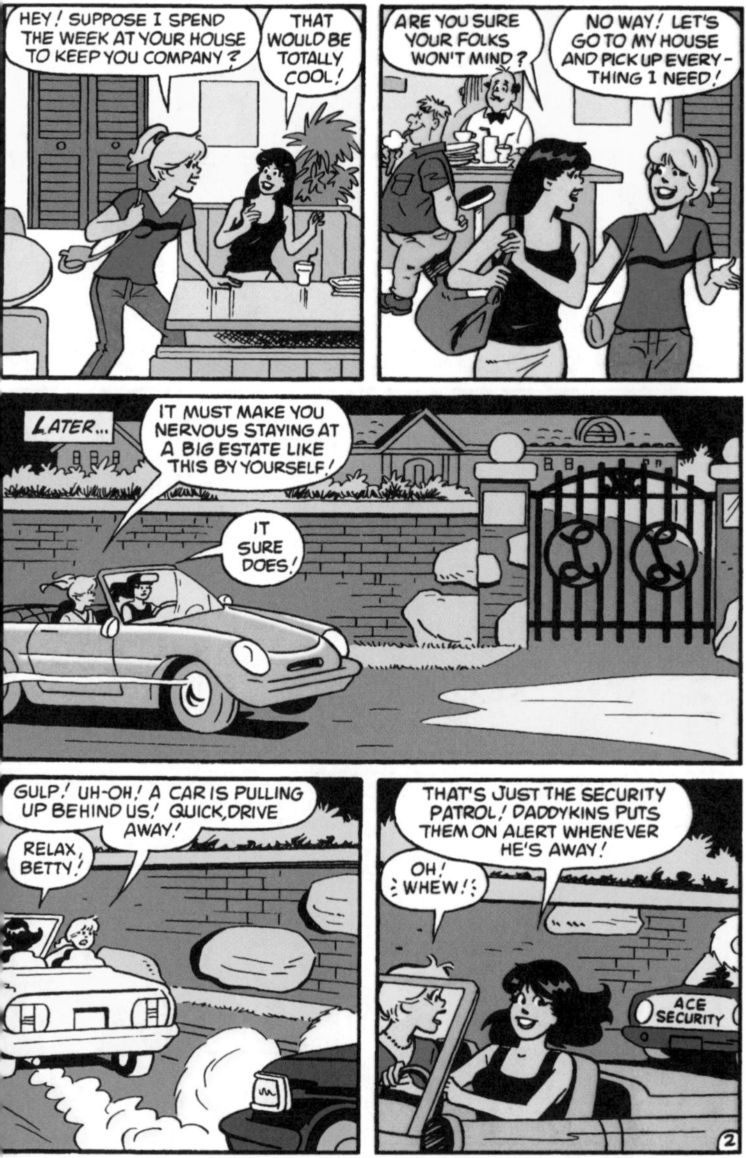
HEY! SUPPOSE I SPEND THE WEEK AT YOUR HOUSE TO KEEP YOU COMPANY?
THAT WOULD BE TOTALLY COOL!
ARE YOU SURE YOUR FOLKS WON'T MIND?
NO WAY! LET'S GO TO MY HOUSE AND PICK UP EVERY-THING I NEED!
LATER...
IT MUST MAKE YOU NERVOUS STAYING AT A BIG ESTATE LIKE THIS BY YOURSELF!
IT SURE DOES!
GULP! UH-OH! A CAR IS PULLING UP BEHIND US! QUICK, DRIVE AWAY!
RELAX, BETTY!
THAT'S JUST THE SECURITY PATROL! DADDYKINS PUTS THEM ON ALERT WHENEVER HE'S AWAY!
OH! WHEW!
ACE SECURITY
2

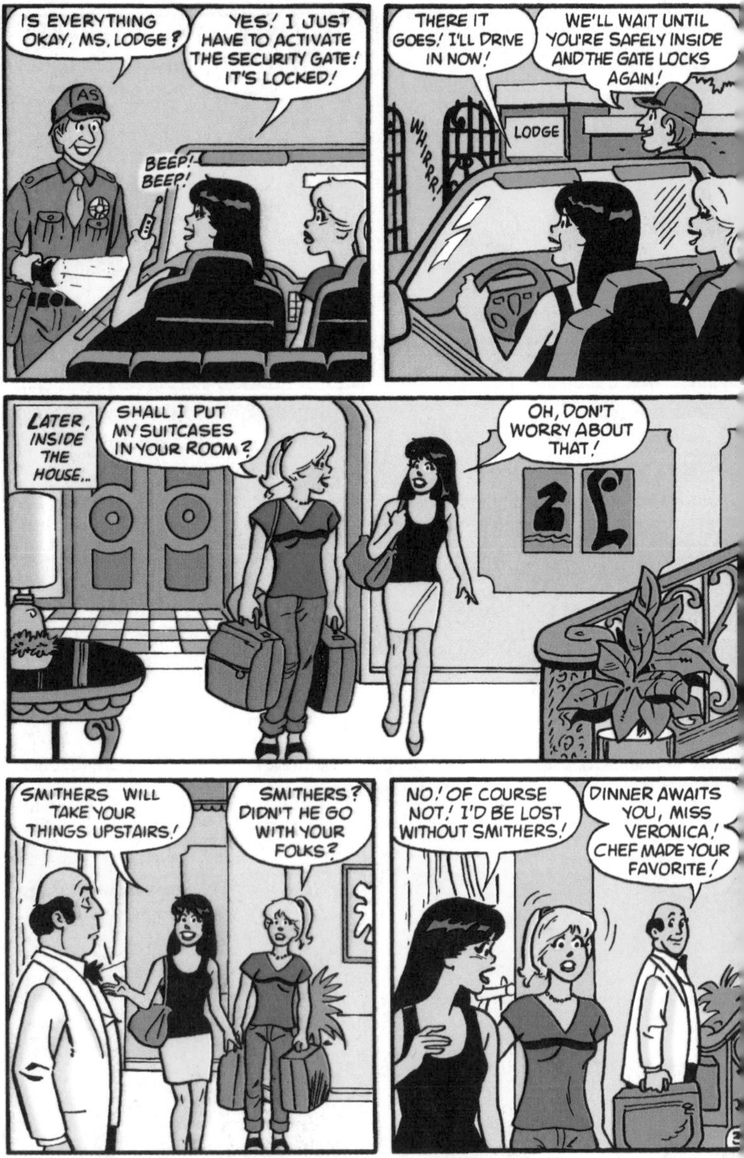
IS EVERYTHING OKAY, MS. LODGE?
YES! I JUST HAVE TO ACTIVATE THE SECURITY GATE! IT'S LOCKED!
BEEP! BEEP!
AS
THERE IT GOES! I'LL DRIVE IN NOW!
WE'LL WAIT UNTIL YOU'RE SAFELY INSIDE AND THE GATE LOCKS AGAIN!
WHIRRR!
LODGE
LATER, INSIDE THE HOUSE...
SHALL I PUT MY SUITCASES IN YOUR ROOM?
OH, DON'T WORRY ABOUT THAT!
SMITHERS WILL TAKE YOUR THINGS UPSTAIRS!
SMITHERS? DIDN'T HE GO WITH YOUR FOLKS?
NO! OF COURSE NOT! I'D BE LOST WITHOUT SMITHERS!
DINNER AWAITS YOU, MISS VERONICA! CHEF MADE YOUR FAVORITE!

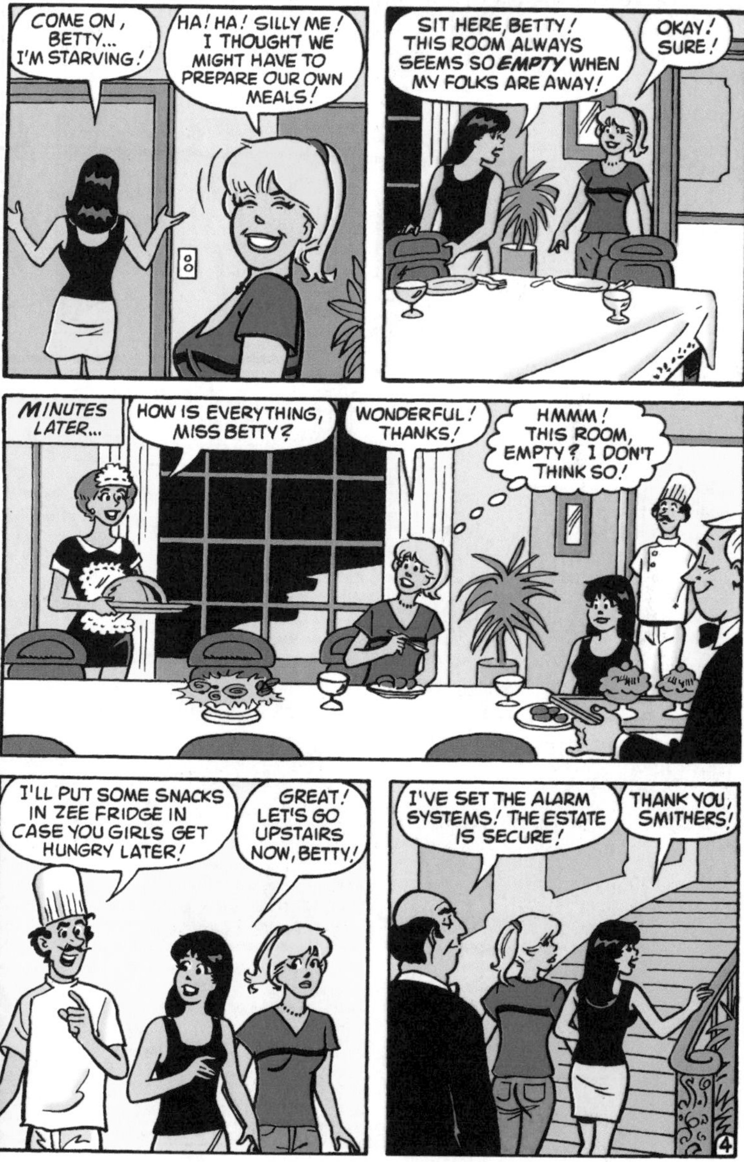
COME ON, BETTY... I'M STARVING!
HA! HA! SILLY ME! I THOUGHT WE MIGHT HAVE TO PREPARE OUR OWN MEALS!
SIT HERE, BETTY! THIS ROOM ALWAYS SEEMS SO EMPTY WHEN MY FOLKS ARE AWAY!
OKAY! SURE!
MINUTES LATER...
HOW IS EVERYTHING, MISS BETTY?
WONDERFUL! THANKS!
HMMM! THIS ROOM, EMPTY? I DON'T THINK SO!
I'LL PUT SOME SNACKS IN ZEE FRIDGE IN CASE YOU GIRLS GET HUNGRY LATER!
GREAT! LET'S GO UPSTAIRS NOW, BETTY!
I'VE SET THE ALARM SYSTEMS! THE ESTATE IS SECURE!
THANK YOU, SMITHERS!
4

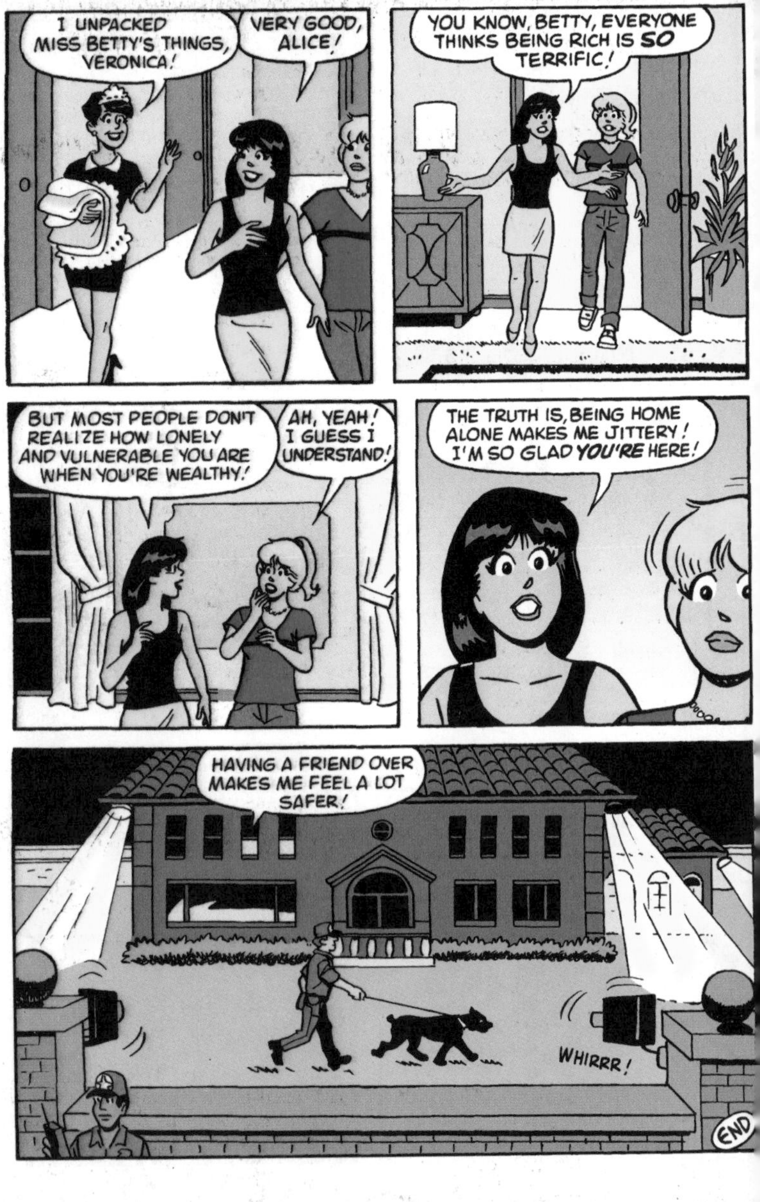
I UNPACKED MISS BETTY'S THINGS, VERONICA!
VERY GOOD, ALICE!
YOU KNOW, BETTY, EVERYONE THINKS BEING RICH IS SO TERRIFIC!
BUT MOST PEOPLE DON'T REALIZE HOW LONELY AND VULNERABLE YOU ARE WHEN YOU'RE WEALTHY!
AH, YEAH! I GUESS I UNDERSTAND!
THE TRUTH IS, BEING HOME ALONE MAKES ME JITTERY! I'M SO GLAD YOU'RE HERE!
HAVING A FRIEND OVER MAKES ME FEEL A LOT SAFER!
WHIRRR!
END